PRAISE FOR *THE HUNTING*

'While shooting first, it does ask a few questions as the extremists and Raj together try to outfox the hunter. Easy action'
The Times

'You'll find yourself getting through this in one sitting'
The Afterword

'I doubt if a more exciting and muscular book will come along this year'
Peterborough Telegraph

STEPHEN LEATHER
THE HUNTING

HODDER

First published in Great Britain in 2021 by Hodder & Stoughton
An Hachette UK company

This paperback edition published in 2021

2

A CIP catalogue record for this title is available from the British Library

Paperback ISBN 978 1 529 34525 4

Typeset in Plantin Light by Palimpsest Book Production Limited,
Falkirk, Stirlingshire

Printed and bound in Great Britain by Clays Ltd, Elcograf S.p.A.

Hodder & Stoughton policy is to use papers that are natural, renewable
and recyclable products and made from wood grown in sustainable forests.
The logging and manufacturing processes are expected to conform to the
environmental regulations of the country of origin.

Hodder & Stoughton Ltd
Carmelite House
50 Victoria Embankment
London EC4Y 0DZ

www.hodder.co.uk

For Alana Jane and Zula

CHAPTER 1

The overhead sun was relentless as it burnt down through the cloudless sky. Jon Van der Sandt had a wide-brimmed hat shielding his face and impenetrable Oakley sunglasses protecting his eyes but there was nothing he could do to make the air that he breathed any cooler. He stopped and took a swig from his water bottle.

'Not far now,' said his guide, as if reading his mind. The guide was in his late twenties, almost half Van der Sandt's age, but he had been born in Botswana and knew every inch of the thirty thousand-acre game farm. His name was Paul Falkner and his family had owned the farm for three generations. He was a good six inches taller than Van der Sandt, lanky with barely an ounce of fat on him, his hair bleached blond by the sun and his skin the colour of polished mahogany. Like Van der Sandt he was sporting a wide-brimmed floppy hat, though there was a racy snakeskin band around his. Both men were wearing olive shirts and shorts and Timberland boots, and hunting vests loaded with ammunition.

'I'm good,' said Van der Sandt. He didn't want the fact that he had stopped for a drink to suggest weakness. He was tired, but after five hours of walking through the bush, who wouldn't be? He knew that many Russian hunters, and lately the Chinese, preferred to be helicoptered in close to their prey. He had even heard stories of them mowing down elephants and rhinos from the air, not even bothering to land. That wasn't the way that Van der Sandt hunted. He went in on foot with only what he could carry. Man against beast and let the strong survive.

He placed the water bottle back in his belt and Falkner began walking again. They were on the track of a small herd of elephants: two males, five females and two juveniles. Falkner was following their trail and figured that they were a mile ahead, maybe less.

Van der Sandt was paying handsomely for the hunt, and he had already been rewarded with a white rhino and three buffaloes, one of which had the biggest spread of horns that he had ever seen. The three-day hunting holiday was costing twenty thousand dollars, which included the necessary licences, but each kill added to the bill. The rarer the animal, the higher the price, and in the case of the buffalo, the massive spread of the horns had meant the kill came with a thirty thousand-dollar price tag. The elephant they were tracking could easily cost more than twice that; it depended on the length of the tusks. According to Falkner, it was a fifty-five-year-old bull that weighed close to seven tons. If that were true, it would be the largest elephant Van der Sandt had killed, and Van der Sandt had killed dozens.

He was carrying his gun and ammunition. Some hunters had a bearer following behind with their gear in the way that golfers used caddies, but Van der Sandt was old school. If he could have done without Falkner he'd have gone into the bush alone, but he wasn't familiar with the area and it would have been foolhardy in the extreme to go solo.

The rifle Van der Sandt was holding was a double-barrelled sidelock made by William Evans of London, and it was his pride and joy. It had been handmade to his requirements and was chambered for the .500 Nitro Express cartridge, the favourite ammunition of big game hunters around the world. The gun had taken almost three years to produce and the action plates and body were engraved with scenes from his favourite hunting grounds in Africa and Asia, with the initials of his wife and children incorporated into the design. He had never told his wife what he had paid for the gun – close to two hundred thousand dollars – but he considered it money well spent. It was perfectly balanced and the eleven-pound weight helped deal with some of the recoil. Not all of it, by any means, and firing the gun meant putting a lot of weight on the front foot and holding the stock tight against the shoulder. It wasn't a gun for amateurs – if you weren't careful you could pull the trigger and end up flat on your back. And if your shot had just missed a seven-ton elephant, a mistake like that could easily be fatal.

A double rifle was vital just in case the first shot wasn't a killing shot. An elephant would charge if it wasn't killed instantly and having the second cartridge ready to fire could be a life saver. The new breed of hunters tended to prefer pump-action guns with five or more cartridges in the magazine, but Van der Sandt was contemptuous of them. If two shots wasn't enough to bring down your quarry, you had no business being a hunter. And it wasn't unknown for pump-action guns to jam. A double never jammed. You pointed it, you braced yourself, and you pulled the trigger. Job done. And you had a back-up shot ready to go. Van der Sandt had requested double triggers. He could have gone with a single trigger but the mechanism was more complicated and more likely to fail.

Van der Sandt's gun had twenty-four-inch barrels, shorter than the twenty-six or twenty-eight inches that most hunters went for. The longer the barrels, the less the tendency for them to rise up after firing, but the shorter barrels were easier to manoeuvre through thick bush. Van der Sandt's gun had a V-type open rear sight with twenty-four-carat gold inlay. Some hunters used telescopic sights but Van der Sandt was also contemptuous of that – if you were so far away that you needed a telescopic sight you weren't really hunting. The whole point was to get up close and personal and to look your quarry in the eye as you pulled the trigger.

Big game animals were only dangerous when they were close up. If an elephant was a hundred metres away and it spotted a hunter, it would probably amble off. But if it was just ten metres away, it would throw out its ears and charge. Same with buffaloes, which were actually way more dangerous than elephants. At a hundred metres a buffalo was as docile as a dairy cow, but bump into one in the tall grass and it could be deadly.

Van der Sandt wouldn't even consider taking a shot at an

elephant if he was more than twenty-five metres away. The same went for rhinos. The rhino he had killed the previous day had only been twenty metres away when he had pulled the trigger.

He had a dozen cartridges affixed to his hunting vest. The minimum legal calibre for hunting game in Africa was a .375 belted rimless Nitro Express – also known as the .375 H&H Magnum, manufactured since 1912 by a London gunmaker, Holland & Holland. The bullets ranged from seventeen grams to twenty-three grams. But Van der Sandt's gun was built to take the much larger .500 Nitro Express, which had a jacketed bullet of thirty-seven grams, almost one and a third ounces of lethal lead. The cartridges cost more than ten dollars each. Van der Sandt had shot with the .500 Nitro Express across Africa and had used it to good effect hunting brown bears and polar bears in the wilds of northern Canada. One of his best hunting trips ever had been the nine hours he had tracked a huge male polar bear across the frozen Arctic Ocean, culminating in a single kill shot to the brain. The Americans had banned the hunting of polar bears for anyone other than Alaskan natives in 1972, but it was still allowed in Canada, and since the Americans had banned the importing of polar bear trophies in 2008, Van der Sandt had to ship his trophy back to his mansion in London. The British had no qualms about big game hunters putting their trophies on show, probably because they were the country that had invented the concept of killing for sport. The same would go for the tusks of the elephant Van der Sandt and Falkner were hunting. The ivory was valuable – it had peaked at more than two thousand dollars a kilo in 2014 but had since fallen back to seven hundred dollars. But even at that price the tusks of a serious bull elephant could be worth more than one hundred and twenty-five thousand dollars. But it wasn't about the money, it was about the trophy. A way of remembering the kill. Of honouring it.

Falkner bent down and examined the tracks. On his back was a bolt-action Winchester Safari Express chambered for the .375 H&H Magnum. It was a nice gun with a polished walnut stock. Falkner had added a scope because his role was tracking and protection; he had to be able to neutralise any threat at a distance if an attack looked imminent. While it was the elephant they were after, the bush was still home to lions, cheetahs and hippos, any one of which might decide to attack them. The Winchester was almost three pounds lighter than Van der Sandt's gun, but the small cartridges caused less recoil. It had a five-round magazine which, with one in the chamber, gave Falkner six shots to play with.

Falkner straightened up. 'We're close,' he said.

Van der Sandt flashed him a tight smile. To their left was a dried-up creek and beyond it a sandstone rock on which were sitting three female lions. The male was probably sitting in the shade somewhere. Van der Sandt wiped his forehead with his sleeve as he stared back at the lions. He had killed more than a dozen over the years, all males, but there was little sport in killing a lion. Lions were light-boned and soft-skinned and you could pretty much hit them anywhere and bring them down. Elephants and rhinos, and even buffalo, were much harder to kill and required a more advanced skill set. One of the lionesses yawned as if showing contempt and he smiled and raised his gun. He aimed at her and mimed pulling the trigger. 'Bang,' he said. She yawned again, and then studiously licked her paw.

Falkner was already walking away and Van der Sandt hurried after him. They spotted a leopard in the distance, sitting on a low branch of a baobab tree, difficult to see against the pinkish-grey bark. Usually at this time of the year the tree would be covered with large white flowers, but like all the vegetation it was suffering from the lack of water.

Falkner held up his hand in a clenched fist and Van der Sandt stopped. The guide pointed off to the right. 'A couple of hundred metres,' whispered the guide, taking his rifle off his back. 'If you listen really hard you can hear them feeding.'

Van der Sandt cocked his head on one side and concentrated. Off in the distance he could hear a whispered rustle. Falkner started walking again, toes first and then the heel, his boots crunching softly on the spiky undergrowth. Van der Sandt followed. They moved through a patch of brambles that tugged at their boots and socks, then across a dried-up creek. As they reached the top of the bank they saw the herd, standing in a thicket of shrubs. The animals were ripping the shrubs apart and shoving the vegetation into their mouths with their trunks.

The two juveniles were sticking close to the females. Some distance away was a male but it wasn't the target; it was only about ten feet tall, still an adolescent, maybe sixteen or seventeen years old.

Baby elephants took milk from their mothers until they were between five and eight years old but were taught how to feed themselves. Usually they took only the softest vegetation but the drought meant there was little of that about and the youngsters were clearly having trouble chewing the dried-up twigs and branches.

The male looked over in their direction and flapped its ears. It was probably due to leave the herd and either fend for itself or join up with a group of other young bulls. Elephant families were matriarchal, led by an older female. She was usually accompanied by her sisters, though sometimes non-related females were allowed into a herd. The males came, mated, and went.

The elephant flapped its ears again, then gathered a clump of sandy soil in its trunk and flicked it towards them. Falkner had his finger on his trigger but the elephant was just posturing – there was no real danger of it attacking. It nodded and snorted and threw several more snoutfuls of soil towards them. The largest female – presumably the matriarch of the herd – looked over at the male, then turned to look at the hunters. She tilted her head on one side, trumpeted, and then went back to helping one of the juveniles rip apart a shrub.

Van der Sandt stood next to Falkner. The two men looked around, trying to locate the trophy bull. Van der Sandt knew that he would be close by.

They heard a branch cracking off to the right and then they saw it. Van der Sandt grinned. It was huge – one of the biggest elephants he had ever seen. It would certainly be the largest he had killed. It was close to thirteen feet tall and its tusks must have been at least eight feet long. It was attacking a spreading baobab tree, using its massive tusks to strip away the bark and chewing on it contentedly. Elephants spent eighteen hours a day feeding, and during that time a fully grown animal could put away more than four hundred pounds of vegetation. Despite being herbivores, elephants weren't able to digest cellulose so most of what they ate passed through undigested. They preferred to graze on brush and grasses, but the drought meant they were in short supply, so these elephants had no choice other than to attack the trees and bushes they found.

Falkner nodded and motioned for Van der Sandt to go forward. It was to be Van der Sandt's kill so he was to take the lead, but Falkner had his gun at the ready just in case.

Van der Sandt felt his heart pounding in his chest – literally the thrill of the hunt. He breathed evenly as he moved slowly across the brush. Brambles scraped against his boots but he ignored them, totally focused on his quarry. They were a hundred feet away from the bull but it seemed to be unaware of their presence as it ripped away the bark.

There was another trumpeting from the lead female. Was she trying to warn the bull? Probably not. Her only concern was the females and the calves – the bulls came and went and were totally replaceable.

Falkner moved to the side, switching his attention back and forth between the herd and the trophy. Van der Sandt had his finger outside the trigger guard but had the barrels up. His heart was still beating fast and his hands began to shake as his body reacted to the adrenaline that was coursing through it. The elephant turned so that its back was full on to them and its tail twitched as it continued to attack the tree. The baobab tree had a long lifespan and there were examples that were more than two thousand years old, but by the time the elephant had finished, this tree wouldn't last much longer. It wasn't only the drought that was killing the habitat.

Van der Sandt began moving to the side. The best place,

possibly the only place, for a quick kill was to shoot the elephant between the ears, four to six inches below the eyes. The instinctive reaction would be to shoot above the eyes but there was too much protection there and even the Nitro Express round would have difficulty penetrating the skull at that point.

He was now about fifty metres from his quarry. Falkner had moved with him so that he could keep the herd in view but could also shoot the trophy if it charged. Falkner nodded his encouragement. Van der Sandt swallowed. His mouth had gone dry and he licked his lips. He really wanted a drink from his canteen, but now was not the time to be sating his thirst. The elephant turned its head as if sensing their presence for the first time. It was upwind of them so it hadn't smelt them, and they were moving quietly so Van der Sandt was pretty sure it hadn't heard them either. There was another instinct at play, an animal sense that was warning the elephant there was danger nearby.

Van der Sandt kept walking. Forty metres. His right foot brushed a rock and a large snake slithered away into the bush. Botswana was home to more than seventy species of snakes, including venomous ones like the black mamba, the puff adder and the Mozambique spitting cobra, but he had disturbed a non-venomous rufous beaked snake so he ignored it.

The elephant was slowly turning now, shuffling its massive feet and raising its trunk. Thirty metres.

The elephant threw up its trunk and trumpeted at the two hunters, then flapped its ears menacingly.

Van der Sandt slid his finger over the front trigger. The elephant stamped on the ground raising clouds of dust. Then it threw its head up and down, snorting angrily, and flapped its ears even more. Van der Sandt's mouth was completely dry now but his hands had stopped shaking.

The female was trumpeting again but he ignored it. Falkner was behind him to his left but Van der Sandt ignored the guide, too. The elephant was the centre of his universe. If it charged now he would have only seconds in which to react. Twenty-five metres.

The elephant stamped with both front feet, then pawed at the ground, still flapping its ears. Van der Sandt knew that the pawing was a prelude to a charge so he stopped where he was and raised the rifle. He took a breath, held it for a second, and then braced himself and squeezed the trigger. The round smacked into the bridge of the trunk. The perfect shot. The elephant blinked and then shook its head and flapped its ears. A dribble of blood ran from the wound. Van der Sandt fired again but this time his aim was slightly off and the shot hit the beast above the eyes.

Van der Sandt was already ejecting the two used cartridges as the elephant turned to its right. Falkner was at Van der Sandt's shoulder now but the guide kept his gun down. He knew this was Van der Sandt's kill and he wouldn't interfere unless their lives were in danger. Van der Sandt slotted in two fresh cartridges and snapped the breeches shut.

The herd had scattered and were running away from the sound of the shots, the mothers helping their calves along.

The trophy elephant was walking away and looked as if it was straining to break into a run. Van der Sandt walked quickly, bringing the gun to bear on the animal's left hip. The important thing to do now was to put the animal out of its misery. He stopped, took aim and fired at the animal's rear leg. It buckled and the elephant sagged to the side, its ears still flapping.

Van der Sandt walked around the animal as it slowly sat back on its haunches, giving a wide berth to the trunk that could easily break his leg if the animal lashed out. The elephant's massive chest was heaving now but the eyes were still clear and it watched Van der Sandt as he came to a halt close to its shoulder. The elephant's left eye kept watching him as he pointed the gun at the beast's ear and pulled the trigger. The shotgun exploded and the elephant keeled over. Its chest heaved twice and then went still.

'Nice kill,' said Falkner, clapping Van der Sandt on the shoulder. 'Has to be seven tons at least. And look at the size of those tusks.'

Van der Sandt grinned. It was one hell of a trophy. It was just a pity that he couldn't take the tusks back to the United States.

He took his iPhone from his vest and gave it to Falkner. 'Let's have some pictures,' he said.

He knelt down by the dead animal's head and posed as the guide snapped away with the phone. Van der Sandt had stopped posting pictures of his kills on social media after seeing a number of hunters named and shamed by the public. These days he kept the photographs for personal use, or to show fellow hunters. Van der Sandt had given up trying to bring people around to his way of thinking. He enjoyed hunting and there was no way he was going to give up that enjoyment just because some ill-informed snowflakes didn't like what he was doing.

Falkner took a dozen or so photographs and then gave the phone back to Van der Sandt. He took out his radio and called the support team who were waiting in Land Rovers a mile away. They would cut up the animal, distribute the meat to local villages and transport the tusks back to the lodge. They would also bring with them a chilled bottle of champagne and canapés to celebrate the kill. The two men would be driven back to the lodge to continue their celebrations.

Van der Sandt rested the gun on his shoulder and looked down at the dead beast. It had been a hell of a kill. One of his best.

CHAPTER 2

As Jon Van der Sandt nibbled on foie gras canapés and sipped chilled Bollinger, some six and a half thousand kilometres away eight men were also preparing to go hunting. They weren't carrying handmade double-barrelled rifles that cost six figures; their weapons of choice were Kalashnikov AK-47s, chipped and scarred from years of use and costing an average of six hundred dollars each.

The eight men were in a hotel room, loading rounds in the distinctive curved magazines, each of which held forty rounds. Regular AK-47 magazines held thirty rounds but the men were using larger ones made of polymer that could hold forty. Each man had ten magazines, a total of four hundred rounds each. When they had finished loading them they used duct tape to bind them into pairs, nose to tail, so that reloading was simply a matter of pulling out the empty magazine, twisting it around and inserting the fresh one. Once all the magazines were loaded and taped together, they were placed in nylon backpacks. They worked quickly and efficiently, their movements well practised.

They then checked their weapons. They all had folding stocks which meant they could be placed in the backpacks.

The men had booked two rooms with a connecting door, and once the work was done they took it in turns to wash themselves in the bathrooms and change into fresh T-shirts and shorts. Then they gathered in one room, faced Mecca, and prayed for the next ten minutes.

Four of the men were from England, two were Somalis with Dutch passports, one was Finnish, and one was from Pakistan but with a Belgian passport. All had trained in Afghanistan before fighting for ISIS in Syria. All had neatly trimmed beards and were battle fit, with barely an ounce of spare fat on them. They were warriors and had been carefully chosen for their mission.

After they had finished praying they embraced each other, shouldered their backpacks and headed out.

CHAPTER 3

Laura Van der Sandt's phone buzzed on the table next to her sun lounger and she picked it up. She pushed her Gucci sunglasses onto the top of her head and squinted at the screen, smiling when she realised it was her husband calling on FaceTime. She took the call and waved when she saw him grinning at her. 'Soaking up the sun?' he asked.

'Factor fifty, so I'm good,' she said.

'How is it?'

'Lovely,' said Laura. 'What about you? Is everything okay?'

'Perfect,' said Van der Sandt. 'Shot a seven-ton elephant this afternoon with tusks that must have been eight feet long.'

Laura's face tightened and her husband was quick to pick up on it. 'Don't be like that,' he said.

'Like what?'

'You know like what. Like I was doing something wrong.'

Laura sighed. 'Honey, you're killing an animal for sport.'

'And there's nothing you like more than a rare fillet steak with all the trimmings.'

'But you're not eating the elephant, are you?'

'It's pest control,' said her husband. 'There's a drought here in Botswana and the elephants are destroying crops and damaging property as if there was no tomorrow.'

'They're trying to survive,' said Laura.

'And so are the people here,' said Van der Sandt. 'That's why they're issuing licences to kill them. I'm doing them a favour. And the people here do eat elephants, honey. The one I killed will literally feed a hundred people.'

Laura sighed. It was an argument she and her husband had

had many times and one that she had never won. 'Honey, so long as you're having fun, that's all that matters,' she said.

'And the kids are good?'

'Glued to their phones as always. But they've been sailing and waveboarding and Karl seems to have found himself a girlfriend.'

Van der Sandt laughed. 'He's seven.'

'He's starting young, like his dad.'

Van der Sandt roared with laughter and blew her a kiss. 'So I'll leave here tomorrow morning and see you tomorrow evening, right? I'll fly in and pick you up and then we'll have a few days in London before heading back to the States.'

'You said we could visit Paris?'

'Really? You want to go back there?'

'I love Paris, honey.'

'It's a shithole these days. And the kids are never happy there.'

'We can take them to Disneyland.'

'We can do that in the States. And they can see the real thing and not just a French copy.'

'Please, honey. Just two days.' She pouted and saw immediately from the look in his eyes that she had won.

He laughed. 'Okay, you didn't complain about my Botswana trip so the least I can do is let you have a couple of days in Paris. I'll book the hotel you like. The Lancaster.' He blew her a kiss. 'Love you.'

Laura laughed. 'Love you more.'

He ended the call and she put down her phone. Off to her right, two jet skis were heading towards the beach. She shaded her eyes with her hand to get a better look. Jet skis had been barred from coming too close to the shore as they were a danger to swimmers and snorkelers. Karl had been pestering her to take him jet skiing but that would have meant leaving the resort and she preferred to stay put. The resort was five star and her every whim was catered for, but outside there were areas that looked less than safe.

'Mum, can I have chicken wings?' asked Sophie. The ten-year-old was lying on the sun lounger next to Laura's. She was wearing a yellow bathing suit and a large floppy hat that provided shade for her phone.

'We'll be having dinner soon,' said Laura.

'How soon is soon? I think you mean soooooon.'

Laura laughed. 'A couple of hours,' she said.

'I'm hungry now.'

'How can you be hungry? You had all that spaghetti for lunch. And I seem to remember a chocolate lava cake. With vanilla ice cream. And strawberries.'

'I'm still growing,' said Sophie seriously, then she pouted. Laura laughed as she realised it was the exact same facial expression that she had used on her husband. 'What?' said Sophie.

'Nothing,' said Laura. She looked around for a waiter. 'And an iced tea,' said Sophie. 'Peach.'

Laura smiled to herself.

'Mum, they've got jet skis,' said Karl. He was sitting up on the sun lounger on the other side of Sophie, peering out to sea.

'I don't think they're from the resort,' said Laura. She shaded her eyes again. 'Can you see Lucy?'

Fifteen-year-old Lucy had her eyes on a group of Italian teenage boys and whenever they went into the sea she followed them. She was wearing a white bikini which made her easy to spot. Laura waved at her and called her name but was pointedly ignored. The Italian boys were throwing a basketball around and Lucy was clearly hoping it would go in her direction. 'Lucy!' she shouted.

The jet skis were close enough to hear now, buzzing like flies. There were water spouts at the back of each craft. There were four of them now, she realised, with two people on each, and they were heading directly to the beach. 'What are they playing at?' she muttered to herself.

Sophie looked to see what Laura was squinting at. 'What are they doing wrong Mummy?' she asked.

'They're being stupid,' she said. 'They could easily run over a swimmer. Someone could get hurt.'

'The jet skis you mean?'

'Yes. The jet skis.' She waved at Lucy. 'Lucy, come out of the water!' she shouted.

'What's wrong, Mummy?' asked Karl.

'I want Lucy out of the water while those idiots are playing with those jet skis,' said Laura.

'They look fun,' said Karl.

'They're not fun,' said Laura. 'They're dangerous and the people on them are just being stupid. Someone could get hurt.'

The jet skis were fanning out now, aiming at different parts of the beach. The engines accelerated and that made no sense because they were getting closer to the shore. Laura swung her legs off the sun lounger and shouted for her daughter. She had the basketball now and was waving it above her head, teasing one of the Italian boys.

The nearest jet ski was only a dozen metres from Lucy, but she was so involved with the boys that she didn't seem to be aware of it. It roared through the surf and up onto the beach. 'Stupid show-off,' said Laura, standing with her hands on her hips.

The driver of the jet ski and the passenger were Asian, young men with beards wearing T-shirts and shorts. Laura shook her head. They definitely weren't the sort to be staying at the resort. She looked around, wondering where the resort security people were. The men shouldn't be on the beach, it was for resort residents only.

The two men walked away from the beached jet ski, then knelt down and took off their backpacks. Laura gasped as they took out guns. 'Sophie, Karl, come here,' she said. Then she shouted at her daughter at the top of her voice. As she did she heard a series of loud bangs further down the beach, to her left. She turned and her stomach lurched when she saw two men shooting at holidaymakers on the beach. The realisation of what was happening hit her like a blow to the chest. She grabbed her son who was staring in horror at the gunmen. Sophie had dropped to her knees and was crouched behind the sun lounger. 'Sophie, come on,' she said, reaching for her.

There were more shots now, to her right, followed by frantic screams. Laura's heart was beating so fast that she thought it was going to burst. She turned to look back at Lucy but as she did she saw that the two men she had watched ride up onto the beach had slotted magazines into their guns and were aiming them at the Italian teenagers. Laura opened her mouth to scream but before she could utter a sound they pulled their triggers and sprayed bullets at the holidaymakers in the sea. Their tanned bodies were ripped apart and blood splattered over the waves. Lucy screamed and there was another burst of fire. Red blotches appeared on her white bikini and then a bullet hit her in her face and it imploded. Laura screamed in anguish and Sophie and Karl began to cry. Then the two men turned towards them. Their eyes were wide and angry and they began to shout something as they pulled the triggers again. Karl died first, then Sophie, and finally Laura. Her dying thought was that she was supposed to protect her children and that she had failed them.

CHAPTER 4

Falkner was sitting at the lodge's bar on a zebra-skin stool sipping a St Louis Export beer from the bottle when Van der Sandt walked in. The guide had changed into a blue polo shirt with the lodge's logo on the breast pocket, and neatly pressed chinos.

Van der Sandt slid onto the stool next to him and ordered a whisky and ice from the barman. 'Nice work today, Paul,' he said.

'I was just along for the ride,' said Falkner.

'No, you're a first-rate tracker and you know exactly what's needed. I've had guides fuck up big time before.'

'I do my best,' said Falkner, raising his beer bottle.

'You did great,' said Van der Sandt. His whisky and ice arrived and he clinked his glass against Falkner's bottle. He looked around the bar. A couple of Americans were talking loudly on the terrace and there was a group of middle-aged women sitting at a nearby table. From the photographic gear on the table he assumed they were there for safaris. One of the women looked over at him and he smiled and raised his glass. She threw him an angry look and turned away.

'We're going out to shoot giraffe tomorrow morning,' said Falkner. 'You're welcome to come along.'

Van der Sandt shook his head. 'They're no challenge.'

'I hear you,' said Falkner. 'But giraffe, zebra, baboon – they're our bread and butter. Groups of Americans mainly, but the Chinese have discovered hunting and they love it.'

'Russians, too.'

Falkner laughed. 'Yeah, the Ruskies are a strange bunch. They're not really interested in hunting, they just like killing.

They say that one of the game farms in the south lets them shoot zebras from a helicopter with a machine gun.'

Van der Sandt shook his head. 'Unbelievable.'

'We have to take the business where we can,' said Falkner. 'But it's no fun shepherding amateurs. I had a Chinese guy last week, richer than God, runs factories in Shenzhen and his wife is the sister of one of the guys in the National People's Congress. He flew in on a chopper with a security team and a girl who I assumed was his daughter but who turned out to be his mistress. He wanted to shoot an elephant and we arranged that but he fucked it up big time and I ended up having to put the animal out of its misery. He also said he wanted to shoot a tiger, but he didn't seem to grasp the concept that we don't have tigers in Africa. He kept saying that money was no object. Seriously, I think he wanted me to fly in a tiger so that he could shoot it. Mind you, he left me with a thousand-dollar tip, so I can't complain too much.'

Van der Sandt chuckled and reached inside his jacket. He took out an envelope and slid it across the bar towards the guide.

Falkner put up his hand. 'Mr Van der Sandt, I wasn't dropping a hint.'

'I know you weren't,' he said. 'That's just a token of my appreciation for a bloody good hunt. And it's more than your Chinese client gave you.'

Falkner thanked him and slipped the envelope into the back pocket of his chinos. 'So what would you say was your hardest kill?' asked Falkner.

Van der Sandt sipped his whisky as he considered the question. Over the course of his life he had killed thousands of animals and every kill was different. 'You know, I think I'd have to say it was a saltwater crocodile, in Australia. The Northern Territory. They've been protected since 1971 but they issue a limited number of licences each year, mainly to get rid of mankillers. The thing about the croc is that you have to get right up to it. I mean really right up to it, so close that you're better off using a revolver than a rifle.' He sipped his drink. 'This one was a monster, six metres long and weighing close to six hundred kilos. It was about as old as the bull

I shot today. It had killed a child and a few months earlier had dragged a guy off his boat and eaten him alive. They issued an emergency licence to kill it and I got it. I'd killed a few crocs before but this was different. This bastard was cunning. He knew we were out to get him. And that made it really hard because like I said you have no choice but to get right up to him. The only place you can put a round is half an inch behind the ear, straight into the brain. And because he was so wary, we had to use harpoons to get him before the kill. We were in a flat-bottomed aluminium boat, about twenty feet long, pretty much the length of the croc. There was me and a guide who knew the river, and a boatman. They were both born and brought up by the river so I was in good hands.' He sipped his whisky again. 'We started as the sun went down, using halogen flashlights, and it took us the best part of four hours to find him. I had a harpoon attached to a line, but the bastard kept submerging every time I tried to throw it. Eventually I got him in the neck and that's when the fun started. I kid you not but he pulled the boat with the three of us in it. There was no way we could pull him in, all we could do was hang on. He pulled us up and down the river for two hours. Strong as an ox. But eventually he started to tire and we could pull him in. When he was close to the boat I ended it with a shot from my Magnum. But he was fighting right up until the end.' He raised his whisky glass in salute. 'It was a good death.' He drained his glass and waved at the barman for a refill. 'Do you know what the most fierce animal in the world is?' asked Van der Sandt.

'The hippo,' said Falkner. 'They kill five hundred people a year.'

Van der Sandt laughed. 'If that's your criteria, then the mosquito kills millions.'

'I figured insects didn't count,' said Falkner. 'Okay, crocodile maybe. They're as dangerous as hell.'

Van der Sandt shook his head. 'Wrong again,' he said. 'You've got to be pretty stupid to get attacked by a croc. They keep to themselves.' He took a long pull on his glass of whisky. 'It's the honey badger. Even the *Guinness Book of Records* has it down as the World's Most Fearless Creature.'

'You haven't hunted them, have you?'

'They're tiny fuckers, not worth hunting,' said Van der Sandt. 'Just over a foot tall. But they'll attack anything that moves. You've seen them, right?'

'Sure. But I'm not sure how dangerous they are.'

'To you and me, probably not. But if a lion cub or a young leopard makes the mistake of trying to catch one, they won't make that mistake again. They've got really loose skin and if they get grabbed they can pretty much twist around inside their skin to fight back. They've got killer claws and a vicious bite. And they'll fight to the death. They're bred to be tough. The mothers start by feeding them venomous animals when they're pups. They start them off on scorpions and then feed them venomous snakes all the way up to puff adders and cobras, building up an immunity to snakebites when they're older. They're as hard as nails.'

Van der Sandt realised there was someone standing at his left shoulder. He turned. It was the woman who had been watching him from the table. She had pale blue eyes and chestnut hair that she had tied back into a ponytail. She was wearing what looked like designer hunting gear: a mesh waistcoat over a pale green blouse, and baggy pants with pockets on them, tucked into polished boots. Van der Sandt flashed her a smile. 'Hi,' he said. 'How are you doing?'

She didn't return his smile and folded her arms. 'Excuse me, but I have to say something to you,' she said. She was American. East coast certainly, probably from Boston.

'I'm always happy to talk to a pretty lady,' said Van der Sandt. He held out his hand. 'Jon Van der Sandt.'

'Yes, sure, whatever,' said the woman frostily. 'I'm told you killed an elephant today.' There was a wedding ring and an engagement ring on her left hand. A big stone, probably four or five carats, and it probably cost more than his gun. He guessed that she had a wealthy husband – or ex-husband – because she didn't seem like a career woman.

Van der Sandt took back his hand but continued to smile. 'I did indeed,' he said. 'Seven tons with a very impressive set of tusks.'

The woman frowned. 'How could you do that? We photographed him only yesterday. He was beautiful. How could you kill a majestic, sentient being, an animal that would never do you any harm?'

'How? Well if you want the specifics, it was one shot to the front of the skull, just below the eyes, one above the eyes and a third shot directly into the brain through its left ear. It was as close to painless as you could wish for.'

The woman's face went white and she gasped, covering her mouth with her hand. Her nails were painted blood red, matching her lipstick. 'That's horrible,' she said.

'That's a matter of opinion,' said Van der Sandt. 'I thought it was magnificent.'

'You killed an innocent animal. An endangered species.'

'Well, taking your second point first, elephants aren't in the least bit endangered. There are somewhere between half a million and seven hundred thousand elephants in Africa, so many that they can't be counted accurately. And when there's a drought they fight among themselves for water and resources. In this country alone there are more than one hundred and fifty thousand elephants, compared with just eight thousand back in the sixties. Hunters like me kill about a thousand a year. And the money we pay – substantial sums I might add – go towards conservation schemes that help ensure that they will be around for a long, long time to come.'

'But you kill them for what? For sport?'

'I'm not denying I get a thrill from hunting big game,' said Van der Sandt. The woman opened her mouth to interrupt but he held up his hand to silence her. 'But on your first point, wherever did you get the idea that elephants are innocent? Watching *The Jungle Book*? Elephants are vermin. Elephants are a huge threat to the African people. They kill and maim hundreds of them a year and destroy fields and crops. You have farmers who have their livelihoods wiped out by a herd of elephants rampaging across their cotton or maize fields. They don't graze, they pillage. They destroy. And who helps the farmer if he has no food to give to his children? Do you think the government gives them rice or cash? No madam, they don't. African governments generally don't give a flying fuck about their people, pardon my language. Anyone who really knows elephants knows that they are a danger and need to be controlled. The media likes to blame poachers when elephants are illegally killed, but in many cases it's local farmers protecting their livelihoods. And what's a better end for the animal – being hacked to death by a group of machete-wielding farmers or shot in the head by an experienced hunter who knows what he's doing?'

'I'm sure the elephant just wants to stay alive,' said the woman.

'I'm sure you're right,' said Van der Sandt. 'How old are you?'

The woman's jaw dropped. 'Excuse me?'

'I'm asking you how old you are. I'm guessing thirty-eight.'

'I'm forty-two,' said the woman. 'Not that that's any business of yours.'

'You look good for forty-two, there's no doubt about that,' said Van der Sandt, and despite her annoyance the woman blushed at the compliment. 'But what about in fifty years' time, when you're getting to the end of your life? How will you end your days? Maybe at home surrounded by family and a couple of Mexican nurses? Holding your hand and giving you their love as you pass away. Or if your family don't want you, maybe you'll pass away in a nursing home, in a soft bed with medication easing your pain.'

'What are you talking about?' said the woman.

'How do you think elephants die in the wild?' asked Van der Sandt. 'I'll tell you. Elephants get six sets of teeth throughout their lives. The way they eat wears the teeth down, and as they wear down they are replaced. But when the final set wears away, they're not replaced. The animal I killed was on its last set and didn't have more than a few months left I'd say. A year maybe. Once that final set is useless, the animal begins to starve to death. As they starve they get weaker and weaker and eventually they are weak enough for the lions or cheetahs to take down. And that's how they die, ripped apart and eaten alive. So tell me, if you were an elephant, which would you prefer? A few months of starvation followed by being devoured by wild cats, or being put to sleep quickly and efficiently by a hunter like me who knows what he's doing?

A hunter who will never forget the elephant he has killed, who will respect and honour the animal's death.'

He glanced up at the television screen. A reporter was standing on a beach and squinting at the camera. A headline across the bottom read: 'MASS KILLING AT LUXURY BEACH RESORT'. Van der Sandt waved at the barman. 'Can you put the sound up?'

'I'm sorry, I was talking to you,' said the woman.

'No you weren't, you were harassing me out of some misguided belief that I'm doing something wrong,' said Van der Sandt, his eyes on the TV screen. 'You've said your piece, now get back to your friends before I say something I regret.'

The woman opened her mouth to reply but then thought better of it and hurried over to her table. She sat down and her friends leant towards her, eager to hear what had happened.

The barman looked around for the TV remote and when he couldn't find it he walked over to the set and pressed the button to boost the sound. The reporter was talking to camera, describing how terrorists had murdered tourists, riding up on jet skis before running amok on a beach and through a hotel. 'The death toll is thought to have reached more than a hundred,' said the woman.

Van der Sandt had a cold feeling in the pit of his stomach. He swallowed and almost gagged because his throat had gone dry. He reached for his glass and gulped down some whisky.

'ISIS have already claimed responsibility on social media for the killings,' said the reporter. The image of the beach was replaced by a picture of a tweet from an ISIS account, praising the actions of the terrorists and warning that there would be more attacks to follow.

The picture of the tweet disappeared and they were back with the reporter. She was walking down a path, shadowed by the camera, pointing out the route the terrorists had taken from the beach to the hotel. Her way was blocked by police tape but in the distance there were bodies hastily covered by sheets and uniformed police officers were moving around. The colour drained from Van der Sandt's face as he recognised the resort. It was where his family was staying.

'Are you okay, Mr Van der Sandt?' asked Falkner.

Van der Sandt shook his head but didn't say anything. He took out his mobile phone and called his wife. It went straight through to voicemail. All his children had phones and he called them one by one. First Lucy, then Sophie, and then Karl. All three went through to voicemail.

He looked back at the television. A terrorism expert was being interviewed by an anchorman. The expert was an American in his fifties, grey-haired and peering through horn-rimmed spectacles. He was explaining that the attack was an example of ISIS changing its tactics now that it had been virtually defeated militarily. The terrorist group was now attacking westerners, and in particular Christians, around the world. There was now nowhere that could be considered safe.

The headline at the bottom of the page now read: 'ISIS ATTACK IN NORTHERN CYPRUS KILLS 118 HOLIDAYMAKERS'.

'Mr Van der Sandt?' said Falkner.

Van der Sandt held up a hand. 'My family are at that hotel,' he said quietly.

'Oh my God,' said Falkner. 'I'm so sorry.'

Van der Sandt's private jet was at Francistown International Airport, some sixty kilometres from the game farm. The two pilots and the flight attendant were in a hotel in the city. He phoned Toni Cooke, the senior of the pilots, and told her that they needed to leave within the next couple of hours. 'Where to, Mr Van der Sandt?'

'Cyprus,' he said.

'Are we collecting your family?'

Van der Sandt ended the call without answering her question. 'Is there anything I can do for you?' asked Falkner.

Van der Sandt shook his head. 'Just get me a car to the airport.'

'I'll arrange that now,' said the guide. 'I'll get the trophies prepared and we'll store them until you're ready to take delivery. Don't worry about the payments, we'll sort everything out down the line.'

Van der Sandt stood up and drained his glass. He turned to leave but then waved at the barman. 'Maybe one for the road,' he said. 'Fuck it, make it a double.'

CHAPTER 5

By the time Van der Sandt's Gulfstream jet had landed at Ercan International Airport in Northern Cyprus, the local police had confirmed the death toll at one hundred and twenty-six. Van der Sandt had received the devastating phone call, confirming his worst fears about his family, just before he had boarded the plane. They taxied to the general aviation terminal and Van der Sandt waited on board until an immigration official arrived. He was accompanied by Rauf Konuk, who ran a security company in Nicosia, about fifteen kilometres from the airport. Konuk was a former cop who had moved into the private sector a decade earlier. He was in his early fifties, broad-shouldered and shaven-headed, and he was wearing a Hugo Boss suit and a gold Cartier watch. Konuk's company was partly cerebral – running due diligence for companies doing business in Cyprus and Turkey – and partly physical, offering close protection services for visiting VIPs. The corporate intelligence part of the business meant that he had a network of agents around the world supplying him with information, and on some issues he was better informed than many government leaders. Van der Sandt had invested several million dollars in Northern Cyprus and Konuk's intelligence had been invaluable.

Konuk stayed at the door to the plane while the immigration official dealt with Van der Sandt's passport and the passports of his flight crew. As the official left, Konuk slipped him a brown envelope which quickly disappeared inside the man's jacket.

Konuk approached Van der Sandt and forced a nervous smile. 'I am so sorry for your loss, Mr Van der Sandt,' he said. 'Your wife was a lovely lady, and your children . . .' He shook his head. 'I am so, so, sorry.'

'Thank you, Rauf,' said Van der Sandt. He held out his hand and Konuk shook it, but Konuk's grip had no strength to it.

'I hold myself responsible,' said Konuk. 'I should have had men with them, I should have taken better care of your family.'

Van der Sandt held up his hand to silence the man. 'Rauf, no, stop right there,' he said. 'My wife insisted that there be no security with her or the children at the resort. She was adamant about that. Your brief was to collect them from the plane and deliver them to the resort, and that you did. None of this is on you.'

'But if my men had been there . . .' He looked down at the floor.

'There's nothing to be gained from "ifs" or "buts". What happened, happened. We have to deal with that. My wife said that the resort was the safest place on the island, and I agreed with her. It was our decision, hers and mine, so I'll hear no more of this.'

Konuk nodded. 'Thank you,' he said.

Van der Sandt patted the man on the shoulder. 'Can you take me to my family?'

'Of course, of course,' said Konuk.

He stepped aside to allow Van der Sandt to leave first and followed him down the steps. There was a white Mercedes with tinted windows waiting next to the plane, and the driver opened the rear door as Van der Sandt and Konuk approached. They climbed into the back.

'So what happened at the resort?' asked Van der Sandt as they drove out of the airport.

Konuk explained what had happened, his voice a dull monotone. Eight terrorists had arrived on jet skis from a small village around the coast. The police had found the hotel they were using as their base but that had not yet been released to the media. There was CCTV at the hotel and that was being studied. Almost all the dead were tourists; the terrorists had gone out of their way to avoid killing hotel employees or locals. Having killed almost everyone on the beach they had moved into the hotel. A dozen died in the lobby, and then the killers made their way up the stairs to the first floor and then the second. The attack only seemed to come to an end when the terrorists began to run low on ammunition. They carried spare magazines in backpacks and kept reloading. By the time they were running back to the beach, the floors of the hotel were littered with thousands of empty casings and dozens of empty magazines. The men had rushed over to their jet skis and headed out to sea. By the time the first police arrived on the scene, the jet skis were long gone. When Konuk had finished he smiled apologetically as if it was somehow all his fault.

'How far is the nearest police station from the resort?'

'Ten minutes' drive.'

'Do you know why it took them so long to get there?'

Konuk shrugged. 'The police in the Turkish Republic of Northern Cyprus are not the world's most efficient.'

'Even so – with reports of a mass shooting, you'd expect a faster response.'

'I shall ask around,' said Konuk.

'What will happen investigation-wise?'

'A team from the Directorate General for Police in Nicosia will be handling the enquiries, but this is not a crime to be solved, Mr Van der Sandt. ISIS have already admitted responsibility. The perpetrators will already be in Turkey or Syria. The police will probably identify them from the CCTV, but what then? The killers will be back in the ISIS fold, they will be unreachable.'

Van der Sandt sighed.

'The police role will be to identify the dead and injured and to produce a report on what happened,' continued Konuk. 'Yes, they will carry out a forensic examination of the scene but that will be for the sake of appearances.'

'The authorities won't do anything?'

'Mr Van der Sandt, there is nothing they can do,' said Konuk. 'The police here have no authority in Turkey or Syria. And because Northern Cyprus is not recognised by any other country other than Turkey, they do not have access to the resources of

Europol or Interpol. We can expect strong statements condemning the attacks, and I have no doubt they will release names and nationalities once they have them, but they won't be taking any action.'

Van der Sandt nodded grimly. 'I understand.' He stared out of the window with unseeing eyes.

The local mortuary could only hold six bodies, so the gymnasium of a local school had been commandeered for the victims of the attack. There were two armed policemen guarding the door but they both recognised Konuk and he and Van der Sandt were waved through.

The corpses had been placed on trestle tables and covered with white sheets. Any belongings had been put in cardboard boxes underneath the tables, with a handwritten number on them.

Portable cooling units had been brought in to keep the temperature down but they were struggling and the air was cool rather than cold.

There were only three forensic specialists in the room, wearing white overalls and blue shoe covers, and they were using old-fashioned ink and paper to collect fingerprints from the dead. Van der Sandt frowned when he saw what they were doing. 'They don't have an electronic system?' he asked.

Konuk shook his head. 'This is Northern Cyprus,' he said. 'And the DNA samples they are taking will take weeks to be analysed. They will have to be sent to a lab in Istanbul. But identification won't be a problem; all the victims were guests at the hotel. They are going through the motions.'

He took Van der Sandt to the middle of the room and stood next to a sheet-covered body. 'This is your wife, Mr Van der Sandt,' he said. 'I am so sorry.'

Underneath the table was a cardboard box with the number 39 on it. 'What is the significance of the number?' Van der Sandt asked.

'It's just a number they were given at the scene,' said Konuk. 'Anything they had on them was placed in the box.'

Van der Sandt bent down and took out the box. There was an

iPhone, a pair of Gucci sunglasses, a Lee Child novel and a bottle of sunscreen. He recognised the phone and the sunglasses. He put the box back on the floor. 'There is no need to identify your wife's body, Mr Van der Sandt,' said Konuk.

'I need to see her,' said Van der Sandt. He pulled back the sheet. His wife's eyes were closed and she looked as if she was sleeping. The bullets must have hit her body. He bent down and kissed her on the forehead. 'They'll pay for this, honey,' he whispered. 'I swear.'

He straightened up. The body on the next table was smaller and the number on the cardboard box was 40. There was an iPad in the box with a Pokémon cover. His son's. Van der Sandt's stomach lurched and for a few seconds he went weak at the knees. Then he pulled back the sheet. Karl's eyes were open and his teeth were bared in an animal snarl. Van der Sandt had seen the look before on the face of a lion that he had killed and he gritted his teeth. Karl was seven. Seven years old, his whole life ahead of him. Why would anyone kill a seven-year-old boy? His hand began to tremble and he fought to control himself. Had Karl been facing his killers when he died? Or had he been shot in the back, fleeing for his life? Van der Sandt was sure that Karl's first instinct would have been to protect his mother and his sisters. He knew that if he pulled the sheet back he'd be able to see if his son had been shot in the front or the back, but he let it fall back over the boy's face. Better not to know.

He could tell by the shape under the sheet on the next table that it was Lucy. Van der Sandt ran a hand over his face. Tears were pricking his eyes but he blinked them away. Tears served no purpose. He flinched as he felt Konuk grip his elbow. 'Mr Van der Sandt, please. Can I suggest you don't look at your elder daughter. She was in the water when the attack occurred, she was very close . . .' Konuk stopped speaking and let go of Van der Sandt's arm.

Van der Sandt turned to look at him. 'Thank you for your concern,' he said coldly.

'It's just, I think, you know, you'd want to remember your

daughter the way she was, not the way . . .' Konuk dried up again and looked away, embarrassed.

Van der Sandt reached for the sheet that covered his darling Lucy, but then he stopped. Konuk was right. If he lifted the sheet and looked at her, it would be the last image he had and it would be an image he would never forget. He kissed his fingertips and placed them on the sheet, then walked over to the final table. The box had 42 written on it and inside there was an iPad with headphones attached, an iPhone, a pink scrunchie, and a small toy elephant that he'd given Sophie when he got back from his last hunting trip in Africa. He picked up the elephant and held it against his cheek, then sniffed it, hoping to pick up her scent, but all he could smell was the sea.

He slowly drew back the sheet. Sophie looked at peace, like her mother, and that gave him some consolation. Hopefully it would have been quick. She was small so she would have bled out quickly, and at least she had been with her mother. It was a small consolation, minuscule, but at the moment it was all he had. He took the toy elephant, tucked it next to her neck, and covered her up again.

He turned to face Konuk. 'I need to take my family back to the States,' he said.

Anyone but Konuk would have pointed out that the bodies were part of an ongoing investigation and that there was no way the police would release them, but Konuk was a man who solved problems, rather than described them. 'Of course,' he said.

'No matter what it costs, pay whoever needs to be paid and have the bodies delivered to the airport as soon as possible.'

'I will get that done, Mr Van der Sandt.'

Van der Sandt patted him on the shoulder. 'Thank you,' he said.

Konuk bowed his head in acknowledgement, but said nothing.

CHAPTER 6

The eight men were sitting cross-legged on carpets in a large tent that was open at the sides to allow what breeze there was to blow through. They were sitting in a circle around a dozen or so plates of food. It was simple fare – kebabs, hummus, mashed eggplant, green beans, stuffed vine leaves, and Arabic bread – and there were jugs of water and watermelon juice.

'Why can't we eat?' asked one of the men. His name was Jaffar Dawood and he had a north-of-England accent. During the attack on the holidaymakers in Cyprus he had been wearing a T-shirt and shorts, but now he was wearing a plain white kaftan.

'We must wait for the imam,' said the oldest man in the group. His name was Faaz Mahmud. He had a Finnish accent, though he spoke fluent Bengali, the result of having parents from Bangladesh. He was in his forties with a greying beard, and was wearing wire-framed spectacles with circular lenses, and a long tunic over baggy trousers. 'It would be disrespectful to begin eating before he arrives.'

Erol Nazzar – who like Jaffar had been born in Bradford – looked at his wristwatch, a cheap black Casio. He was clearly eager to eat but held his tongue. The other men also kept quiet. They were all tired. Immediately following the attack on the resort they had fled on their jet skis around the bay to a beach, where a speedboat was waiting for them. The speedboat had taken them out to sea where they had transferred to a small Syrian freighter. They had hidden in a compartment in the hold, barely big enough for all eight of them. They had been given bottles of water but no food.

It had been dark when they had arrived at Latakia, Syria's

main port. The area was under Russian control and the port was close to Khmeimim Air Base, where the Russians had an electronic eavesdropping facility. The men were hustled off the freighter and into a truck, this time into a secret compartment behind boxes of olive oil.

A local driver had driven them through areas controlled by Russian and Syrian troops, then reached ISIS-controlled territory where the truck had headed into the hills. The jihadists had remained in their cramped hiding place until the truck had driven into a compound, a collection of concrete buildings, wooden shacks, and tents. They had climbed out of the truck and had been taken to a concrete shower block where they had showered and changed into clean clothes, before joining the rest of the camp for morning prayers.

After prayers they had been taken to the tent where the food had been put out on rugs, and they had been waiting almost half an hour.

'What do you think they'll get us to do next?' asked Mohammed Siddiq. Siddiq was the only white member of the group. He had sandy brown hair, and a soft blond fuzz around his cheeks and chin, his best attempt at cultivating a beard. Mohammed Siddiq was the name he'd been given by the imam at the west London mosque where he had converted, though most people called him Sid. He had been christened Gary Wilkinson. His father was an Amazon delivery driver and his mother sold health supplements online from their home in Kilburn. His parents had disowned him after he had become a Muslim in his late teens, and had gone as far as reporting him on the terrorist hotline. MI5 had put him on their watchlist but by then he had already left the country, heading initially to Pakistan where he had crossed the border into Afghanistan and been accepted into an ISIS group.

'Bloody hell, Sid, we've only just got back,' laughed Amer Qasim. Amer had been in the camp in Afghanistan with Sid, and was also from London, and the two men had bonded immediately.

'We need to keep the momentum going,' said Jaffar. 'Strike while the iron's hot. Come on, bruv, you know I'm right. Look at all the kafirs we killed and we don't have a scratch on us, Allah be praised.'

'It was wicked, no question,' said Erol. 'I got fifteen. Ten men and five bitches.'

'You were counting?' asked Sid.

'Fuck, yeah. Weren't you?'

Sid shook his head. 'I was just firing you know?' He mimed putting an AK-47 to his shoulder and firing, *bang-bang-bang*.

'I was counting,' said Abdullah Rarmoul, a lanky Somalian with a shaved head and a baleful stare. 'I got nine.'

'Only nine?' laughed Erol. 'What the fuck were you doing?'

'They were running by the time I got my gun out of my bag,' said Abdullah. 'Running like the dogs they are. And by the time I got to the hotel everyone was dead. It was only when I got up to the second floor that I found kafirs to shoot and then I ran out of ammo.'

'It is not a competition, brothers,' said Faaz. 'We were a team. And we were a successful team. That is all that matters.'

An old man with a straggly grey beard and a knitted skullcap on his head appeared at the tent entrance. He was wearing a grey-and-white-striped kaftan and was holding a chain of Muslim prayer beads. Faaz leapt to his feet and the others quickly followed. The imam smiled and embraced Faaz. '*Subhan Allah, Alhamdulillah, Allahu Akbah*,' he said. 'Glory to Allah, all praise belongs to Allah, Allah is the greatest.'

'We are honoured to serve Allah in all his glory,' said Faaz.

The imam patted Faaz on the cheek. His eyes were burning with a fierce intensity. 'This is only the start,' he said. He hugged Faaz again, and then the imam embraced the other seven men in the tent one by one. 'You have done Islam a great service,' he said. 'You have killed the infidels and shown the world the power that men of pure heart can wield. You should take pride in what you have achieved, and know that you will be blessed by your actions.'

'We want to do more,' said Jaffar. 'Send us out again. We're ready, we're as ready as fuck.'

Faaz held up his hand. 'Brother, you need to contain your enthusiasm.'

The imam smiled and patted Faaz on the shoulder. 'That's all right, Faaz,' he said. 'You are all excited, I understand that. Your mission was a complete success, a perfect victory. The adrenaline will be coursing through your veins. But yesterday was a success because it was planned to perfection. It was perfectly executed, true, but the planning took months. We will not rush into another mission because when we rush, we make mistakes. Another mission is being planned, and trust me brothers, you will not be waiting long. We want to punish the Europeans for helping the Americans murder our people and you will help us to do that.'

Jaffar punched the air. 'Yes!' he said.

'And while we wait we will continue with your training. We need to widen your expertise. We shall be showing you how to construct explosive devices, for example.'

Erol grinned. 'Cool,' he said.

'We also need you to pass on your knowledge to the others about how you were so successful in Cyprus. There are always lessons to be learnt and you have much to teach.'

The men nodded respectfully.

'I will leave you to your meal now, brothers,' said the imam. 'You have earnt it.' He smiled, revealing yellowed teeth and gums speckled with small sores, then turned and left.

Jaffar sat down, grabbed a lamb kebab and began to gnaw on it hungrily. The others also sat down and began reaching for food.

'You know what I really want?' said Abdullah.

'KF fucking C,' said Salmaan Yousif, who was Abdullah's cousin. Both men had been born in war-torn Somalia but had Dutch passports and had lived for many years in London. Salmaan – known as Sal – was shorter than his cousin and his left cheek had a wicked scar running from his eye to his jaw. 'It's all you ever fucking want.'

'KFC is halal so I don't see why they can't sell it in Syria,' said Abdullah. 'The food here is shit.'

'We're not here for the food, Jaffar,' said Mohammed Elsheikh. He was a Pakistani but travelled on a Belgian passport. 'We're here for jihad.'

'I know that, Mo. I'm just saying, would it kill them to open a few KFCs?'

'We've got chicken,' said Faaz, pointing at a dozen or so cubes of white meat on a tin plate.

'How do you know that's chicken?' asked Abdullah, squinting at the plate. 'That could be cat or dog for all I know. Have you seen any chickens in the camp? Because I haven't.'

Faaz sighed. 'We have proper cooks here, they would not serve us cat or dog.' He picked up a piece of meat, popped it into his mouth and chewed it.

Sal grabbed a lamb kebab. 'At least I know this is lamb,' he said, and took a bite.

Sid barked like a dog and everyone except Abdullah and Faaz laughed.

'Brothers, you should not be making fun of the food we have been given,' said Faaz. 'It is disrespectful.'

The men stopped laughing and concentrated on eating.

'Where do you think they will send us?' asked Sid.

'They will not tell us until the last moment,' said Faaz.

'Sure, but he said Europe,' said Mo. 'He doesn't mean England does he?'

'It would be harder to get the guns in the UK,' said Jaffar. 'I think mainland Europe is what he meant. The south of France, maybe. Lots of tourists there, easy pickings.'

Amer shook his head. 'Spain,' he said. 'It'll be Spain. Marbella. Full of rich white kafirs, and Morocco is only a few kilometres across the sea.'

'Gibraltar's even closer,' said Jaffar. 'And it's British.'

Faaz held up his hand. 'Brothers, it is not for us to predict where we will be used, it is our role to carry out the tasks we have been given to the best of our abilities.' He waved his hand at the food. 'Eat, we will need our strength for what is to come.'

Amer grabbed another lamb kebab. He took a bite and then

frowned. 'The imam said we'll be training with explosives. What do you think he means?'

'The stuff that goes bang,' said Jaffar. He mimed an explosion with his hands.

'Yeah, but what sort of explosives is he talking about? We've already done loads of training with bombs. Does he mean suicide vests?'

'That'd be wicked,' said Erol. 'Fucking blowing kafirs into the next world.'

Amer put down his kebab. 'Bruv, there's no way I'm doing the shahid thing. I joined to fight, not to fucking die.'

'No one said anything about dying,' said Jaffar. 'What was it the imam said? Construct explosive devices, that's what he said. And yeah, I'm up for that.'

'What if they want you to wear a vest and blow yourself up?' asked Amer.

Faaz held up his hands. 'Brothers, we are all here to serve Allah as best we can. It's not for us to query the instructions we are given, it is to carry out those instructions as professionally as we can. Now is not the time for second-guessing our betters. It is time to eat, and to celebrate our victory.'

'Fuck yeah!' said Jaffar, punching the air. He lowered his hand when he saw Faaz's eyes narrow disapprovingly. 'Sorry,' he muttered, and reached for a stuffed vine leaf.

CHAPTER 7

Van der Sandt stared out of the window, his face a blank mask. 'Mr Van der Sandt?' It sounded as if the woman's voice was underwater. He felt a gentle touch on his arm and he turned to see Kimmy looking at him anxiously. Kimmy Lee was officially a flight attendant but she was more of a flying PA. She made sure he was fed and watered during his flights, but also handled incoming and outgoing calls and had access to his address book, containing the numbers of the richest and most powerful men in the world. Kimmy was Korean. She was forty years old but could pass for half that. She was wearing a black suit and had sensible flat shoes on that kept her just below five feet tall. She flashed him a worried smile. She had spent the flight at the rear of the plane, leaving him alone with his grief. 'Toni asked me to tell you that we're coming up to the closest we'll get to Paris. On our left.'

'Thank you, Kimmy.'

He looked out of the window. He could make out lights in the distance.

'Shall I serve the champagne?'

'Yes, please, Kimmy.'

She went back to the galley. He stared at the lights. Laura was in the hold, with Sophie, Karl and Lucy. Konuk had managed to arrange coffins despite the short notice and they had been delivered to the airport in four hearses. There had been no paperwork; the bodies had been removed unofficially and everyone who needed paying had been paid. Van der Sandt had watched as the coffins had been placed in the hold by men in dark suits and he had waited until they had driven away before climbing the steps and settling into his seat. Part of him had wanted to put the coffins in the cabin, but the hold would be colder and that would slow the decomposition. He felt tears well up in his eyes and he blinked them away. He could barely believe what had happened. Every time he turned around he expected to see Laura and the kids. He took a deep breath and exhaled slowly.

Kimmy appeared at his shoulder with a bottle of Krug in an ice bucket. It was Laura's favourite champagne. She placed two glasses on the table, and suddenly the tears came. He wiped them and Kimmy looked away as she deftly popped the cork. She poured champagne into both glasses and then left him to it. He picked up one of the glasses and raised it to the window. 'I love you so much, honey. I should have spent more time with you in Paris. I'm sorry. God bless.' He sipped his champagne as tears ran down his cheeks. 'I can promise you one thing,' he said quietly. 'I will make the bastards pay. Every single one of them.'

CHAPTER 8

Sid said the final words of his prayer, touched his forehead to the prayer mat, and got to his feet. Back in Kilburn he had prayed maybe once or twice a day, but at the camp everyone had to fulfil the full quota of prayers. They started with Fajr, the dawn prayer, then that was followed by Zuhr, the early afternoon prayer, Asr, the late afternoon prayer, Maghrib, the sunset prayer, and finally the night prayer, Isha'a. After the night prayer they went to the barracks to sleep. There were no fires and no electricity and even if there had been power they were forbidden from switching on their phones. It had been explained to them that the Americans could track all phones and they could use them to target the Hellfire missiles fired from killer drones high up in the sky. That was how the Americans liked to fight, from a distance. It was the coward's way, the imams always said. Real men, real warriors, looked their enemy in the eyes when they killed them. Cowards fought from the safety of their desks, thousands of kilometres away from the battlefield. That was why the West would eventually lose the fight and Islam would win.

Life in the camp was tough, but Sid had known it would be before he joined up. The men showered first thing in the morning and before Isha'a prayers, and washed with a wet towel for the rest of the prayers. Water was pumped from an underground well and was in relatively short supply. Food and other supplies came in on a truck once a day, or when new fighters arrived for training. The meal they had been given when they returned from Cyprus had been a celebration feast; usually they ate twice a day – a piece of meat, some bread, yoghurt and fruit.

Days were filled with praying, physical fitness, being taught about the Koran, and military training. It was only the training that interested Sid. He prayed because he had to pray and did it so many times that his mind almost always wandered as he went through the motions. Fitness training was fine, but Sid was already as fit as the proverbial butcher's dog. He could do sit-ups and press-ups by the score, and as with praying his mind would wander freely as he toiled away.

He had to be more focused during Koran studies, as the imams were expert at spotting anyone who wasn't giving their full attention. Teaching took place in the tent where they had had their victory feast, usually in groups of between ten and twenty. The imams were all in their sixties and seventies. They had long beards and skin as dark as molasses from exposure to the fierce Syrian sun, their faces and hands mottled and wrinkled. But while their bodies were aging, their minds were sharp and they knew every word of the Koran by heart. They tended to be selective in their teachings, though, concentrating on those passages that encouraged violence against disbelievers. According to the imams, the disbelievers were filthy and untouchable and impure and were destined for hell. It was the duty of every Muslim to fight and kill all disbelievers until Islam was the only religion. They seemed to relish one particular phrase – that all Muslims should 'slay or crucify or cut off the hands and feet of the unbelievers, that they be expelled from the land with disgrace and that they shall have a great punishment in the world hereafter.'

The imams made it clear that they were never to befriend a non-believer. A theme that came up again and again was that the Koran wanted good Muslims to strike fear into the hearts of their enemies and that jihad was not a matter of choice, it was compulsory.

There were no women in the camp and there was a distinct misogynistic tone to the teaching. They were left in no doubt that the book of Allah regarded women as inferior to men and that if they were disobedient they could be beaten. Sid had suppressed a smile at that – he knew plenty of Muslim sisters back in London who would not react well to having a finger laid on them. The jihadists were free to have four wives, but they could have sex with as many slave maids or captives as they wanted, and it was permitted – in fact encouraged – for soldiers to rape the women of any country they subdued. The imams had explained that it was the duty of every good Muslim to have sex with as many kafir girls as possible and to impregnate them.

Sid struggled to pay attention and to even appear to be interested in the lectures – in reality all he cared about was the military training. That was why he had come to Syria in the first place, to acquire the skills he needed to fight and kill for Islam. They trained with various pistols and with AK-47s, and they were drilled in the use of RPGs, though they had never been allowed to actually fire one. They were taught how to storm houses, and how to defend them. They were shown the best way to kill close up, and how to ensure the maximum number of casualties when attacking a group. Much of the training was done without ammunition as supplies were running low, but they had been assured that more bullets were on the way. There had been extensive training in explosives, too. Grizzled ISIS warriors had showed them how to construct bombs from generally available substances such as weedkiller and fuel oil, but they had also been taught how to use Semtex and C4, how to use commercial detonators and how to set up trip wires and timers. It was all good stuff, and while Sid was happy enough in Syria he looked forward to the day when he could use the skills he had acquired against his own country.

Sid and his comrades had given lectures of their own, telling and retelling the story of their operation in Northern Cyprus, how it was planned and put together, how they got in and out of the country, and describing the killings. They were asked the same question every time: 'What did it feel like, killing the kafirs?' The answer was always the same: 'Good. It felt fucking good.' But in his heart of heart, Sid was having second thoughts. He had been so caught up in the euphoria of planning the operation that he hadn't given much thought to what he would find on the beach. He knew he would be attacking kafir holidaymakers but it was only when he had climbed off his jet ski that it had hit home that many of the targets were women and children. He shuddered at the memory and tried to blot it out, or at least push it to the back of his mind. He stretched and arched his back. Amer patted him on the shoulder. 'You okay, bruv?'

'All good, bruv,' said Sid, faking a smile.

'You know we're doing suicide vests soon?'

'Yeah?'

'For sure. They've sent some hot shot in who's been doing it in Kabul. He's a fucking legend apparently and I heard that next time we're going to be doing a hotel in Spain. The suicide bombers will be going into the hotel and when the survivors run out, we pop them.'

'Where did you hear that?'

'Jaffar, I think.'

'No one tells Jaffar nothing,' said Sid.

'Nah, bruv, he said he got it off one of the imams.' He patted him on the shoulder again. 'Come on, get a move on. If you're late for breakfast all the good stuff will have gone.' He hurried over to the tent where the morning meal was being served. Sid hurried after him. If what Jaffar had heard was true, plans were being made for another attack. His heart began to race and he tried to calm himself down. Hopefully Amer was wrong and this time he would be attacking a military target and not women and children. But whatever was being planned would take time – the ISIS chiefs never rushed into anything.

CHAPTER 9

Van der Sandt checked out his suit and tie in the mirror. Black suit, white shirt, black tie, black shoes. There wasn't much leeway when it came to dressing for a funeral. He smiled as he imagined Laura looking at him, tilting her head on one side as she always did when she was being critical. 'Are you sure you're going to wear that tie?' she'd ask, usually with one eyebrow raised.

He'd always smile and say the fact that he'd knotted it around his neck was probably a clue, then she'd tut and go to his tie rack and choose the one that she thought would suit him better. She was always right, of course. About pretty much everything.

He saw movement in the mirror and whirled around. There was a drone about fifty feet from the house. A white one, a couple of feet across with a small camera underneath it. 'Fucking vultures,' he muttered under his breath. He stormed out of the bedroom and along the corridor to his gunroom. It wasn't far off the size of a basketball court, the walls lined with the trophies that he had been allowed to bring into the US before the government had banned the importation of trophies. There were two stuffed tigers and a stuffed lion, and easy chairs and sofas made of the hides of his kills. There were half a dozen hides and skins on the floor, including a polar bear and a cheetah with the head still intact, staring at him glassy-eyed. There was also the largest crocodile he'd ever killed, a monster that had been stuffed and mounted with its jaws wide open.

His gun cabinet was at the far end of the room and he walked quickly over to it. The guns were hidden behind wooden doors that were lined with steel, and he had to place his thumb on a reader to open them. He put his hands on his hips as he surveyed the two dozen weapons on display. His pride and joy – the William Evans double-barrelled sidelock – was on a rack in the middle of the display, but he knew that an elephant gun was not the weapon of choice for a drone. He picked up a Purdey 20-Bore Sporter over-and-under shotgun, manufactured by the London firm in partnership with Perugini & Visini. It had been built to his specifications, with a longer barrel than usual for greater accuracy and a Turkish walnut stock, and was one of several guns that he used when he went pheasant shooting, usually with royalty, in the Scottish Highlands.

He grabbed two cartridges and loaded the weapon as he walked back down the corridor to his bedroom. He held the gun in his left hand as he opened the window with his right. The drone was still hovering, the camera pointed at the entrance to the house. Van der Sandt shouldered the weapon, aimed, braced himself for the recoil and pulled the trigger. There was a satisfying bang and the drone disintegrated into a dozen pieces that scattered over the lawn. Van der Sandt lowered the weapon and looked around for a second target, and when none was to be found he closed the window and took the shotgun back to the gunroom. He ejected the cartridges, put the unused one back in its box and the used one on a shelf. He smiled at the thought of mounting the smashed drone on a plaque, along with the cartridge. It'd be a talking point, once he felt like talking again.

He locked up the guns and went downstairs. His PA was there, in a black dress and black heels. Catherine Shirley had worked for him for the best part of fifteen years and she had never let him down. Her salary had risen in line with her professionalism and she now earnt more than many company chairmen, but she was worth every penny. Over the years she had developed the knack of anticipating his every move, to the extent that sometimes it felt as if she was reading his mind.

'The car's ready, Mr Van der Sandt,' she said quietly.

'Thank you, Catherine,' he said. 'Will you ride with me? I'd appreciate the company.'

'Of course, Mr Van der Sandt.'

He flashed her a smile and walked across the marble-tiled hallway, under the massive crystal chandelier that Laura had imported from Milan, and down the stone steps to where a black Bentley was waiting. The liveried chauffeur already had the door open and waited until Van der Sandt was seated before closing the door and hurrying around the vehicle to open the door for Catherine.

Van der Sandt took slow, deep breaths as the car drove away from the house. He had lived there with Laura for almost twenty years and all three of their children had been born at the local hospital. Laura had always complained that the house was far too large – it had twenty-two bedrooms, a ballroom, and a dining room that could host a dinner for forty people. The landscaped grounds included a tennis court, a helicopter landing pad next to a large metal hangar, an orchard and a vegetable garden that alone required three full-time gardeners to keep in order. In all there were a dozen men and women working full time to maintain the grounds. The estate, surrounded by a high wall topped by CCTV cameras, was close to forty-five acres – which Van der Sandt liked to boast was larger than the grounds around Buckingham Palace – including a three-acre lake stocked with trout. Van der Sandt owned another twenty thousand acres of forest, stretching almost all the way to the Canadian border.

The main gate was half a mile away from the house and as they drove towards it Van der Sandt looked over at a herd of deer that roamed free among the trees. Laura had insisted on the deer, and made him promise never to raise a gun against them. She had also drawn up a programme to introduce wolves into the surrounding forest, as if that would in some way compensate for the animals he killed.

There was a security block by the entrance and a man there opened the gates electronically. There were six security people on duty day and night, overseen by a former Seattle police captain. The men and women on the security team had special dispensation to carry handguns, but on Laura's instructions they had to be casually dressed and the guns had to remain hidden at all times.

'How many will be there?' he asked Catherine, as the Bentley slowly pulled away onto the main road.

'Thirty-seven,' she said.

Van der Sandt grimaced. He had wanted the funeral to be a private family affair and as he had no relatives to speak of, that meant Laura's parents, her brother and his wife, and a handful of cousins that she had always been close to. Nine mourners, ten at the most. But he knew that many of his friends and business associates would take it as an insult if they weren't allowed to pay their respects. He understood – it wasn't that they wanted to intrude on his personal grief, it was because they wanted to show that they cared and, more importantly, that they would support him. Without being asked, Catherine began to run through the names of those who would be at the church. There were four members of the British Royal Family, one former US president, three senators, and the chief executives of eight Fortune 500 companies. All of Laura's friends in the fashion world and Hollywood had stayed away, probably because they knew that their presence would detract from the solemnity of the occasion, and he was grateful to them for that.

'We have three security perimeters in place,' said Catherine, anticipating the next question. 'There are police checkpoints on the roads to the church turning away most people. They have no legal right to refuse access, so if someone insists, they have to be allowed through. Obviously the ones who have insisted so far, I'm told, are the journalists, TV crews and paparazzi. Inside is a second perimeter of our own security people who are offering financial incentives for them to turn back. Quite a number of the paparazzi and the freelance journalists have taken the money. The TV crews have apparently continued on, along with several of the paparazzi, but they have been prevented from entering the grounds of the church by the third perimeter, which is again local law enforcement. They will arrest anyone who sets foot on the church grounds. So far as them getting pictures, we have erected barriers around the church, using foliage and trees wherever possible. All the guests have been driven to the church in cars with tinted windows and they can access the church at the rear without being seen.'

Van der Sandt nodded his approval. 'Nice job, Catherine.' He settled back and closed his eyes. He rode the rest of the way to the church in silence and didn't open his eyes until the car slowed close to the entrance to the church grounds. There were a dozen men in weatherproof gear holding cameras and they crowded around the Bentley. There were three camera crews also jostling for position. 'Vultures,' muttered Van der Sandt again under his breath. 'Actually, they're worse than vultures. At least vultures serve a purpose in the grand scheme of things.'

The Bentley had to slow to a crawl to avoid hitting the cameramen, which gave them the opportunity to crowd even closer. There were four uniformed policemen wearing hi-vis jackets at the gateway to the car park. One of them was holding a clipboard and he checked that the registration number was on the list before nodding at a colleague to open the gate. The Bentley drove in and its tyres crunched across the gravelled drive. Tall fir trees in large tubs had been lined up either side of the driveway and as the car turned to the right towards the church the trees blocked the view from the gate. The police closed the gate and stood with folded arms, glaring at the photographers with undisguised contempt.

There were more than twenty black limousines with tinted windows already parked. The Bentley came to a halt. The driver got out and hurried around to open the door for Van der Sandt, but Van der Sandt beat him to it and the driver opened the door for Catherine instead.

Van der Sandt walked to the rear entrance of the church. It had been built almost a hundred years ago; the stone had weathered and was mottled with moss. It was the church he and his family had used ever since he had bought the estate, though Laura and the children were there far more often than he was. As he walked, Catherine followed close by. There were two of

Van der Sandt's security team standing either side of the arched door wearing black suits and wraparound dark glasses, with earpieces connected to whatever radio system was keeping them in the loop. Both men stood as still as statues with their hands clasped together over their groins.

The oak door was open and Van der Sandt walked through to a flagstone corridor that opened into the nave of the church. The mourners filled less than a third of the pews and all eyes turned towards him as he walked to the front and sat down.

The service took less than an hour. The coffins came in with the priest, and there were readings from the Bible, and two hymns. It was a Catholic service so there was no eulogy, and Van der Sandt was grateful for that. There was no way he could talk about the lives of his wife and children without mentioning what had happened and what he planned to do about it. Far better just to say goodbye. After the service the coffins were taken out to the graveyard. Van der Sandt was one of six men who carried Laura's coffin. The others were Laura's brother, two of her cousins, the former president and a British prince.

The coffins were interred but Van der Sandt was barely aware of the committal service. He stood staring at the coffins, willing himself not to cry until it was all over.

Once the service was done, Van der Sandt shook the priest's hand and thanked him, then began shaking hands with the mourners. He could see the concern and sympathy in their eyes but he met their glances with a grim smile and a firm handshake. He accepted their condolences with a nod, and he thanked them for their offers of support, should he need it. They knew that he didn't need help from anyone, but he appreciated the offers and knew that they were genuine.

As Van der Sandt shook the hand of the last of the mourners, a man in his forties with prematurely grey hair walked over. It was Neil Thomas, head of security for Van der Sandt's company. 'I'm so sorry about your loss,' said Thomas. He was wearing a black coat over his black suit and tie, and there was no way the casual observer would know that he was missing his right leg below the knee, the result of an IED explosion in Iraq that had ended his military career. Thomas had been a master sergeant in Delta Force, with twelve years under his belt, when the vehicle he was in was hit by a barrel of explosive in a culvert under the road. Two of his comrades were killed instantly in the blast, and Thomas was only saved because there was a US helicopter nearby that was able to airlift him to a medical facility.

Van der Sandt shook hands with him. The left side of his face was peppered with small scars and the ear was ragged, a result of the blast.

'Thank you for coming,' said Van der Sandt.

Thomas gestured over at the entrance to the churchyard. 'I'm sorry we couldn't keep the media away, but the church is on a public road so our options are limited.'

'They'll get their pictures one way or another,' said Van der Sandt. 'I shot down a drone this morning.'

Thomas chuckled. 'That'll teach them,' he said.

Van der Sandt shook his head. 'No, they'll keep coming. The public has an insatiable craving for gossip and the media feeds it. "Billionaire financier loses family in terrorist attack" becomes clickbait. It's the way of the world.'

Van der Sandt looked over at Catherine. 'I'll ride back with Neil,' he said.

'Of course, Mr Van der Sandt.'

Van der Sandt and Thomas walked over to a black stretch Mercedes limousine and climbed into the back. Van der Sandt pressed a button to raise the privacy screen as the car headed out of the churchyard.

'So, where do we stand?' he asked Thomas.

'The men are all presently at an ISIS training facility in Aleppo Province in Syria,' Thomas replied. 'US Forces have been active in the area but that part of north-west Syria is still very much a safe haven for ISIS. They've been using the camp to train their people and plan attacks in the region and beyond.'

'You can get to them?'

'Subject to being allocated enough resources, yes.'

'Money is no object,' said Van der Sandt.

'Then we can get to them, for sure,' said Thomas.

'I don't want them killed, Neil,' said Van der Sandt. 'Not in Syria, anyway. I want them brought here.'

Thomas frowned. 'You want to put them on trial in the States?'

Van der Sandt smiled thinly. 'Not exactly. Where are they from?'

'They're a mixed bag,' said Thomas. 'Four of them are British. Home-grown jihadists, born in the UK but radicalised at some point. Of the four, two are from Bradford, in the north of England, and two are from London. They were known to the UK anti-terrorism police and were under surveillance before they slipped off the grid and reappeared in Syria.'

Van der Sandt shook his head. 'It's an island, how hard is it to stop people leaving?'

'The Brits tend to be good at surveillance but not quite so good at taking action,' said Thomas. 'Often their law enforcement agencies are shackled by political correctness. We've got excellent sources in MI5 and the Metropolitan Police so we have full details on all four men. They've been behind a number of beheadings of journalists and NGO workers in Syria and are very active on social media.'

'I don't get this whole home-grown terrorist thing in the UK,' said Van der Sandt. 'These people fight to get into a safe country and once they're in they turn against it. It doesn't happen in the US, does it? When was the last time you heard about a jihadist with a US passport?'

'These guys were never refugees, they were all born in the UK,' said Thomas. 'The problem seems to be the British mosques, where they recruit disaffected youth and groom them to be jihadists. And the internet, of course.'

'The internet's worldwide, but we don't see American Muslims being converted,' said Van der Sandt. 'The Brits need to get their act together.'

'No argument from me,' said Thomas. 'Anyway, two of the others are Somalians with Dutch passports. The Dutch government gave them asylum and fast-tracked them to citizenship. As soon as they got their Dutch passports they moved to the UK. We've done some digging and it looks as if they weren't your run-of-the-mill asylum seekers fleeing a war zone. Their uncle was a warlord behind several ship seizures ten years ago.'

'A pirate?'

'Responsible for ransoms totalling more than twenty million dollars. The story I'm told is that the uncle paid for the nephews to get to Holland.'

'And the Dutch never checked?'

'Most of Europe are known to be lax when it comes to assigning refugee status,' said Thomas. 'Anyway, the two Somalians dropped below the radar at the same time as the Brits, and then resurfaced at a training camp in Syria. And then there are two more,' Thomas continued. 'One is a Pakistani with a Belgian passport. He claimed to be from Afghanistan and on the run from the Taliban, but we've spoken to family members in Pakistan and there's no doubt it's him. Then the final guy is from Finland. His parents are from Bangladesh but he was born in Finland. He left the country more than fifteen years ago and has been with ISIS for more than a decade. He was the oldest of the group so there's a good chance he led the attack.'

'And they're all in the same training camp now?'

Thomas nodded. 'According to the intel we have, they went straight there after the attack. They're instructing other jihadists on the techniques they used. But we have no idea how long they'll be there.'

'So you go get them now, Neil. Money no object. Just do what needs to be done.'

'Not a problem, Mr Van der Sandt. I already have a team in place and I have guys working on the logistics as we speak.'

'And what about the attack itself? Did they have help?'

'We think so but we don't have any hard intel as yet. As you probably know, the north of the island is a very grey area under international law. It's only recognised by the Turks, because they invaded back in 1974. Most Turkish Cypriots are Sunni Muslims, and some are pro-ISIS. Intel suggests that ISIS has been using Northern Cyprus to get its people from Syria in and out of Europe. Foreign fighters from Europe can fly straight to the south of Cyprus, then cross the border into the north and fly from there to Turkey, Syria or Iraq.'

'So they had help from locals?'

'Maybe, maybe not,' said Thomas. 'They rented the jet skis themselves using fake Turkish passports. And they used the same passports to register at the hotel they were staying in. If they were being helped they would probably have stayed under the radar completely and avoided hotels. The thing is, they probably don't care that their identities are known. The opposite in fact; there are several gloating videos that keep appearing on Facebook and YouTube. They get taken down but they're like cockroaches – you stamp on one and two more pop up.'

'How did they leave the island?'

'They weren't on any scheduled flights and so far as we can tell they weren't on a private flight, so we're assuming they left by boat. Either to Turkey and then on to Syria, or maybe to Syria direct.'

'What about the lack of police response?' asked Van der Sandt.

'We're looking at that,' said Thomas. 'More than a dozen calls were made to the emergency services, some within a few seconds of the first shots being fired. But the police didn't arrive until after the shooters had left. The chief of police is a Muslim but then so is most of the force.'

'The police station is ten minutes away from the resort, right?'

Thomas shrugged. 'But it's not an efficient police force by any means. The question is whether or not anyone in the cops helped facilitate the attack and we're looking at that. The difficulty is that if they did help it would probably have been for ideological reasons rather than for money, so there's no paper trail. I'm on the case, Mr Van der Sandt. If they were helped by someone locally, we'll know eventually.'

They arrived at the entrance to Van der Sandt's estate. The gates opened and a female member of the security team came out of the gatehouse and waved them through. 'Will you be going over?' asked Van der Sandt.

'I've a first-class operator in Turkey who will run the operation in Syria,' said Thomas. 'Colin Bell, former lieutenant colonel with Delta. He's a contractor these days but has all the contacts we need. He doesn't need me looking over his shoulder.'

'Sounds like a plan,' said Van der Sandt. 'Let me know if you need more funding. And come straight to me. I know you often deal with Catherine Shirley but on this you deal with me direct.'

'I understand, Mr Van der Sandt.'

'This Colin Bell, and his team – they know this is to be done on the QT?'

'The amount they're being paid, they won't say a word to anybody.'

Van der Sandt smiled thinly. 'Thanks for this, Neil.'

'No need to thank me, Mr Van der Sandt. Those bastards deserve what's coming to them.'

The limousine pulled up outside the mansion. Van der Sandt climbed out. He bent down and spoke to the driver. 'Take Mr Thomas wherever he needs to go,' he said. The driver saluted and Van der Sandt closed the door, then watched as the car drove away. He turned and looked up at the house. He'd sell it, eventually. There was no way he could live there without Laura and the children. There were too many memories. But that was down the line. First there were things he needed to do, and the house and the estate would play a crucial role in his plans.

CHAPTER 10

There were more than a hundred men at Zuhr prayers, the early afternoon worship, and those that couldn't fit into the main tent performed the ritual outside, their prayer mats on the desert floor. As usual Sid prayed on autopilot, spending most of the time thinking about the killings he'd seen early that morning. A group of ISIS fighters had arrived in a pick-up truck, with two bound and hooded kafirs in the back. The prisoners were American journalists who had been captured at an ISIS checkpoint. The men were freelancers and the decision had been taken to not bother asking for a ransom but to kill them immediately.

They were beheaded in front of the shower block. An ISIS flag had been nailed to the wall and the two men had been given orange jumpsuits to wear before being forced to kneel down and to beg their president to stop killing Muslims around the world. Their appeals were filmed on a small video camera, then two men, their faces covered with scarves, used machetes to hack off their heads. The way the men struggled and the blood spurted down their chests as their eyes had bulged in terror was something Sid would never forget.

When the prayers were over, Amer came over, clearly excited about something. 'Bruv, that vest guy is here. The suicide vest expert. He's going to be showing us what to do.'

'Cool,' said Sid.

Amer patted him on the back. 'Show some more enthusiasm, bruv.'

Sid grimaced. 'I don't like the whole explosives thing,' he said. 'We're fighters. We're warriors. Bombs are . . . cowardly.'

'There's nothing cowardly about a suicide bomber,' said Amer. 'Blowing yourself up to kill infidels – that takes balls.'

'Bruv, the shahids are usually borderline retarded. They get talked into it. Or forced to do it. I heard that sometimes they ply them with drugs before they do it.'

Amer lowered his voice and put his face closer to Sid's. 'Don't let the imams hear you talk like that, bruv.'

'I'm not stupid,' said Sid. 'But I don't believe everything I've been told.'

Amer opened his mouth to say something, but then he turned his head away.

'What?' said Sid. 'Something on your mind?'

Amer shifted his weight from foot to foot. 'I saw what you did on the beach, bruv,' he said quietly.

'What do you mean?'

Amer looked around to make sure that no one was within earshot. 'You know what I mean. You fired high.'

'I did what?'

'You fired high, bruv. You had a bead on that woman and her kids and you lifted the gun before you pulled the trigger and the rounds went high. Then Jaffar fired and they went down and you ran up the beach to the hotel.'

'Are you on something, man? Why the fuck would you say that?'

'Because I saw it with my own eyes.' He lowered his voice and put his head closer to Sid's. 'Don't worry, I haven't said nothing to nobody. But I saw what I saw.'

Sid grabbed Amer by the elbow. 'If you tell anyone, I'm fucking dead.'

'Hell, bruv, you think I don't know that? I'm just saying I know, that's all.'

'I couldn't shoot kids,' whispered Sid. 'Or their mum. I just couldn't do it.'

'I hear you.'

'That's not what I signed up for. I thought I'd be fighting troops, like a soldier. Not butchering women and children.'

'It's about inspiring terror, bruv. It's nothing personal. And at the end of the day, a kafir's a kafir.'

Sid released his grip on Amer's arm. 'Yeah, you're right.'

'Look bruv, I understand, I do. You're a brother, but on that day you were killing your own. Most of the people on that beach were white, like you. If we'd been attacking Asian holidaymakers then maybe I'd be feeling the same.'

'I'm a Muslim first, Amer.'

'I know you are. No one's saying you're not. It's no biggie, you killed your fair share of kafirs that day, no one's complaining.' Amer patted him on the back, put his arm around him and the two men walked towards the training area at the edge of the camp. There was a shooting range and an obstacle course that they had to complete several times a week. Several dozen fighters had already gathered there.

They saw Faaz talking to Sal and went over to join them. 'Bruv, how long do you think they will keep us at the camp?' Amer asked Faaz.

Faaz smiled and patted him on the shoulder. 'Your impatience is admirable, brother, but there is no need to rush.'

'I'm as trained as I need to be,' said Amer. 'I'm wasting my time here.'

'Training time is never wasted time, brother,' said Faaz.

'I don't need to be taught how to make suicide vests,' said Amer. 'We need to be on the offensive. We need to keep striking fear into the hearts of the kafirs.'

'We will, brother. And soon. But in the meantime, better to train than to just sit idle.'

An elderly man with a white beard and thick-lensed spectacles walked over from the admin block. He was holding a large cardboard box and behind him was a younger man in a white thobe who was carrying a mannequin. Fighters gathered around them, intrigued by the mannequin. The elderly man put the box on a wooden trestle table and pulled out a brown canvas vest with multiple pockets. He put it on the mannequin. Sid saw Amer approach the man and talk to him. Sid grinned at Amer's obvious enthusiasm.

'We should get closer and hear what he has to say,' Faaz said to Sid.

They walked towards the crowd. There were more than fifty men there and more were heading that way from the barracks. Amer was stroking the vest, and saying something to the old man, when all of a sudden there was a flash of light and a deafening bang – and then the sound of men screaming in pain and terror.

CHAPTER 11

The woman was bleeding to death and there was nothing Raj Patel could do about it. And her unborn child was in an even worse state. He stared down at the gaping wound in the woman's abdomen and at the bullet lodged in the head of the baby. 'I don't know what to do,' he said. He looked at the half dozen masked faces, all staring at him and waiting for a decision. The woman had been wheeled into the operating theatre ten minutes earlier, the victim of a sniper who had taken to shooting pregnant women in the stomach. The anaesthetist had put her under right away, they had put her on a blood drip and Raj had opened her up. But as soon as he saw the internal damage, Raj realised there was nothing he could do. The bullet had tumbled through the woman's liver before destroying the baby's brain. The liver was beyond repair and that meant removal was his only option, but there was no dialysis equipment in the hospital and no chance of a transplant. The baby's chest was still moving and its heart was still beating but the damage to the brain meant that even if he could keep it alive, it would never leave the hospital. The faces staring at him were blank. At first Raj didn't recognise them but then one by one he realised who they were. His mother. His father. Dr Williams, his mentor back at St Mary's Hospital in London. Ricky, his childhood friend who had died from leukaemia when he was at primary school and whose death had set him on course to being a doctor. Raj looked at his blood-stained hands. He wasn't wearing surgical gloves, he realised. Or a mask. In fact he wasn't wearing anything. He was naked. Stark bollock naked. The baby was crying, and Raj looked down at it. Its bloody hands were reaching up to him. 'Help my mother, Dr Raj. Please help her Dr Raj.'

Raj opened his mouth to scream but then he woke up, gasping for breath. A Syrian nurse was standing over him. 'Dr Raj, I'm sorry,' she said. 'Dr Eloias needs you in the theatre.'

'Right, yes, sorry.' He sat up. His face was bathed in sweat and his mouth was bone dry. The nurse was Amira. She had been with the hospital from the day it had opened for business, six years earlier. She was in her forties and had a no-nonsense approach. She always spoke her mind, which was unusual in a society where women were generally subjugated. 'What's happening, Amira?' he asked. He looked at his watch. It wasn't yet midday and he had dropped down onto his cot bed at nine in the morning after sixteen straight hours in the operating theatre.

'We've had three casualties brought in and Dr Eloias is on his own.'

'Where's Ahmed? He's on call.'

'He's gone out to deal with two children who were hurt in an explosion. They can't be moved. Dr Mahdi and Dr Karam are in the surgery and there are dozens of patients waiting. There is only you, Dr Raj, I'm sorry.'

There were just seven full-time doctors at the hospital and two had been injured in a bombing three days earlier. That left only five and five was barely enough to handle the emergency cases. Up until three months ago there had been twenty doctors, but after a spate of bombings and an increase in sniper attacks, all the foreign doctors with the exception of Raj had left. He understood why. The day-to-day conditions were bad enough, but most of the doctors who had left had families and the increase in attacks meant it had simply become too dangerous for them to be there.

Raj swung his legs over the side of his cot. He hadn't bothered to undress and was still wearing his stained T-shirt and scrubs. Amira held out a bottle of water. He grinned, took it from her, and gulped some down, then slipped on his sandals and followed her out of the cupboard-sized room that the medics used as a crash pad. They walked down the tiled corridor to what was laughably referred to as the operating theatre. It was a window-less room with an air conditioner. The room was powered by a generator, necessary because they were always being hit by power cuts. There were two operating tables and a decent lighting system, courtesy of a crowdfunding appeal organised by a group of Syrian doctors who were now working for the NHS in London. The equipment had arrived with much-needed medicine on two trucks that had driven across Europe to the Turkey–Syria border. The medicines had long gone but the lights still worked.

There was a small washing area outside the theatre and Raj quickly but efficiently washed his hands and arms. A nurse helped him on with his gown and he pulled on a mask and gloves. Eloias looked up from his patient as Raj walked in. He was a big man, his shaved head covered with a surgical hat and mask. 'Sorry, Raj,' he said. 'I know you must be exhausted.'

There were two nurses assisting Eloias and a third dealing with the anaesthetic. Three more nurses were standing at the second operating table, waiting for Raj. 'Gunshot wound,' said Eloias, gesturing with his surgical scissors at the second table. 'It needs handling now.' Raj stopped and a cold hand gripped his heart as his dream flashed back to him, but then he saw that the patient was a man and he relaxed. 'Left thigh,' said Eloias. He was the hospital's most experienced doctor and had been its director for the past year, ever since the previous holder of the post had given up and gone back to Turkey.

'Fuck,' said Raj. 'Are you kidding me?' There had been six thigh wounds so far that week and it was only Wednesday. The previous week most of the sniper wounds had been to the left shoulder. It was as if the snipers were having some sort of competition between themselves. It would have been just as easy to shoot their victims in the head, but the snipers wanted to leave them alive to put the hospitals under pressure. Neither side in the conflict respected the neutrality of hospitals – they were bombed and attacked as much as government buildings or rebel strong-holds. Hospital staff had painted over the red crosses on their ambulances as they had clearly become targets, and doctors and nurses never went outside wearing medical outfits after several nurses had been shot leaving the hospital.

Raj went over and looked down at the thigh wound. It was bad. Someone had put a tourniquet above the wound but even so the man had clearly lost a lot of blood. Blood was always in short supply at the hospital, as were most things. The only thing they had a regular supply of was patients.

The bullet was a big one and had broken into at least four pieces that he could see. The thigh bone was shattered and several blood vessels were mangled. The nurse on his left handed him a pair of tweezers and he smiled his thanks. He dug out the fragments and placed them in a metal tray, then asked for suction to clear the blood that was pooling in the wound.

Raj flinched at the sound of gunfire. It sounded as if it was coming from inside the hospital. Automatic fire, probably a Kalashnikov. He looked over at Eloias. The older doctor looked anxious, but Raj bent back down over his patient.

Raj looked over at the door, then carried on working on the damaged blood vessels. There was a rapid footfall on the concrete outside and then the door was shouldered open. A young man, bearded with a grey skullcap, stood in the doorway holding an AK-47. For a second, Raj thought he was going to spray the room with bullets, but then he stepped aside to let another man walk in. He was white with sun-bleached hair, and was also carrying an AK-47. He had a black-and-white checked keffiyeh around his neck and had shielded his eyes with wraparound sunglasses. 'Who's in charge?' he barked in Arabic, in what sounded like an English accent.

After almost a year in Syria, Raj's Arabic was good enough to hold a conversation, but he knew that any native speaker would know he wasn't local. He took a quick look over at Eloias who was about to speak but silenced him with a stare. 'That'd be me,' Raj said to the man, in English.

The man looked at him. 'You're English?' he asked, taking off his sunglasses to reveal pale blue eyes. He had a sprinkling of freckles across his snub nose and old acne scars on his cheeks.

Raj nodded.

'Where are you from, bruv?' asked the man.

'Maida Vale. West London.'

'I know where Maida Vale is bruv, I'm from Kilburn, just down the road.' He put the glasses back on. 'What's your name?'

'Rajesh – Raj.'

'All right, Raj, mate. My name's Sid. You run the show, yeah?'

'I'm the hospital director.'

'But you're a doctor, right?'

Raj held up his scalpel and tweezers. A third man appeared in the doorway. He was wearing a baggy grey shirt and pale green baggy trousers and was also holding a Kalashnikov. 'What's the problem?' he asked.

'No problem, Jaffar, keep your knickers on,' said Sid. He waved his gun at Eloias. 'Who's he?' he asked.

'He's a local,' said Raj. 'A nurse. He's getting the patient ready for me.'

'You're the only doctor here?'

'We've one doctor out on a job and two were injured in an explosion yesterday. Why, do you have a casualty with you?'

Sid shook his head. 'We need you at our camp. We've got a lot of guys hurt there.'

'Bring them here,' said Raj.

'Nah, bruv, you're one Mohammed that's going to have to visit the mountain.'

'My name's Raj, not Mohammed. And I have to finish these patients first.'

The man called Jaffar stepped towards the operating table and looked down at the unconscious patient. Then in one smooth movement he raised his AK-47 and shot him three times in the chest. The man twitched and went still and blood began to pool over the table. 'He's finished,' said Jaffar.

'Jaffar, what the fuck!' shouted Sid.

'We don't have time to piss around!' shouted Jaffar.

'Bruv, you need to calm down and take your finger off that trigger,' said Sid.

Jaffar gritted his teeth as he stared at Sid, but then he relaxed and slid his finger out of the trigger guard. 'We need to get back to the camp, Sid. Our guys are dying.'

'I hear you, but we don't kill people for the fun of it, bruv.'

'It wasn't fun, I was showing him we're serious.'

Raj's ears were ringing from the gunshots and the cordite was stinging his eyes. Jaffar took a step towards Eloias's patient and raised his gun. 'Bruv, don't!' Sid shouted, but Jaffar ignored him and sighted on the patient's chest.

'No!' shouted Raj. 'I'll come with you.'

Jaffar turned to look at him. 'Good call,' he said. He lowered his Kalashnikov and grinned at Sid. 'See, now he sees sense.'

Raj put down his scalpel and tweezers and stepped away from the table. 'Can I at least change?' he asked, taking off his mask and gloves.

Jaffar shook his head. 'We've got clothes in the camp,' he said. He gestured with his gun. 'Outside.'

Raj took off his gown and dropped it on the table. He threw Eloias a last worried look, and they headed out. The three armed men took him down the corridor and into the main reception area where a fourth man had herded a dozen patients into a corner and was covering them with his gun.

'Bring painkillers and shit,' Sid said to Raj.

'We need all our medicines here,' said Raj. 'We don't have any to spare.'

Jaffar levelled his AK-47 at Raj's stomach. 'Bruv, I'll quite happily put a bullet in you now and see if your colleague can follow instructions without mouthing off.'

'Okay, okay,' said Raj. He grabbed a backpack and went along to the supply room. He grabbed a selection of painkillers, then threw in some bandages and dressings.

They went outside where a rusting pick-up truck was waiting, its engine running. Another armed man stood by it, his Kalashnikov at the ready. 'Get in,' said Sid.

Raj climbed into the back of the truck. The armed men got in after him. The guy who had been waiting for them got into the front passenger seat and the truck drove off in a cloud of dust.

CHAPTER 12

There were forty men in the hangar, chatting and joking, the buzz of their conversations echoing off the metal walls. They were all wearing military fatigues but without any markings. They had handguns and tasers in holsters and most had Heckler & Koch carbines in their hands or on their backs. They fell silent as the man leading the operation walked in. His name was Colin Bell and he had served in Delta Force for almost two decades before losing a hand to a sniper's bullet in Afghanistan. His left hand was replaced by a prosthesis or a more serviceable hook, depending on his circumstances. Today he had installed the hook. He walked over to three whiteboards at one side of the hangar, which was part of Incirlik Air Base, thirty kilometres inland from the Mediterranean Sea in the city of Adana. The airbase had a single three thousand-metre runway and hardened aircraft shelters and was where America stored tactical nuclear weapons in case they were needed in the region. There were about five thousand US airmen at the base, but the men in the hangar didn't work for the military. They were all contractors and their CVs covered many of the world's most dangerous spots, including Iraq, Afghanistan and Syria.

Bell surveyed them with his cold blue eyes, then flashed a tight smile. He wasn't a man to waste time on small talk or preamble and he got straight to the point. 'You will be working in ten groups of four, with call signs Alpha through Juliett. Each group of four will have two men with tasers. The aim of this operation is to bring the eight targets out of the camp and back here. There are more than a hundred men in the camp, but we will be there in darkness with full night vision gear so we will have the advantage.'

He walked over to a satellite map of the area which had been taped to a whiteboard, and tapped it with his hook. 'There is a hill behind the camp. Day and night there are sentries on the hill, keeping watch. There are four and they do three-hour shifts. They stay in the same places each night and they do not have night vision gear. Groups Alpha, Bravo, Charlie and Delta will have one sniper each and they will approach first to take out the sentries. Once the sentries have been neutralised the groups all move in.'

He went over to another whiteboard where there was a hand-drawn map of the camp, with the main buildings labelled. He pointed at four small circles on the periphery of the camp. 'There are no fences or walls around the camp, but these four sentry placements define the perimeter. They are manned day and night and need to be taken out with silenced weapons or knives before we move into the camp itself.'

He tapped a square on which had been written 'ADMIN', the hook making a loud click that carried across the room. 'This is where the leaders stay most of the time, and it also serves as a medical facility and weapons storage area. We've no interest in a softly-softly approach there. Hotel and India groups will take out the occupants of this block, with no need for tasers.' He pointed at another, larger square. 'This is a barracks and is probably where our targets will be. There are two entrances, front and back. We haven't been able to see inside but at night there are eighty or more men in there. We don't know if they have beds or bunks or if they sleep on the floor. Echo, Foxtrot, Golf and Juliett are to take this block. It'll be sixteen against eighty but it'll be pitch dark in there and we'll have the element of surprise. Once those teams are in, Alpha through Delta can join them. Use tasers to take them down, zipties to bind them and once the block is secure, separate the wheat from the chaff.'

One of the men raised his hand. 'What about the chaff, Colonel? What do we do with them?' Even though Bell had left Delta Force five years earlier, the men who had worked with him still used his rank.

'Leave them bound. We'll be picked up by the chopper so they won't be a threat. But remember, these are hardened ISIS fanatics; there's no need to use kid gloves and no one will care about casualties on their side. This is not a military operation, it's not about racking up bodies, we just want the targets. Do you all have the cards?'

The men nodded. Several held up sets of small plastic cards on which were printed the faces and details of the men they were after. There were eight in all. On the back of each card was the name of the target and any details that might help identify them.

'Seven of the men are the standard ISIS profile – young, male, brown-skinned and bearded,' said Bell.' A few have scars, which are mentioned on the cards. One is Caucasian. His real name is Gary Wilkinson but he now goes by the name of Mohammed Siddiq. Just to be clear, this isn't an intelligence-gathering operation, so don't bring anything other than the targets. No phones, no belongings, just the men. Don't answer any questions they have, keep all communication to a minimum. Once we have the camp under our control I will call in the chopper to evacuate us back here. Any questions?'

He was faced with shaking heads and shrugs. 'Excellent.' He looked at the rugged Breitling on his wrist. 'Right, the night is darkest between 11 p.m. and 2 a.m. and the camp is a ninety-minute flight from here. Our drop zone is eight kilometres downwind of the camp so they won't hear us coming. I'm assuming that even in the dark and over rough terrain we'll cover the distance in about ninety minutes, so we'll be leaving here at twenty-two hundred hours. In the meantime check all your equipment over, paying particular attention to the batteries of the tasers and the night vision goggles. And just to remind you, this mission is one hundred per cent covert. No selfies, no trophies, and when it's over, no war stories. You've all signed non-disclosure agreements, I know, but if anyone starts blabbing, it won't be lawyers you have to deal with.'

Several of the men laughed uneasily, and Bell grinned, but it was crystal clear that he wasn't joking.

CHAPTER 13

The pick-up truck turned off what passed for a main road onto a single track that was rutted and pot-holed. They slowed down but the air around the back of the truck was still full of dust. 'So what brought you to Syria, Raj?' asked Sid. He had wound his black-and-white scarf around his mouth and nose to keep out the worst of the sand being kicked up by the tyres.

'I just wanted to help,' said Raj. 'The people here need it.'

'It's a shithole, that's true. But yeah, respect to you for doing that.' He took his right hand off his weapon and made it into a fist. 'Respect,' he repeated, and fist-bumped Raj. He gestured at the man sitting next to him. 'This is Salmaan, we call him Sal. He's from Somalia but says he's Dutch, but don't hold that against him.' Sal also fist-bumped Raj. 'His mate Abdullah is in the cab, he's a Dutch Somalian as well. Or is it Somalian Dutch?' He laughed. 'Who gives a fuck, right?'

The two other men introduced themselves. One was Erol. The other was Jaffar. They both leant over and fist-bumped Raj.

'You're from England, too?' Raj asked them.

Sid laughed. 'They're from Bradford, not sure that counts as England any more.'

Erol and Jaffar laughed.

'And you're what, ISIS?'

Erol grinned. 'Fuck, yeah.'

'So you're here to fight the Syrian government?' Raj frowned. 'Why would you do that?'

'It's not about fighting the government here. It's about fighting for Muslims everywhere in the world. Our faith is under attack and we have to defend it.'

Raj shrugged but didn't say anything.

'You're Muslim, right?' said Erol. 'You know what it's like.'

Raj stayed silent. He wasn't a Muslim, he was a Hindu. Religion had never played a large part in Raj's life, even less so once he'd become a doctor, but he figured now wasn't the time to own up to not being a follower of Islam.

Sid leant over and patted Raj on the knee. 'Mate, don't worry. No one's going to hurt you. We just need you to patch up our brothers and then we'll take you back to your hospital. It's all good, innit?'

'You give me your word?' Even as the words left Raj's mouth he knew that there was nothing that Sid could say to reassure him. They had shot an innocent man on the operating table, they wouldn't think twice about putting a bullet in Raj's head out in the desert.

'Of course, bruv,' said Sid, patting him on the knee again. 'It'll be fine. Trust me.'

Raj didn't trust the man at all but he forced a smile. 'So tell me what sort of injuries they've got,' he said.

'They were standing next to a suicide vest when it went off,' said Sid. 'There was a lot of metal flying around and the guys nearest it were blown to pieces.'

Raj shook his head. 'What the hell were they thinking?'

'Bruv, they were thinking that they were going to learn how a suicide vest works. They had no idea it was going to go off. One of my mates was standing right by it when it exploded. Amer. He was from Kilburn, too. I don't think he even knew what happened. One second he was looking at the vest, the next . . . gone.'

'Somebody fucked up?'

'Obviously,' said Sid. He looked over his shoulder. 'We're nearly there.'

'What sort of facilities have you got?'

Sid looked back at him, frowning. 'Facilities?'

'Medical facilities.'

'There's a first aid room. With the basics. Bandages and antibiotics.'

'That's it?' said Raj. 'Mate, I'm not going to be able to treat bomb victims with bandages and antibiotics.'

'We've no choice, bruv, we can't take them to a hospital. The government troops will finish the job with bullets.'

Ahead of them was a hill and in front of it a collection of concrete buildings. Raj shaded his eyes with his hand. 'That's it?'

'That's the camp,' said Sid.

'How do you manage for water and sanitation? Electricity?'

'There's an underground well they pump water up from. Sanitation is a hole in the ground. Electricity comes from generators. It's not a fucking resort, it's a military camp.'

The truck drove by a sentry block where two sentries holding Kalashnikovs waved a greeting. Sid waved back and the driver beeped his horn. They pulled up in front of a single-storey block where there was a line of men lying on blankets.

A man in his forties with a greying beard, wearing a knitted skullcap and a grey thobe, was standing by the entrance. He walked over as they climbed down from the back of the truck. 'This is Faaz,' said Sid.

The driver climbed out of the cab and Sid gestured at him with his Kalashnikov. 'And this is Mohammed Elsheikh. We call him Mo.' Mo nodded and grunted.

'You are a doctor?' Faaz asked Raj.

'I am. How many casualties do you have?'

'There are the twelve you see here. We have eight dead, but obviously they don't concern you. The most serious are inside. The ones who weren't seriously injured we have patched up and sent to the barracks.'

'How are we placed regarding blood if we need transfusions?'

'We have no stocks because we don't have refrigeration. But almost everyone here has been blood-typed so we can get blood as and when we need it.'

'Plasma?'

'No.'

'You have an operating theatre?'

'We have a room where you can operate.'

'Sterile?'

Faaz waved his arm around the camp. 'We are in the desert, my friend. Nothing here is sterile. But we have antiseptic and we can boil as much water as you need.'

Raj walked along the line of injured men. Most had shrapnel injuries and were holding bandages or strips of material over their wounds. One man had a bandage over his eye. Raj moved it to get a better look. The eye had a piece of metal sticking out of it. The injury wasn't life threatening but it would take a miracle for the man not to lose the eye. Raj patted him on the shoulder. 'We'll get to you soon,' he said.

Several of the men were burnt and would have hideous scars, but most of the wounds just needed cleaning and dressing. Once he had checked the victims outside, he went into the building with Faaz.

There were three wounded lying on blankets on the floor of a corridor. One was unconscious, two were in shock. The unconscious man had lost most of his left hand. A tourniquet had been applied just below his elbow. Raj looked at the bloody stump and loosened the tourniquet. 'I have some injectable morphine. And some oxycodone and fentanyl. And anti-inflammatories,' Raj said to Faaz. 'What do you have here in the way of painkillers?'

'Paracetamol, and morphine pills,' answered Faaz. 'And some heroin.'

'You use heroin as a painkiller?'

'Morphine is difficult to acquire. Heroin is easy to get.'

Raj gestured at the three casualties. 'What have you given them?'

'All three have had a morphine tablet each.'

Raj checked the other two casualties. One had severe burns on his face and neck but didn't seem to have any shrapnel wounds. Raj had seen countless IED injuries and sometimes, as here, they defied logic – the man had been close enough to the explosion to get burnt but hadn't been hit by any shrapnel. The third man hadn't been so lucky – bits of metal had ripped through his chest and abdomen. A large dressing had been taped across his chest and it was soaked in wet blood. 'This one is going to need blood, what's his blood type?'

'We will find out,' said Faaz. 'It will be in his records.'

'If you get a match, we'll get him hooked up. If you don't have a match, get blood from someone with O negative. In fact, right now get everyone in the camp who has O negative to start giving blood. Are there any others?'

'This way,' said Faaz. He led Raj down the corridor to another room. There were three tables and three camp beds, each of which had a victim lying on them, and Raj cursed when he saw the state the casualties were in. They had all clearly been close to the explosion. One was missing his right arm, another's face had been completely obliterated, two had gaping chest wounds, one had half a dozen deep gashes across his face and had lost an ear, and another was missing a leg.

'Do you have any nurses? Anyone with any medical training?'

'Most of our fighters have had first aid training,' said Faaz.

'So the answer is no?' Raj cursed under his breath. There was a sink by the door and next to it a table with a box of latex gloves and surgical masks. He hung his backpack on a hook and began to wash his hands. 'You know basic first aid?' he asked Faaz.

'Some,' said Faaz.

'Wash your hands and get gloves on. I don't suppose you have any scrubs or surgical gowns?'

Faaz shook his head. 'We have nothing like that.'

'Get some clean clothes that we can wear. Even clean T-shirts and trousers will be better than what we're wearing.' He looked over at Sid who was standing by the door, still holding his AK-47. 'Sid, everyone else has to stay outside. And ask around, see if there's anyone out there who has had medical experience. I'm going to need help, even if it's just a pair of hands.'

'I'm on it, bruv,' said Sid, and he headed back down the corridor.

Raj turned and looked at the casualties. He knew that he would do his best to save them, but he also knew that his best almost certainly wouldn't be enough.

CHAPTER 14

The Chinook stayed low as it crossed the border into Syria. Syrian radar was patchy at best and virtually non-existent below a hundred feet. The two pilots were wearing night vision goggles and had no problem keeping the massive helicopter on course. The Boeing-made CH-47 Chinook was a workhorse helicopter used by armies around the world. It was capable of carrying loads of up to ten thousand pounds and there was more than enough room in its massive cargo bay for Bell and his team and all their equipment. It was flying at close to its top speed of nearly two hundred miles per hour as it sped across the desert.

Fifty minutes after it had crossed the border, the helicopter slowed to a hover and then landed. The rotors continued to spin as the rear ramp slowly came down. Bell led his men down the ramp to the desert floor, and they switched on their night vision goggles. The goggles gave them a greenish view of the landscape around them as they lined up in their ten groups. They performed a final inspection of their equipment and then Bell gave the order for them to move out.

CHAPTER 15

It was just after midnight when Raj finished working on the final casualty. It was an imam and the man had insisted on being treated last. He had two deep shrapnel cuts on his right arm and a superficial cut by his eye. The cut on his face only needed a dab of antiseptic but the arm wounds required a dozen stitches between them. The imam had refused any anaesthetic, saying that medical supplies were limited and he didn't want any wasted on him. He was in his seventies but was as hard as nails and didn't even flinch as Raj closed the wounds. When he'd finished, the imam thanked Raj for his work and suggested that he stay on at the camp. 'We are in need of a skilled doctor,' said the imam.

'I came to Syria to help civilians,' said Raj.

'We are all warriors in the cause of Islam,' said the imam. 'If we do not fight the infidels, they will wipe us from the earth.'

Raj continued to smile, though he knew that the imam would only have to snap his fingers to end his life. He thanked him for the offer, and said that he would be happy to visit the camp when he was needed. The imam took Raj's refusal in apparent good grace and left the treatment room.

Sid was standing at the doorway, cradling his Kalashnikov. 'That's the lot,' said Raj, stripping off his bloody latex gloves and dropping them in a bin. 'Can I go now?'

Sid looked at his watch and grimaced. 'It's too late to start driving around the desert without night vision gear,' he said.

'Mate, you promised.' Raj took off his blood-splattered shirt and hung it on a hook on the wall. He removed the baggy trousers he'd been given and put them next to the shirt.

'And I'm sticking to it,' said Sid. 'But not right now. First thing in the morning, right? You can do Fajr prayers with us and then we'll drive you back.' He handed him a clean T-shirt and trousers. 'You can wear these.'

'You don't have night vision gear?' Raj went over to the sink and washed his hands and face, then changed into the clothes that Sid had given him.

Sid laughed. 'Bruv, we're short of everything out here.' He patted Raj on the arm. 'Look, Doc, you're knackered, grab some rest in the barracks and we'll have you back at your hospital first thing tomorrow.'

Raj could see there was no point in arguing with the man. Sid had a point. There was virtually no moon and navigating in the desert at night was asking for trouble. Plus he was dog tired and could do with a few hours' sleep.

Sid took him out of the treatment block and over to a larger cement block building. He pushed open a door. Inside were ranks of wooden bunk beds and lines of camp beds. Most were occupied, and more men were sleeping on blankets on the floor. Raj wrinkled his nose at the smell of stale sweat and flatulence, but he was so tired he just fell onto a free camp bed and was asleep within seconds.

CHAPTER 16

Bell signalled for his men to come to a halt. In the distance they could just make out the outline of the ISIS training camp. Behind the camp was a hill but they couldn't see the guards that they knew were stationed there. The rest of the teams waited with Bell as Alpha, Bravo, Charlie and Delta teams moved ahead. Their snipers needed to get close enough to be sure of a killing shot.

Twenty minutes after the teams had left, Bell got his first call over the radio. The first sentry had been dispatched. Three more calls came in within the following five minutes. All four sentries were dead. Bell waved for the men to start moving again.

As they got closer to the camp, two teams moved forward, each team splitting into two. They approached the sentry placements that marked the perimeter of the camp, moving slowly but confidently, knowing that their night vision gave them a deadly advantage. The four sentries were killed quickly and efficiently with next to no noise.

The eight men in Hotel and India group moved towards the admin block, which also served as the sleeping quarters for the imams and the senior ISIS officers. Echo, Foxtrot, Golf and Juliett headed towards the barracks, tasers at the ready. Echo and Foxtrot went to the front entrance of the block while Golf and Juliett hurried around to the rear. They entered simultaneously, the men with tasers first, the men with carbines following.

CHAPTER 17

Raj jumped awake. There were figures moving around him in the darkness, and crackling sounds followed by dull thuds. He looked around, blinking, but all he could see were dark silhouettes. To his right there was the crackle of electricity and the sparks provided enough light for him to catch a glimpse of a helmeted soldier thrusting a taser at Faaz. Faaz slumped to the ground. A man leapt off the top of one of the bunk beds and grabbed one of the attackers but he was knocked unconscious with the butt of a carbine.

A man stood over Raj and there was the crackle of a taser but as the man struck Raj rolled off the bed. He hit the concrete floor and rolled again, then came up in a fighting crouch. There were men with tasers everywhere, and men with carbines, all wearing night vision goggles, moving like ghosts in the darkness. The man who had tried to taser him walked around the camp bed. The taser crackled again. Raj kicked out and caught the man in the hip, then he stepped forward and punched him in the chin, sending him sprawling. A man with a carbine appeared in front of Raj and pointed his weapon at Raj's chest. He was about to pull the trigger when a taser crackled behind Raj and he went into spasm, falling to the floor.

When he came to, he was being dragged face down across the desert floor, his bare feet scraping through the sand. He gasped for breath. It was pitch dark outside but he could just make out the squat bulk of a Chinook helicopter, its twin rotors turning slowly. 'Guys, I'm on your side,' he gasped. His captors ignored him. He tried to speak again but there was so much sand in the air that he began to choke and cough. The two men dragged him over to the ramp at the rear of the helicopter, and then hauled him to his feet. The interior of the Chinook was lit by red bulbs and he could make out Erol and Jaffar sitting on seats bolted to the sides, flanked by soldiers. 'Guys, listen to me, I'm a Brit, I'm not . . .' He heard the crackle of a taser once more and he passed out.

This time when Raj regained consciousness he was harnessed into a seat and his wrists had been ziptied. The noise from the twin turbines was deafening. He looked left and right. The men either side of him were wearing military fatigues but with no markings to say who they were with. Navy SEALs, maybe, or Delta Force. They were wearing Kevlar helmets with night vision goggles attached, and again there were no markings. The two men were staring straight ahead and both were chewing gum. Raj knew that there was nothing he could say to them that would change the outcome of what was happening. At some point he was sure that someone would listen to him and understand that a mistake had been made, but now wasn't the time.

They had removed his watch but it felt as if they had been in the air for less than an hour when the massive helicopter began to descend. It landed with a double thump, then the rotor slowed and the rear ramp was lowered. The prisoners were taken from their seats and manhandled down the ramp. Overhead, with a roar of its engines, a jet was taking off. They were at an airfield, Raj realised. A military airfield by the look of it. They were prob-ably in Turkey, he thought. Incirlik Air Base, maybe.

When he reached the bottom of the ramp, he stopped and spoke earnestly to the man who was gripping his right arm. 'Listen, my name is Rajesh Patel. I was born in London.'

'Half the foreign ISIS fighters out here were born in London,' growled the man.

'You've got the wrong fucking guy.'

The man took a set of plastic cards linked with a metal ring from his pocket. He flicked through it and then held up one of the cards next to Raj's head. 'That's you,' he said.

'Show me.'

The man showed the card to Raj. On it was an image of an Asian man with a close-cropped beard and piercing brown eyes. There was a likeness, Raj could see that, but it definitely wasn't him. 'That's not me,' he said.

'It fucking looks like you.'

The man read the name on the back of the card. 'Amer Qasim,' he said.

'What?'

'Your name. It's Amer Qasim.'

'I told you my name. It's Rajesh Patel. Raj.'

'Where's your ID?'

'In my wallet.'

The man began to pat down Raj's trousers.

'It's not there,' said Raj. 'It's back at the hospital.'

'What hospital?'

'The hospital I work at.'

'You work at a hospital but you sleep at an ISIS training camp?' The man laughed harshly. 'Do I look fucking stupid?' He grabbed Raj's shoulder. 'Get on the plane.' He gestured at a Gulfstream G550, parked on the tarmac fifty metres away from the Chinook.

Another man led Sid from the helicopter ramp towards the plane. Raj gestured with his chin at Sid. 'Ask him, he'll tell you. He'll tell you who I am.' The man ignored him so Raj shouted over at Sid. 'Sid, mate, tell him I'm not with you.'

Sid tried to speak but the man escorting him pushed him in the small of the back. Sid stumbled forward. The man pushed him again. 'No talking!' he barked.

Raj flashed his own escort a pleading look. 'He'll tell you who I am,' he said. 'Just ask him.'

'You know him?'

'His name's Sid, He's from London, too.'

The men sneered at Raj. 'So you know his name's Sid, he knows you, you're both from London and we grab you both from an ISIS training camp in Syria. But you're not really a terrorist?'

Raj opened his mouth to speak but the man backhanded him, hard. Raj tasted blood and his ears were ringing. He tried to speak but the man slapped him again. 'You say one more fucking word and I'll drag you unconscious onto that plane.' He grabbed Raj by the throat, squeezed hard and then thrust him towards the Gulfstream.

There were now four of the men that had been taken from the camp standing at the steps leading up to the hatch of the plane. Four men in fatigues were standing guard holding Heckler & Koch 416s with the barrels aimed at the tarmac. The HK416 was the favoured weapon of American Navy SEALs and Delta Force but they didn't look like special forces to Raj. Most of the special forces guys that Raj had met in the past had been super fit and usually under thirty. These guys seemed older and heavier, so Raj figured they were former soldiers working in the private sector. But for whom?

He joined the queue at the bottom of the steps. The Asian guy at the front of the queue was being handed a white adult disposable nappy, the sort they gave to patients in hospitals who were at risk of soiling themselves. The man was told to remove his pants, put on the nappy and then put his pants back on. It was Sal, Raj realised. One of the Somalians. Sal was struggling to follow the instructions, his bound hands making it difficult to remove his underwear.

Raj turned to look at his captor but the man grinned before he could even phrase the question. 'It's going to be a long flight.'

'Why can't we use the toilet?'

'Because you're going to be hooded, shackled and handcuffed,' said the man.

'Where are you taking us?'

The man's grin widened. 'You don't get the concept of the hood, do you?'

Raj opened his mouth to reply but the man raised his hand and glared at him as if daring Raj to speak. Raj sighed and averted his eyes.

Sal was taken up the stairs. A man at the top shackled his ankles and led him inside the plane.

More prisoners were brought from the Chinook and forced

to line up behind Raj. One by one the three in front of him were made to put on the nappies, hooded and taken up the steps. Erol. Then Jaffar. Then Abdullah.

When it was Raj's turn, he refused the nappy with a shake of his head. 'I've got control of my bladder,' he said to the man.

'You don't know how long we'll be in the air for, and the hood and the shackles aren't coming off until the wheels touch the ground so shut the fuck up and put on the diaper.'

Raj leant closer to him. 'Mate, I know you won't listen to me man to man, but can I at least appeal to you soldier to soldier?'

'What the fuck are you talking about? Either put the fucking diaper on now or we'll taser you and put it on while you're unconscious.'

'Listen to me, I was a Royal Marines Commando, pretty much the same training as you went through. I served in Afghanistan, I'm one of the good guys.' He nodded at the gun which was in the nylon holster on the man's hip. 'Your weapon is a Glock 19, which pretty much replaced the SIG Sauer P226 as the sidearm of choice for SEALs. It only has thirty-four parts and it will still fire with eleven of those parts missing. When I was with the Marines I was issued with a Glock 17, which replaced the Brownings that we used to use. We had seventeen rounds in the magazine as opposed to yours which only has fifteen in the clip, but I guess it's not how many rounds you have it's what you do with them, right? Look, I was a soldier, the same as you.'

Raj heard a crackling sound to his right. Before he could turn the prongs of a taser were pressed against his neck and he collapsed onto the tarmac in a senseless heap.

CHAPTER 18

When Raj regained consciousness he was sitting in a comfortable seat with his hands bound in front of him and a hood over his head. He moved his legs and felt the chain binding them tighten. He was breathing quickly and starting to feel light-headed, so he forced himself to slow his breathing down. There would be enough air seeping through the hood to keep him alive, but not if he began hyperventilating. His feet were sore from where he'd been dragged across the ground and his right side and neck ached, presumably the result of being tasered. He could hear the hum of the Gulfstream's engines and there was a faint vibration coming through his feet – they were definitely airborne, but where were they going?

The Gulfstream – like the lack of markings on the men's uniforms and equipment – suggested it wasn't a military operation, but the men had operated with military efficiency. Who were they and what were they up to? If it had been a military operation then presumably they would have just gone in with their guns blazing. The whole tasering business made no sense.

He sat back in his seat. Perhaps there was a reason why their captors needed them alive. For a trial, maybe. Was that the plan? To take them back to face some sort of war crimes tribunal? But if that were the case, why were they being so selective about who they were taking? Raj closed his eyes and pictured the men he'd seen being taken to the Chinook and then boarding the plane. Erol and Jaffar, the Bradford boys. Sid, from London. Mo from Belgium, and Faaz, the Finn. And the two Somalians, Abdullah and Sal. Seven in all. He opened his eyes again. And they thought that he was Amer Qasim. Amer had been Sid's friend, killed when the vest had exploded. So all the men they had taken were connected to the group that had seized him. But what in particular had they done that would result in them being extradited? Or renditioned? Raj wasn't sure what the difference was, but being hooded and shackled and put on a plane sure felt like rendition.

He swallowed and almost gagged because his throat was bone dry. 'Hey, can I have some water?' he shouted. 'Please,' he added as an afterthought. When no one responded, he shouted again. 'I need a drink here.'

There were footsteps to his left, then the hood was loosened around his throat and a straw was pushed in. Raj opened his mouth and sucked greedily. After a few seconds the straw was pulled away. 'I need the bathroom,' he said.

'That's what the diaper's for,' growled a voice.

'Seriously, you expect me to piss myself?'

'Piss, shit, fart, the diaper'll take care of it. Now shut the fuck up or I'll taser you again.'

'Okay, okay,' said Raj. The way they were being treated suggested this wasn't a government operation. This was something else. But what?

He had lost all track of time and had no way of knowing if it was day or night. Despite his predicament, he nodded off, then woke up with a start. Someone was shouting off to his right, screaming obscenities and demanding to be released. There was the crackle of a taser and the shouting stopped. Raj dozed again.

During one of the periods when he was awake he tried to work out where they were being taken. Most long-range private jets had a range of between ten thousand and fourteen thousand kilometres. Anywhere in Europe was well within that distance. The United States was about ten thousand kilometres from Syria, Australia was closer to thirteen thousand. South America was some ten thousand kilometres away. Raj had no way of knowing which direction they were heading, nor did he have any idea how long they had been in the air. But the fact that his captors were American suggested that the United States might be their ultimate destination.

A sudden thought hit him. Guantanamo Bay. Cuba. He closed his eyes and tried to visualise a globe. Cuba was probably about eleven thousand kilometres from Syria. Was that where they were being flown to? Guantanamo Bay? Raj remembered reading an article in *The Guardian* about the detention camp, where America held its terrorists, usually without trial. President Obama had promised to close the camp but Donald Trump had vowed to keep it open indefinitely. At its peak the camp had held around seven hundred inmates but so far as Raj could recall, there were now just forty or so detainees. Was that the plan, to fly them to Guantanamo Bay and torture them? Raj's pulse began to race. Would they believe him when he told them who he was and why he was in Syria? It would be easy enough for the Americans to check, but he had read countless stories of innocent men who had been held without trial for years and subject to all sorts of abuse and torture. And if they were being taken to Guantanamo Bay, why were they using private contractors and not troops?

He drifted into sleep again. He had no idea how many hours had passed when he awoke, his ears popping and the plane clearly starting to descend. It landed and taxied for a while before stopping. The hatch opened and he felt a hand groping around his waist to undo his seat belt. He heard the others being taken to the front of the plane and then he was grabbed roughly by the shoulder and told to get to his feet. His arm was gripped tightly as he was led forward. 'Watch your feet, you're going down the steps,' growled a voice. Raj resisted the urge to tell the man there was no way he could watch his feet because he was wearing a fucking hood, but decided that his best option was to remain quiet. He was taken down the steps, his leg chain rattling on the metal, then he was walked across tarmac. The hood made it difficult to tell the temperature but it felt warm.

He couldn't hear any planes so it probably wasn't an airport or an army base. In fact it was unnaturally quiet, the only sound was that of leg chains scraping across the ground and the occasional grunt.

'There are steps ahead of you, and watch your head,' said his captor. Raj was manhandled up some stairs and into a seat, and a seatbelt was clipped around his waist. A few moments later, he heard a helicopter turbine kick into life and a rotor start to whirl.

CHAPTER 19

Van der Sandt heard the helicopter before he saw it. It was his company sixteen-seater H175 Airbus, flying in from his private airfield, fifty kilometres away. He was standing at the entrance to his house and as the helicopter came into view he walked across the lawn so that he could get a better view of it landing. He was dressed for hunting – lightweight trousers with Timberland boots and a camouflage shooting jacket, with a pair of sunglasses sitting on the top of his head.

The helicopter landed smoothly and the pilot cut the engine. As the rotors slowed, the side door opened. Neil Thomas and half a dozen armed men in fatigues were standing around the helicopter pad. The men had arrived in two black SUVs that morning, with bulging kitbags. Thomas's regular security team had left, as had the entire house staff. A coach had arrived at dawn to take away the housekeepers, cooks, drivers and gardeners, along with the security guards. Catherine Shirley had left with them, but under protest.

Three men in fatigues climbed out of the helicopter. One of them, grey-haired and holding a carbine, walked over to Thomas and shook his hand.

Two more men in fatigues climbed out, and then they dragged out a hooded man wearing baggy clothing and pushed him away from the helicopter. Another hooded man followed. Then another. As they walked away from the helicopter they were taken towards the hangar. Van der Sandt kept counting until all the prisoners were off the helicopter. Eight. He smiled. All present and accounted for.

Thomas and the grey-haired man walked over to Van der Sandt. 'Mr Van der Sandt, this is Colonel Bell,' said Thomas, by way of introduction.

Van der Sandt offered his right hand, then realised that the other man's hand had been replaced with a hook. The Colonel grinned at his discomfort. 'It's all right, Mr Van der Sandt, we can still shake. It won't come off.'

Van der Sandt shook the hook. 'Thank you for this,' he said. 'It can't have been easy.'

'Actually it went off without a hitch,' said Bell. 'We were well briefed with first-class intel, and we met with virtually no resistance.'

'And you have all eight of the terrorists – excellent.'

'We do,' Bell replied. 'Mr Van der Sandt, if it's okay with you I'll wait for you in the hangar.'

'Of course,' said Van der Sandt. As the Colonel headed off to join his men, Van der Sandt turned to Thomas. 'Neil, thank you for everything you've done, but I think it best you leave now.'

'I'm happy to stay, sir.'

'I know, and I'm grateful for your loyalty. But Colonel Bell and his team should handle everything from now on.'

Thomas smiled tightly. 'I understand.'

Van der Sandt offered his hand and they shook. 'I'll always be grateful to you for your help and support. I'll call you when this is over.'

Thomas headed to his car. As the men in fatigues took the prisoners into the hangar, Van der Sandt walked back across the lawn and into the hallway of his house. He had left his gun on a Victorian oak table, an antique that Laura had bought at auction in London and shipped over along with another dozen pieces soon after they had bought the house.

Van der Sandt had thought long and hard about which gun to use, and had settled on his Ambush 300 Blackout, a gun that he had last used to hunt feral pigs in Georgia. The irony of using a gun that had killed pigs being used to execute Muslim terror-ists was not lost on him. The weapon usually fired 110-grain subsonic bullets, but for the pigs he had used subsonic 220-grain rounds, heavier and deadly up to two hundred metres or more. He would use the same for the jihadists, he'd decided. The Ambush had a camouflage pattern and a threaded sixteen-inch barrel into which he had screwed a bulbous Wave suppressor. The suppressor weighed more than a pound, but if anything it added to the balance of the weapon.

He cradled the gun as he walked along a corridor to the rear of the house and into the kitchen. The kitchen had been Laura's pride and joy. She had worked with an architect for weeks to get the perfect design, and all the appliances had been imported from Europe. She had flown to Italy to choose the marble work-tops and the cabinets were all handmade. The floor tiles were also Italian, and made by hand. Laura loved to cook, and they had eaten most meals on the kitchen table, looking out over the gardens through the floor-to-ceiling windows.

Van der Sandt walked out onto the terrace with its BBQ pit – the only cooking he ever did – and across the lawn to the hangar. The Colonel was standing at the massive sliding doors at the entrance to the building. 'So what happens now, Mr Van der Sandt?' asked Bell.

'We'll use the helicopter to drop the terrorists out in the forest. We've identified a clearing just under forty kilometres away. Once they have been dropped the helicopter will return and fly you and your men back to the airport. You can take the jet to wherever you need to go.'

Bell nodded. 'Sounds like a plan.'

Bell stepped to the side to allow Van der Sandt into the hangar. The eight jihadists were lined up. Their diapers had been removed but they were still hooded, their wrists bound by plastic zipties. Van der Sandt motioned with his gun for the hoods to come off, and one by one they were removed. The men stood blinking, trying to focus their eyes.

'This is what's going to happen,' Van der Sandt said to the men. 'You're going to be taken back onto the helicopter and dropped into the woods. Then I'm going to come looking for you.'

'Fuck that, man,' said one of the men.

Van der Sandt held up his gun. 'I'm going to come looking for you, and one by one I'm going to kill you the way you killed my family on the beach. One by one.'

'You cannot do that, we have rights,' said the oldest member of the group. He was wearing a baggy shirt and loose trousers and had a black-and-white scarf around his neck.

Van der Sandt walked over to him and stared into his watery brown eyes. 'You're the Bangladeshi, right? The leader of the group? Faaz Mahmud.'

'I am just a servant of Allah,' said Faaz, staring back at him. 'And I am a citizen of Finland. I insist that I be allowed to speak to my embassy.'

'That's not going to happen,' said Van der Sandt.

'You need to hand us over to the police,' said Faaz.

Van der Sandt took a step back, pointed his gun at Faaz's bare left foot and pulled the trigger. The foot burst open and Faaz screamed in pain. He hopped back and then fell to the concrete floor. The rest of the men stared in horror as Faaz writhed in agony. 'There's been a small change of plan,' Van der Sandt said to the terrorists. 'Mr Mahmud can stay here. Once I've dealt with him, I'll be coming after you. You're going to have about as much chance as you gave my family and the others you killed that day.' He took casual aim at Faaz's right knee and shot him again. Faaz screamed and then began to sob as blood pooled on the floor.

One of the men raised his hands. 'Sir, there's been a mistake. I'm a doctor, I shouldn't be here.' He was in his early thirties, his beard neatly trimmed, but all Van der Sandt saw was a murdering bastard who was going to get what was coming to him. 'I was in the camp taking care of casualties,' said the man. 'I'm not a terrorist.'

'Me neither!' shouted another of the men. 'I work for an NGO, I was helping people, I'm not a terrorist.'

'Yeah, I'm with an NGO too!' yelled another of the men. 'Save the Children. I was helping kids, this is all a mistake.'

Then all the men started shouting and yelling, proclaiming their innocence. Van der Sandt fired a shot into the ceiling and they fell silent. He swung his gun around, his finger on the trigger. 'If you want, you can die here like this piece of shit. Or you can go outside where you'll have a chance. Not much of a chance, but then you didn't give my family much of a chance. So it's your call. Anyone who wants a bullet now, just raise your hand and I'll oblige.'

He glared at the men one by one and they all looked down, avoiding his stare, except for the one who was claiming to be a doctor. The man stood with his head up as if he wasn't fazed by the gun. 'I am not a terrorist,' said the man. 'I don't know what the fuck is going on here, but I'm not with them. They were holding me . . .' One of the guards walked up behind the man and slammed the stock of his carbine against his head. The man slumped to the ground. 'Anyone else have anything to say?' asked Van der Sandt.

One of the men looked up. It was the only white guy in the group. 'I didn't kill your family,' he said. 'I was there but I swear that I didn't harm your family. I didn't shoot any kids.'

Van der Sandt walked over to him, his steps echoing around the hangar. He stopped in front of the man. 'You're white – what are you doing with these animals?'

'I'm a Muslim,' said the man. 'I'm fighting for my religion. But I swear I did not harm your family.'

'So you're a convert? You became a Muslim? By choice?'

The man nodded cautiously.

'What are you, fucking retarded? Do you actually believe that there's a god who doesn't want you to eat bacon? Who thinks that paedophilia is okay and that gays should be thrown off roofs? You had the choice and that's the religion you chose?' The man opened his mouth to reply but Van der Sandt silenced him with a shake of his head. 'You think I care who actually pulled the trigger?' said Van der Sandt. 'You're all scum and you all deserve what's coming to you. But you, my little white friend, you I am going to take particular pleasure in killing. You weren't born into this savagery, you chose it; you embraced it. You've got nobody to blame but yourself.' He turned to Bell. 'Colonel, if you would be so good as to put them on the helicopter and take them to the drop zone.'

Bell waved at his men to round up the captives. 'Let's get this show on the road!' he shouted.

CHAPTER 20

When Raj came round he was sitting in one of the helicopters again. His neck was burning and it hurt when he breathed. The thudding of the rotors and the roar of the turbine was loud but far from deafening. This time he was sitting on the starboard side of a row of three seats. Next to him was Sal and on the other side of Sal was Mo. They were both staring fearfully out of the window. The helicopter was flying just above the trees, the leaves rippling below like the waves of a green sea.

Judging from what Raj could see inside the helicopter, it looked like an Airbus H175. He twisted around. There were three armed men sitting on the back row. One of them prodded him with a taser. 'Eyes front or I'll zap you again.' Raj did as he was told. The rear-facing seats at the front were occupied by three of the men in fatigues. The one on the starboard side was grey-haired and older than the rest. His right hand had been replaced by a steel hook. Raj figured he was the guy in charge. Raj got eye contact with the man but there was a coldness to his stare that made it clear there was no point in saying anything to him. The two men sitting with him were cradling their Heckler & Koch sub-machine guns.

The four seats in the row in front of Raj were occupied by Erol, Sid, Jaffar and Abdullah. In front of them were three more men in fatigues, facing forward. So nine of them, all armed. Raj looked down at his ziptied wrists. He had nothing. They'd taken his watch so he had no idea of the time, and he had no shoes. All he had were the clothes Sid had given him at the camp. The leg shackles had been removed but even if his wrists weren't bound he couldn't take on nine armed men.

The trees below flashed by. The sky was a cloudless blue. Raj couldn't see the sun out of either side of the helicopter, which suggested it was high overhead. That meant it must be somewhere between eleven o'clock and three o'clock. He looked down at the trees below, trying to work out where in the world they were. Europe, maybe. North America, perhaps. Not Asia, he was sure of that. Probably not South America. Most of the trees looked evergreen. Firs and cedars. But he wasn't an expert.

Sal caught his eye. 'What are they going to do with us?' he whispered.

'You heard what that guy . . .'

'No talking!' shouted one of the men behind Raj and he felt the metal prongs of a taser press against his neck. He flinched but there was no searing pain, just pressure. 'Okay, okay,' he said.

Raj's mind raced. The man in the mansion had talked about hunting them and clearly it wasn't an idle threat. At some point they were going to be dropped into the forest and he'd come after them. One man with a gun against seven unarmed men, hungry and thirsty and dressed for the desert. It wasn't going to be a fair fight, but then fairness seemed to be the last thing on the man's mind. If Raj was going to stand any chance of surviving this he was going to need a weapon, but he doubted that they planned to give him one.

The engine noise changed and the helicopter slowed. Raj peered through the window. Ahead of them was a clearing, a couple of hundred feet across. The helicopter approached the clearing and slowly descended. Raj assumed they were going to land, but once the helicopter was about ten feet above the grass, it went into a hover. The men in fatigues undid their harnesses. The one nearest the door let his carbine swing on its strap and he used both hands to slide the door back. The noise from the engine was deafening with the door open. The grey-haired man pointed at Erol with his steel hook. Then pointed at the open door. 'Out!' he shouted.

'Fuck that!' shouted Erol.

'Out!' shouted the grey-haired man, and when Erol shook his head one of the men took out his taser, leant forward and thrust it against Erol's chest. Erol went into spasm as the man continued to press the taser against his chest. The man put the taser back in its holster, undid Erol's harness, and then manhandled him towards the door. With the help of the man who had opened the door, he tossed Erol out.

The man with grey hair pointed at Sid. 'Now you.'

Sid stared at the open doorway. 'Can you go down further?' he shouted.

The guy opposite reached for his taser. 'Okay, Okay, I'll jump,' said Sid. He undid his harness, then held on to his seat as he edged closer to the open door. The grey-haired man drew back his right leg and pushed Sid out with his foot. Sid shot out of the helicopter, screaming and waving his arms frantically.

Jaffar was next, followed by Abdullah. Both jumped out without saying anything.

It was Mo's turn next but he had frozen in his seat, his eyes wide and staring. When he ignored the grey-haired man, the man sitting behind him leant forward and tasered him in the neck. The man by the door went over and undid Mo's harness and together with the grey-haired man carried him over to the doorway and threw him out.

Sal undid his own harness and shuffled over to the door. He gave the finger to the grey-haired man, told him to fuck off, and jumped out of the door. Now only Raj was left. The grey-haired man pointed his hook at him. 'Come on, we don't have all fucking day.'

Raj undid his harness and shuffled across the row of seats to the door.

'Come on, come on, or do you want us to zap you?' shouted the guy by the door.

'It's okay, I'll jump,' said Raj. He took a step towards the doorway and he looked out. They were now fifteen feet above the ground. Twenty maybe. He flashed the man by the doorway a worried look. 'Can't we go lower?'

The man opened his mouth to speak but before he could say anything, Raj grabbed him by the shoulders and pushed him out of the doorway. Raj kept a tight grip on the man's shoulders as they fell, twisting his body so that the man stayed underneath him and bracing himself for the impact. They hit the ground hard but the man under him took most of the fall. Raj rolled off him and found himself staring up at the helicopter. The grey-haired man was looking down at them, shouting something, but his words were lost in the roar of the turbine.

Raj sat up. The man he had pushed from the chopper seemed to be unconscious and his left leg was twisted at an unnatural angle, almost certainly broken. Raj grabbed at the man's carbine, checked that the safety was off and in the single shot position, and then lay back and aimed it at the helicopter. He fired at the hatchway and the grey-haired man ducked away. There was very little recoil and Raj knew that the rounds wouldn't do any real damage to the helicopter, but pilots never liked being shot at. He fired again, two single shots, and the helicopter banked to the left. Raj knew that he didn't have long so he placed the gun on the ground and pulled off the man's boots and socks. Then he took off the man's belt. There was a transceiver in a holster on it. As Raj started to remove the man's fatigues his eyes fluttered open. Raj punched him, hard, and the man went still.

Raj heard a noise behind him and he turned to see Sid. 'What the fuck did you do?' asked Sid.

'We're going to need gear if we're going to get through this,' said Raj.

Sid reached for the carbine but Raj grabbed it. 'The Heckler's mine,' he said.

'You're just a medic.'

Raj pointed the barrel at Sid's chest and tightened his finger on the trigger. 'It's mine,' he said. 'I got it, I'm keeping it.'

Sid raised his hands. 'Okay, okay,' he said. He gestured at the Glock in the man's holster. 'Can I have the handgun?'

Raj nodded. 'And strip off his vest. And shirt. We need everything we can get.'

Sid pulled the Glock from its holster and stuck it in the waistband of his pants.

There was a survival knife in a sheath on the man's right leg and Raj undid the straps and took it.

Abdullah came over and undid the vest and pulled it off. He put it on over his shirt.

Sal grabbed the transceiver and hurried away with it.

As Sid began unbuttoning the unconscious man's fatigues, Raj heard the roar of the helicopter's turbine and he looked up to see it heading back towards him. There was a man leaning out of the door with a carbine. Raj grabbed his gun, shouldered it and fired two quick shots at the doorway. The man pulled back and the helicopter flashed overhead. Abdullah and Sal ran off to hide in the trees.

Raj put the gun back on the ground and helped Sid strip off the man's fatigues. He unclipped the man's watch, a black Casio G-Shock, and put it on his own wrist. Erol was sitting up, groaning. Mo was about twenty feet away, lying on his side. His chest was moving so he was still alive, albeit stunned.

Raj took the fatigues from Sid. 'Sid, see if you can get Mo up. We need to get away from here.'

Sid rushed over to the injured man.

Raj pulled on the socks and the boots. They were loose but he could wear them. He tied the knife scabbard to his leg. The helicopter was banking overhead, preparing to head back in his direction.

He stood up, threw the fatigues over his shoulder and ran over to Erol, the Heckler in his right hand. 'You okay?' he asked.

Erol frowned. 'I think so.'

'Nothing broken?'

Erol shook his head and Raj helped him to his feet. Erol put his weight on his right foot and yelped in pain.

Sid had thrown Mo over his shoulder. 'Come on, we need to get into cover,' said Raj. He headed into the trees with Erol. Sid followed.

The helicopter banked overhead and bullets ripped across the clearing, tearing through the vegetation and kicking up divots of earth.

Erol was limping badly and had to lean on Raj with most of his weight. Jaffar came over and helped Raj with Erol. Together they got him out of the clearing. Jaffar stared up at the helicopter. 'Motherfuckers!' he shouted.

'They just want us away from their guy,' said Raj. 'We'll be okay here.' He set Erol down on the ground. Sid had propped the unconscious Mo up against a tree and was staring up at the helicopter. He pulled the Glock from the waistband of his trousers. 'Don't bother, Sid!' shouted Raj. 'The rounds will just bounce off it.'

Sid nodded and put away the gun.

CHAPTER 21

Colonel Bell tapped the pilot on the shoulder with his steel claw. 'Pull around and get ready to land on the south side of the clearing,' he said.

'Roger that,' said the pilot, and he put the helicopter into a right-hand turn. The treetops flashed below them.

Bell turned back to address his team. 'Right, we're going to land and retrieve Nick. We'll do a fly-by at low speed and I need Barry, Chris and Charlie to bail out and move across the clearing to the north to establish a perimeter. The only firepower they have is Nick's Heckler and his Glock, and if they have any sense they'll be running and not looking back.'

Barry, Chris and Charlie nodded. They were all Delta Force veterans who had worked with the Colonel in trouble spots around the world for the last five years.

'As soon as the clearing is secure we'll land near Nick and retrieve him, then you three return to the heli and we're out of there.' Barry opened his mouth to speak but Bell beat him to it and silenced him with a wave of his claw. 'This is not a search and destroy mission, our client wants those men alive so lay down covering fire but that's as far as it goes.'

Barry tightened his grip on his carbine. 'Roger that, sir.'

The helicopter pulled a tight turn, then swooped down to the south side of the clearing. The pilot hovered a few feet above the ground and Bell shouted for the men to go. Barry, Chris and Charlie jumped down and immediately fanned out, firing short bursts towards the trees.

The pilot took the helicopter up and headed south. Bell peered out of the open doorway and saw the three men moving determinedly across the clearing. From the look of it they weren't taking any return fire.

He could see Nick, lying on the ground. He'd been stripped down to his boxer shorts. Bell couldn't see any blood, but the man wasn't moving.

He heard the cracks of the Hecklers as the three men continued to move, fanning out so they were now more than thirty feet apart. He tapped the pilot on the shoulder. 'Down we go!' he shouted.

The pilot put the helicopter in a sharp turn, then he approached the clearing from the west, into what little wind there was. He put the helicopter into a hover about twenty feet away from Nick. Bell jumped out and ran away from the helicopter, bent double at the waist even though there was plenty of clearance. Two more men followed him, carbines at the ready.

The helicopter's rotors continued to spin, kicking up dirt and grass. Bell knelt down besides Nick and grabbed his hand. 'Nick, are you okay?' he shouted.

Nick squeezed his hand but didn't answer.

'We're going to get you out of here, buddy,' said Bell. Nick squeezed again. He was breathing shallowly, his chest barely moving, and he kept his eyes closed. There didn't appear to be any bones protruding through the skin but there was no way of knowing what the internal damage was.

'Let's get him to the heli,' said Bell.

The two men let their carbines swing on their slings as they bent down and grabbed Nick's feet and shoulders. Bell kept his Heckler at the ready as they carried Nick to the hovering helicopter. The pilot had taken the helicopter so low that its skids were just a few inches above the rocks.

Barry, Chris and Charlie were continuing to fire sporadic bursts into the trees but there was still no returning fire. Bell took a quick look over his shoulder. The two men were lifting Nick into the helicopter and the men inside reached for him. Together they lowered him to the floor. One of them gave Bell the 'okay' sign.

Chris and Charlie turned and ran back towards the helicopter, keeping low, as Barry laid down covering fire.

Once Chris had covered twenty metres he looked and started shooting at the tree line as Barry turned and ran.

For the next thirty seconds they took it in turns to lay down covering fire as they crossed the clearing. Bell waited for them by the door. Barry and Charlie climbed in and took their seats as Chris fired a final salvo into the trees. Then Chris climbed in and Bell followed him and the helicopter's engine roared as it leapt into the air. The pilot banked to the left and headed south-east.

CHAPTER 22

Raj peered out from behind the tree and watched as the helicopter flew off. 'Have they gone?' asked Sal from behind him. He was standing next to Erol who was sitting with his back to the tree, his legs outstretched. They had moved further into the forest when the helicopter had landed, but all the covering fire had gone high, ripping through the upper branches.

'Yeah, they picked up their injured guy and took him away,' said Raj.

Sid appeared at Raj's shoulder. 'Shit, I really thought they were going to come for us,' he said. 'I thought it was over.'

Raj looked at Sid. 'How's Mo?'

'He's awake but his leg hurts like hell. I think he's broken it.'

Jaffar looked at the clearing. 'Why did they stop?' he asked. 'Why didn't they keep shooting?'

'That man in the house, he wants to kill us and they work for him,' said Raj. 'That was just about retrieving their guy. The first three guys were establishing a perimeter so that the helicopter could land safely. They weren't trying to kill us, they just wanted to make sure that we kept our heads down.'

'What happens now?' Jaffar asked.

'That nutter with the rifle is going to come looking for us,' said Sid. He held up the Glock. 'But he's got a fucking surprise coming.'

Raj shook his head. 'How good are you with that?' he asked. 'Twenty feet? Thirty? On a good day I'm accurate up to about fifty feet with a Glock. I'm pretty sure the gun he was holding was some variant of an M4 carbine, which means with the right cartridge he can be accurate up to a couple of hundred metres.

And it was fitted with a suppressor, which means at that distance you wouldn't even know where he was.'

'Suppressor?' asked Sal. 'What's a suppressor?'

'A silencer,' said Raj. 'It cuts down the noise the gun makes when it fires. The point I'm making is that we're outgunned so the last thing we need is a shoot-out.'

Sid gestured at the carbine that Raj was holding. 'That's a Heckler, that can shoot a couple of hundred metres easily.'

'Sure, but I'm out of practice and it's not as if we can pop down to the range to hone our skills is it?' He ejected the magazine and squinted at it. 'I've got eighteen rounds left.' He gestured at the Glock. 'How many rounds have you got?'

Sid ejected the magazine. 'It's full.'

Raj nodded. 'So fifteen rounds.'

'Do you think he's going to come after us on his own?' asked Jaffar. 'Or will he bring others with him?'

'That's a good question,' said Raj. He stood up and cradled the Heckler. 'He seems to be taking it all very personally.' Raj looked at Sid. 'He said you killed his family. What did he mean?'

'How the fuck would I know, bruv?'

Raj smiled thinly. 'Sid, mate, that guy, whoever he is, sent a team of former special forces mercenaries into Syria to kidnap us from an ISIS camp and then fly us halfway around the world in a private jet to fuck knows where. That couldn't have cost him less than a million quid. And you saw that house? He's loaded, obviously, and he seems to be holding you – and me – responsible for the death of his family. A guy like that wouldn't be spending that sort of money unless he was sure of his facts, so you need to stop fucking around and tell me the truth. Who is he?'

Sid put his hand on his chest, above his heart. 'Bruv, I don't know the guy. Never seen him before in my life.'

Raj's eyes narrowed. 'But you know what happened to his family.'

Sid looked away and didn't say anything.

'We recently carried out a mission in Cyprus,' said Jaffar quietly. 'It's possible that his family died there.'

'Mission? What mission?'

'We were tasked with killing kafirs at a luxury resort. We killed tourists, we did not harm the locals and we did not harm Muslims. We killed only kafirs.'

'So it's possible his family were there?'

Jaffar shrugged. 'Yeah, it's possible.'

'So you killed women and children?'

'We killed non-believers,' snarled Jaffar.

Raj gritted his teeth in frustration. His life was on the line because a group of trigger-happy jihadists had thought it was somehow acceptable to kill innocent holidaymakers. To butcher women and children? For what? To prove that their religion was somehow superior? Raj didn't have a wife or children, but if he did and if Faaz and his misguided moronic jihadists had harmed them, he'd probably not have thought twice about exacting his own revenge.

'Bruv, what's done is done,' said Sid. 'It doesn't matter what set this guy off, does it? What matters is us getting the hell out of here.'

'We don't even know where "here" is,' said Abdullah, waving his arm around. 'We don't even know what country we're in.'

'It's the US, right?' said Sal. 'The guy's a Yank. So were the men who brought us here.' He nodded. 'It's America, for sure.'

'Which means we have rights, here,' said Jaffar. 'We need to find the police. We need to get to a town or a city and there will be people who will help us.'

Mo groaned. Raj went over to the injured man and knelt down next to him. He put the Heckler on the ground as he examined the man's leg. It was clearly broken below the knee. He heard movement behind him and as he turned, Abdullah was bending down, reaching for the weapon. Raj grabbed it and leapt to his feet. He aimed it at Abdullah's chest and tightened his finger on the trigger. Abdullah threw his hands into the air. 'I just wanted to look at it,' he said.

Raj swung the gun around, covering them all. 'Let's make one thing clear right from the start,' he said. 'This is my gun. Mine. If anyone tries to take it from me, I'll shoot them. Are we all absolutely clear on that?' He glared at them defiantly but no one answered. 'I said are we clear on that?'

One by one the men muttered that yes, they understood.

'Back off, Abdullah,' said Raj, gesturing with the gun.

Abdullah walked away, lowering his hands. 'I only wanted a fucking look,' he said.

Raj waited until Abdullah was well away from him before kneeling down and checking Mo's leg. He was wearing sandals and Raj carefully removed them. He was conscious so was able to describe his pain, and after a few seconds of prodding and twisting Raj was pretty sure that the tibia and the fibula had both broken. Mo didn't appear to be in shock – his skin wasn't clammy or blue, and he didn't appear to be confused or breathing rapidly. The breaks were clean and a decent splint would have him mobile if not exactly pain free. The problem was they were in a forest, so medical splints were out of the question. He grinned and patted Mo on the shoulder. 'Don't worry, we'll get this fixed,' he said. He grabbed his gun and stood up. 'Sid, we need something to tie a splint in place. Can you cut some lengths of material off the shirt you took from the guy.' He pulled the survival knife from its scabbard and gave it to Sid.

Raj gestured at Abdullah. 'Can you and Sal have a look around for something we can use as a splint? Two branches, each about eighteen inches long. They need to be about two or three inches wide. We might be able to cut one branch down the middle. See what you can find, yeah?'

Abdullah frowned as if he didn't understand.

Raj let the Heckler hang from its sling so that he could use his hands to show Abdullah how long the piece of wood needed to be. 'This long will do it.'

'What the fuck do you think you're doing, bruv?' asked Abdullah.

'We're going to fix Mo's leg so that we can move.'

'Fuck that. It's his own fault for falling wrong. He'll just slow us down.' He waved at Sal. 'Come on, Sal, let's go.'

'Go where?' said Raj.

'The hell away from here because here is where that guy's going to come looking for us.'

Sid had sat down and was using the knife to cut strips of cloth from the sleeves of the fatigues. 'That's your plan?' he asked Abdullah.

'Do you have a better one?' asked Sal. 'Seems to me we need to get as far away from here as possible. And Abdullah's right, he'll just slow us down.'

'Where are you going to go?' asked Raj. 'You've no idea where we are.'

'That's the way the helicopter went,' said Abdullah, pointing over Sid's head. 'If we go that way, we'll find the house. And a road. Once we find a road we can find a town.'

'That's a great plan, except I didn't see any town when we were on the helicopter, and if you head towards the house you'll run into the guy with the gun. Our best chance is to stay together and to work as a team.'

'Yeah, well that's easy for you to say because you've got a gun,' said Abdullah. 'Me and Sal have got fuck all and it looks to me like your plan is for you and Sid to carry the guns while me and Sal and the rest carry Mo and Erol.'

'I can walk,' said Erol.

'You're limping already,' said Abdullah. 'You haven't even got shoes, bruv. A couple of kilometres and you'll be begging to be carried.' He shook his head. 'Nah, it's every man for himself. If we stay together, we die together. If we all take care of ourselves, some of us might make it.' He waved at Sal. 'Come on, Sal, let's bounce.'

'You're making a big mistake,' said Raj.

'Maybe, but at least it'll be my mistake,' said Abdullah.

'Brothers, I think Raj is right,' said Jaffar. 'We're stronger together.'

'No, we're a bigger target, easier to hit,' said Abdullah.

Sal nodded. 'He's right. We can move faster alone.'

'Except you don't know where you're going.' Raj shook his head bitterly and waved them away. 'You know what? Do what you want to do.'

Abdullah and Sal spoke to each other in their own language. They didn't appear to be arguing. Eventually Sal raised his hand. '*Ma'a as-salaama*,' he said. Goodbye.

'Yeah,' said Sid. '*Ila-liqaa*'.' Until we meet again.

Raj pointed at the transceiver in Sal's pocket. 'You should leave that with us,' he said.

'Fuck that,' said Sal.

'There are more of us.'

'So?'

'Just give it to me, Sal.'

Raj held out his hand but Sal shook his head. 'I'll swap it for the Glock.'

'That's not going to happen,' said Sid.

'Then we're out of here,' said Sal. The two Somalians disappeared into the forest. For a few seconds the rest of the men heard the crunch of their feet in the undergrowth, and then there was only the sound of the birds in the treetops.

Raj looked over at Jaffar. 'Can you look for wood for a splint, something we can use to bind Mo's leg?'

Jaffar nodded. 'Sure.' He started walking around, looking through the undergrowth.

Raj went over to Erol who was sitting down and massaging his ankle. 'How are you feeling?'

Erol grimaced. 'Abdullah was right, I don't think I'll be able to walk much.'

Raj knelt down and examined the swollen ankle. 'It's sprained, not broken,' he said. 'I'll bind it and we'll find you a stick to walk with. You'll be fine.' He patted Erol on the shoulder and went over to Sid.

Sid had prepared six strips of cloth that he had laid out on the ground. 'Okay?' he asked.

'Perfect,' Raj said.

Jaffar came over with two branches that he'd stripped clean of twigs. One was about an inch thick and two feet long, the other was thinner and longer. 'Let me have the knife,' Raj asked Sid and Sid handed it over.

Raj took the thicker branch from Jaffar, put one end against a rock and used the knife to carefully split it into two. He took the two pieces of wood and the strips of cloth over to Mo. He knelt down and placed the two pieces on the outside and inside of the man's broken leg and nodded. It would be a good fit.

'Sid, give me a couple of pieces to use as padding. Wider and longer than the strips you've done.' He tossed the knife over to Sid who started hacking away at what was left of the fatigues. 'Hey, Jaffar, see if you can find some sort of stick that Erol can use to help him walk,' he said.

'Will do,' said Jaffar.

Raj took two of the strips over to Erol and used them to bind his injured ankle. 'It won't be comfortable but it'll ease the pain,' he said.

'Abdullah was right, I'm fucked without shoes. Jaffar too. It's okay for you and Sid, you've got the boots you took off that guy and Sid had his sandals on when they took us. But if we do any walking, my feet will be shot.'

Raj nodded. Erol was right. The undergrowth was covered with twigs and sharp stones and their feet weren't tough enough to cope with a long trek with no shoes. 'I'll sort something out,' he said.

Sid finished hacking out two pieces of the fatigues to use as padding and he gave them to Raj.

'Thanks. Can you cut a few more pieces that Erol and Jaffar can use to wrap their feet?'

Sid went to work again with the knife. Raj took the thicker strips of cloth that Sid had given him and put them between the sticks and Mo's leg, before using the thinner lengths to bind the wood in place. The trick was to make the ties snug, but not too tight that they would cut off the circulation.

Once he'd tied the splint he wrapped cloth around the ankle to minimise any movement. Bending the ankle meant the muscles and tendons put stress on the tibia and fibula and that can lead to pain. 'How does that feel?' he asked when he'd finished.

'It's okay now, but I'm not sure what it's going to be like when I start to walk.'

'We'll take it slowly,' said Raj.

Jaffar returned from the forest with two branches, both about five feet long. 'How about these?' he asked.

'Perfect,' said Raj. He took them and offered one to Erol. Erol used it to get to his feet and took a few steps. 'Yeah, that's not bad,' he said.

Raj gave the other stick to Mo. 'Do you think you can walk on your own?' he asked. 'We can fix up a stretcher if we have to, but walking under your own steam will probably be quicker.'

Mo nodded. 'I'll give it a go.' Sid and Raj helped him up. He put his weight on the stick and took a step. Then another. 'It's a lot better than it was,' he said.

'You're going to be in pain, no question of that,' said Raj. 'But both breaks are clean and you'll heal okay.' He held up a hand. 'Right guys, gather around, we need to put together a game plan.'

Erol hobbled over with Jaffar. Sid tossed them several large pieces that he had cut from what was left of the fatigues, along with a few strips to tie them into place. Erol laughed. 'Are you serious?'

'Best we can do,' said Raj. 'But it'll be a lot better than nothing. The forest floor will rip your feet apart.'

'Too fucking right,' said Jaffar. He showed them the sole of his right foot which was bleeding from several cuts.

Erol and Jaffar sat down and Sid helped tie the material around their feet.

'Right, there are five of us and my suggestion would be that we stick together,' Raj said. 'Anyone else got a problem with that?'

Nobody argued, so Raj continued. 'The helicopter that dropped us here was a H175 Airbus which has a cruising speed of about two hundred and seventy-five kilometres an hour. They cold-cocked me so I was unconscious for the first part of the flight – how long do we think we were flying?'

Sid shrugged. 'Ten minutes maybe.'

'No, brother,' said Mo. 'It was eight minutes exactly. Not including the take-off time.'

'You're sure?' asked Raj.

Mo nodded. 'I counted.'

'Good,' said Raj. 'So, eight minutes at two hundred and seventy-five kilometres an hour means we travelled . . .'

'Just under thirty-seven kilometres,' said Mo.

Raj grinned. 'Nice one,' he said. 'Are you a human calculator?'

Mo smiled. 'I have always been good with numbers.'

Raj took the survival knife from its scabbard. There was a small compass set into the hilt and he looked at it, then pointed in the direction the helicopter had gone. 'South,' he said. 'Now assuming the helicopter went as the crow flies and wasn't trying to confuse us, the house is thirty-seven kilometres in that direction. The problem with that is, as I told Abdullah, that's probably the direction the man with the gun will be coming from. Did any of you see a road or a town as we flew here?'

The four men shook their heads.

'Then it looks to me as if the house is our only hope. But we can't go straight towards it. We need to weave around a little more. The obvious thing to do would be to go west or east for a short while, then head south – then turn towards the house when we get nearer to it.' He pointed west. 'The ground seems to be going up there which means we might be able to get a better view of the surrounding area. But obviously going up is harder than going down.'

'With all these trees, I don't reckon we'll ever get a view of the land,' said Sid. 'I didn't see any mountains on the flight here.'

'That's true,' said Erol. 'Just trees.'

'So we'll go down,' said Raj. He had a closer look at the knife. It was good-quality steel and was well balanced. The top of the blade was serrated and it narrowed to a wickedly sharp point. The compass was set into the metal handle. Raj unscrewed it. As he suspected the handle was hollow. Inside was a small black plastic capsule. He put the knife in its scabbard and twisted the capsule open. It contained a small flint for starting a fire, three matches, a fishing hook and a length of nylon fishing line.

Erol peered over his shoulder. 'What about food?' he asked.

'What about it?' asked Raj.

'I'm fucking hungry.' He pointed at the contents of the knife handle. 'There's fishing stuff there, right?'

'Mate, first of all I don't see a lake, and second of all we don't have time to start catching fish. Plus we'd have to cook it and a fire'll give away our position.'

'I'm starving.'

'No you're not. Not even close.' Raj laughed. 'You go by the rule of three,' he said. 'You can survive for three minutes without air, three days without water and three weeks without food. So we've a way to go before food becomes a priority.' He looked at the watch on his wrist. 'I reckon we've got four hours before it gets dark so I suggest we head east for two hours and then we'll set up camp as best we can.' He put the survival gear back in the handle of the knife and looked at them one by one. 'Any questions?'

They all shook their heads.

'Okay,' said Raj, slotting the knife into its scabbard. 'Let's head down and see what we find.'

'I've got a question,' said Sid. 'Where did you learn to shoot like that? You're a doctor, right?'

'I'm a doctor, but I had some military training.'

'Where?'

'We don't have time for a Q&A right now,' said Raj. 'It's getting late and we need to put some distance between us and this clearing before we build shelter for the night.'

Sid stared at him for several seconds and then sighed. 'Yeah, you're right,' he said.

Raj knelt down and scratched at the forest floor. He found a small pebble, then another. He kept scraping at the ground until he had nine. 'What are they for?' asked Sid.

'I'll show you, soon enough,' said Raj.

CHAPTER 23

Van der Sandt heard the helicopter from the terrace at the rear of the house, where he was sitting with a crystal tumbler of his favourite malt whisky in one hand and a cigar in the other. Laura had always insisted that he smoke his cigars outside and he didn't feel like changing that now. The chair he was sitting in had once graced the verandah of the main house of a Burmese rubber plantation owned by a business friend. He'd found it to be the most comfortable chair he'd ever sat in and had been delighted when Laura had presented it to him for his fiftieth birthday. It was known as a planter's chair, made from teak with an inclined seat of cane matting and extensions that folded in and out to provide leg rests. Van der Sandt didn't have the leg rests out – he had propped his feet up on a wooden coffee table carved from a single trunk with a frieze of elephants around the bottom. Another gift from Laura.

He stood up and walked over to the edge of the terrace, and watched as the helicopter turned gently over the grounds and landed in the centre of the concrete pad.

The door slid open and Colin Bell climbed out. He ducked his head as he jogged away from the helicopter, then straightened up and waved to Van der Sandt. Van der Sandt waved his cigar. Bell's men began to exit the helicopter as he approached the terrace, his Heckler 416 on his back. Van der Sandt wasn't a fan of the weapon. He knew that American special forces liked it, but then the requirements of a soldier were very different to those of a hunter. A flick of the selector switch on the side allowed the weapon to either fire on semi-automatic or fully automatic, which was great for a firefight but of little use when trying to bring down an elephant or a rhino. The HK416 fired the standard 5.56 x 44 mm Nato round, which was based pretty much on the .223 cartridge developed by Remington some sixty years ago. It was powerful enough to go through more than twelve inches of flesh, which meant it tended to go in and through a soldier, though if it hit bone it would often fragment and cause serious internal damage. The downside of a bullet going right through a target was that it could take more than a minute for the target to bleed out, during which time he was capable of continuing to fight. That meant that several shots were usually necessary to make sure of a kill; either that or a shot to the head. But it was horses for courses, and not everyone agreed with Van der Sandt's weapon choices.

Bell reached the terrace and climbed the short flight of stone steps. 'There was a bit of a problem, sir,' said Bell. 'One of our men fell out of the helicopter and is quite badly injured.'

'Then get him to a hospital,' said Van der Sandt. Half a dozen of Bell's men were now off the helicopter and were standing in a group a short distance away. Two of them were smoking.

'That's the plan,' said Bell. 'But I wanted to drop off most of my guys and all of the weapons here before we fly to a civilian hospital.'

Van der Sandt nodded. 'There's a good hospital emergency room seventy kilometres to the west, and they have a helicopter pad.' He sipped his whisky. 'So what happened?'

'We were dropping the guys out of the heli, and one of them grabbed Nick and fell on top of him. Nick's just about conscious now but it looks as if his right lung has collapsed and there's a good chance there's more internal damage.'

Van der Sandt waved at the helicopter where another of Bell's men was climbing out. 'Your men are welcome to stay in the staff cottages until you're ready to pull out.'

'There's something else, sir,' said Bell.

'They took his weapons,' said Van der Sandt. He smiled at the look of confusion that flashed across Bell's face. Van der Sandt had always had a talent for reading people. It was clear that the

Colonel had something he needed to get off his chest, and that he feared that Van der Sandt wouldn't take the news well. He guessed that the jihadists had taken the man's weapons and he could see from Bell's reaction that he had guessed right.

Bell nodded. 'His Heckler and his Glock.'

'How many rounds?'

'One clip for the Glock, three for the Heckler. A few shots were fired at the helicopter.'

That news did catch Van der Sandt by surprise and he raised his eyebrows. 'They shot at you?'

Bell nodded. 'The mouthy one, the one that said he was a doctor. He's the one who pushed Nick out and then landed on top of him. He grabbed Nick's Heckler and fired at us. We regrouped, retook the clearing and recovered Nick, though by then they'd stripped him of pretty much everything.'

'Which would be what, exactly?'

'His guns, his knife, his radio, his watch, most of his clothes, his boots.'

'Sounds as if this doctor knows what he's doing.'

Bell smiled thinly. 'He was behaving less like a doctor and more like an ISIS-trained jihadist. I'm sorry about this. I take the full blame for what happened.'

Van der Sandt shook his head. 'Shit happens, Colonel,' he said.

'But in view of what you have planned . . .' Bell shrugged.

Van der Sandt smiled. 'It'll just make it more interesting,' he said. All the men except Nick were off the helicopter now. 'You should be on your way, get Nick to the hospital.'

'What about the heli? When do you need it?'

Van der Sandt looked at his Rolex. 'Sun's up around six fifteen. I'd like to leave here at about five forty-five. There's another clearing about thirty kilometres from here, to the south-west of the first one. In view of what's happened you should drop me there and I'll start tracking.'

'You're sure you don't want any of my guys to go with you?'

Van der Sandt shook his head. 'This is down to me,' he said.

'I understand sir,' replied Bell.

'Can I make a suggestion?'

'Of course.'

'You might want to think about changing out of the fatigues before you get to the hospital. Wouldn't want them to think you were part of some militia group bent on civil unrest.'

Bell grinned. 'I've got civilian clothes in the heli, and we'll leave all the weapons here.'

Van der Sandt raised his tumbler in salute. 'Then God bless,' he said.

Bell turned and hurried back to the helicopter. On the way he handed his carbine to one of the men, then took off his sidearm and gave him that, too. He got back into the helicopter, the rotors began to spin faster as the engine roared, then it lifted into the air and headed west.

Van der Sandt sipped his whisky thoughtfully. The fact that the jihadists had a carbine and a handgun was a wrinkle, but it wasn't a problem. If anything, it made what he was doing more acceptable. The best hunts were always the ones where there was a possibility that the quarry could fight back. If his prey was docile and couldn't retaliate, it was no different to shooting fish in a barrel. Now that the jihadists were armed, the hunt became more of a challenge. The end result would be the same, though. The men who had killed his family would be dead. He took a long pull on his cigar and blew smoke up into the sky. He knew that killing the men wouldn't bring back his wife and children. They were gone forever. And he knew that killing them wouldn't make him miss Laura and the kids any less. The loss would live with him until the day he died. But Van der Sandt believed in an eye for an eye. And tomorrow he was going to get his revenge.

CHAPTER 24

Raj put the last of the nine stones into his pocket. Another one hundred metres and they would have covered a kilometre, the third since they had left the clearing. It was easy enough to count off a hundred metres – about a hundred and thirty-five steps, for the average pace length – but beyond that it was easy to forget, and the stones ensured that he kept track of how far they had walked. Each time he covered a hundred metres he put a stone in his pocket. Nine stones, nine hundred metres. He looked at the compass in the hilt of the knife to check that they were still heading due east.

'I'm knackered, Raj,' said Sid. He and Jaffar were supporting Mo. Mo had tried walking with his makeshift crutch but he had winced at every step and after half an hour had collapsed, unable to go any further. Even with Sid and Jaffar taking an arm each, they were still making slow progress and it would be dark soon. Erol was faring better, but they could only travel as fast as the slowest member of the group, and that was Mo.

'Another hundred metres and we'll make a camp,' said Raj.

They were heading up a slight incline. The forest was so dense that he couldn't see more than fifty metres ahead but there were enough gaps in the branches overhead to see the darkening sky. Raj counted off his steps and when he reached a hundred he stopped and turned round. 'This is it?' asked Erol. 'We're stopping here?'

Raj nodded and Erol sighed and lowered himself to the ground. Raj waited for Jaffar and Sid to catch them up, with Mo between them. They helped Mo sit down against a tree. 'Now what?' asked Sid.

'It'll be dark soon,' said Raj. 'We need to build shelters.'

Sid pointed at the knife on Raj's thigh. 'Does that survival knife have flints in it?'

'Yeah, but I don't want to light a fire. If that nutter is already tracking us he'll see it at night, and the smell will carry for kilometres.'

'It's going to get cold.'

'I know. But we can use leaves and ferns to provide insulation. And we can lie together to share body heat.'

'And we need to pray,' said Jaffar.

Raj looked at him in astonishment. 'You what?'

'Isha'a, the night prayer.'

'Mate, we don't have time to pray,' said Raj. 'We need to get shelters built before it's dark.'

'He's right, Raj,' said Sid. 'We need to pray.'

Raj shook his head. 'No, we need to make shelters.'

'Give me the knife,' said Sid, holding out his hand.

'What?'

'I need the compass, for the qibla. To make sure we're praying to Mecca.'

Raj narrowed his eyes, but then he shook his head contemptuously and gave him the knife, hilt first. 'You don't even know where we are,' he said.

'Mecca is east, that's good enough,' said Sid.

'Well that's the direction we've been walking in, or haven't you been paying attention? And what about Mo? He's in no state to pray.'

'We'll help him,' said Sid. He looked at the compass, then pointed off to the left. 'That way,' he said. 'That's the qibla.'

'Give me back the knife,' said Raj. Sid did as he was told. Raj took it and started looking around. He found a walnut tree with reasonably straight branches and he put the knife in his scabbard and began wrenching a ten foot branch away from the trunk.

Behind him Jaffar and Sid were helping Mo up. Erol got to his feet himself. The four men stood in a line and began to pray.

Raj shook his head and continued to pull at the branch. It splintered next to the trunk and he ripped it away, dropped it onto the ground, and grabbed a second branch.

He heard a yelp of pain and turned to see Mo staggering to the side. He was clearly having trouble getting to the ground to kneel – hardly surprising with the splint on his leg. Jaffar, Sid and Erol were already kneeling, their heads on the ground as they prayed.

Raj pulled the branch away and tossed it on top of the second one. He didn't see any other suitable branches on the tree so he moved further into the forest. He found an ash tree with long straight branches and he managed to pull four away before Jaffar came up behind him. 'We're done,' he said.

Raj gave him the knife. 'Start stripping the twigs off the branches over there. And tell the others to start gathering ferns and leaves. We need large ferns to act as roofing and smaller ones for insulation.'

Jaffar went over to Sid as Raj grabbed another branch and began to twist it away from the trunk.

Once he had six long branches, he broke off six shorter ones, each about four feet long. Once he was done he took them over to Jaffar, who was doing a decent job of stripping the branches clean. Sid came over with an armful of ferns and dropped them onto the ground. 'What's the plan?' he asked Raj.

'We use the shorter branches to make two A frames. Then we run three of the branches from the A frames to the ground. Then we cover them with ferns. It's simple enough. We'll have shelter if it rains and it will trap our body warmth. We can use leaves and ferns to provide insulation from the ground. I figure we can get two in one shelter and three in the other. We need to sleep together to conserve body warmth.'

'How cold do you think it will get?' asked Sid.

'I don't know. Five degrees. Ten maybe. Enough to get hypothermia if we don't prepare for it.' He looked up at the darkening sky. 'We need to get a move on.'

Raj helped Jaffar to strip the twigs off the branches while Sid went looking for more ferns. Erol went with him. Mo was still sitting on the ground.

Once they had stripped all the branches, Raj took the knife from Jaffar and went off in search of vines. He found a redwood that was covered in them and he hacked off a dozen sections, each two or three feet long.

When he returned, he showed Sid and Jaffar how to use the vines to make the A frames. Together they placed ferns on top of the branches to make the roof, then they piled more ferns and leaves underneath. It was almost dark by the time they had finished, and their breath was feathering in the night air.

'I think Mo and Erol should take the smaller one and the three of us take the bigger shelter,' Raj said to Sid and Jaffar.

The two men nodded. 'Sounds like a plan,' said Sid. He and Jaffar went over to Mo, helped him to his feet and walked him slowly over to the shelter. He lay down and they covered him with ferns.

'Erol,' said Raj, gesturing for him to lie down next to Mo. Erol limped over and crawled into the shelter.

'So how come you know all this survival stuff?' Sid asked Raj.

'I'm a big fan of survival shows,' said Raj.

'Fuck off,' laughed Sid. 'Okay, the shelter stuff you could have seen on the TV or YouTube, but the way you handled that gun when they dropped us off . . .' He shook his head. 'That takes training. And not the sort of training me and the guys have had.'

Raj didn't say anything and waited for Sid to get to the point.

'Army, right?' said Sid quietly.

Raj nodded. 'Sort of.'

'I fucking knew it,' said Sid. 'So if you're a soldier, what the fuck were you doing in a hospital in Syria?'

'I had military training and medical training,' said Raj. 'Now I'm just a doctor.'

'How can you be both? It takes years to be a doctor.'

'They trained me as a doctor when I signed up. It's a programme they've got. You join the Royal Marines and they train you as a commando, and you study medicine at the same time,' Raj said. 'It was the medical side I was most interested in. My family didn't have much money and I didn't want to get stuck with a huge student debt.' He shrugged. 'Plus I was bored and the Marines definitely isn't boring.'

'How the fuck does a Muslim end up in the fucking Army?' said Jaffar. 'I don't get it.'

'The Marines are part of the Navy, not the Army. And I'm not going to argue with you, not when we need to get some sleep.' He knelt down and crawled into the larger shelter. The last thing he wanted just then was to explain that he wasn't a Muslim. He wasn't sure how they would react to the news and was in no hurry to find out.

'This is fucked up,' said Sid, and he crawled in next to Raj.

'No argument here,' said Raj.

Jaffar crawled into the shelter and lay down next to Sid. The three men covered themselves with leaves and ferns and then settled down to sleep. Raj had his hand on his carbine as he closed his eyes.

CHAPTER 25

Sal tripped over a tree root, staggered and fell to the ground. He cursed and picked himself up. 'Fuck it,' he said.

'Are you okay?' asked Abdullah, coming up behind him.

Sal wiped his hands on his trousers. 'Yeah.' He looked around. 'We're going to have to rest up. We're going to break something if we keep walking in the dark.' They were heading up a gentle slope, and had been for the best part of an hour. The darkness had crept up on them slowly but now the bits of sky that they could see through the tree canopy were dotted with stars. The temperature had dropped and they could see their breath in the night air.

'What do you want to do?' asked Abdullah.

'Grab some ferns, we can sleep on them,' said Sal. In the distance he spotted a giant redwood that had died and fallen over, leaving its roots exposed. He walked over to it. Much of the bark was rotting and covered in moss, and the roots had dried and were cracking. 'We could sleep in there,' he said. 'It'll block out the wind.'

They gathered armfuls of ferns and threw them under the roots. They made several trips until they had a few inches of makeshift bedding. 'That'll do,' said Sal. He threaded his way through the roots and lay down.

Abdullah joined him. 'Fuck, we didn't pray,' he said.

'We'll pray tomorrow,' said Sal.

'We should pray tonight,' said Abdullah.

'Bruv, I tell you what,' said Sal, 'you don't tell my imam and I won't tell yours. We'll pray tomorrow.'

Abdullah nodded. 'Okay.' He shivered. 'I'm fucking freezing.'

'Lie next to me,' said Sal.

Abdullah moved over so that his side was pressing against Sal's. 'What's the plan, Sal?' he asked quietly. 'What the fuck are we going to do?'

'We're going to get out of here, don't worry,' said Sal.

'We should have taken Raj's gun.'

'He wasn't going to give it up,' said Sal. 'But he's fucked himself. Mo and Erol will slow him down. The guy who wants to kill us is going to get them first. They can't move quickly or quietly, but we can. Either we find help or we get back to the house. There are phones there, we can ring the cops.'

'Do you think you can find the house?'

Sal sighed. 'I don't know bruv, I hope so.'

The two men lay in silence for a while. 'We killed his family, didn't we?' said Abdullah. 'In Cyprus.'

'That's what it looks like.'

'So, family. That means wife and kids.'

'I guess so.'

'Did you kill kids?'

'I shot kafirs. They were all kafirs. Man, woman, child, a kafir is a fucking kafir. We're fighting for our religion and anyone who isn't a Muslim is the enemy.'

'I know, bruv. I know. But I didn't shoot any kids that day.'

'What, and you think he'll take that into consideration?' He snorted contemptuously. 'He don't give a fuck about who you did or didn't kill. He just wants revenge and we fit the bill.'

Abdullah took a deep breath and held it for several seconds before exhaling. 'This guy, I understand where he's coming from, bruv. He wants revenge for what we did to his family. And maybe he's right. Maybe what we did was wrong and we deserve this.'

'You need to shut the fuck up or I'll kill you myself.'

'I'm just saying, what we did . . .'

'I'm serious,' interrupted Sal. 'If you don't stop talking I'll pick up a rock and bash your fucking brains out.'

'Bruv . . .'

'I'm serious. We're in deep shit and you whining about it isn't going to get us out of it. You hear me?'

'I hear you,' whispered Abdullah. He turned his back on Sal and curled up into a foetal ball as tears ran down his cheeks.

CHAPTER 26

Van der Sandt whisked some eggs, then added a splash of milk. He put the mixture into a saucepan and put it on the gas burner. Two slices of toast popped out of the toaster and he buttered them as the eggs began to cook. He stirred the eggs until they were the consistency he liked, then spooned them onto the toast. He topped the eggs off with slices of Forman's London Cure smoked salmon. He had the salmon flown in from London on a regular basis. H. Forman & Son were the oldest producer of smoked salmon in the world, and in Van der Sandt's opinion theirs was the finest by far.

He poured himself a fresh mug of coffee and then carried it along with his breakfast out onto the terrace. Two of Colin Bell's men were standing guard at either side of the terrace, cradling their Hecklers. They nodded and he nodded back. He hadn't asked for the security and he didn't think it was at all necessary, but he figured that at least it would give them something to do.

He sat down and tucked into his breakfast. As he ate, three more of Bell's men came into view, heading from the direction of the staff cottages. They were wearing green shorts and T-shirts and they ran around the perimeter of the grounds before dropping to the grass and carrying out an energetic series of press-ups and sit-ups.

As Van der Sandt was finishing his meal, he heard the buzz of an approaching helicopter off to his left. It got louder and louder and then the Airbus came into view. It did a circuit of the grounds and landed. As its rotors slowed, Colin Bell appeared from the doorway. He had changed out of his fatigues and was wearing a long-sleeved denim shirt and jeans. The men who had been exercising ran over and surrounded him as he walked towards the terrace. He said something to them, they grunted in unison, and then they jogged back to the cottages.

Bell climbed the steps to the terrace. There were dark patches under his eyes and a greyish pallor to his skin. Van der Sandt waved for him to sit. 'How's Nick?' asked Van der Sandt as Bell pulled out a chair and sat down.

Bell grimaced. 'Not good. He's got a collapsed lung and a busted spleen and several broken bones. He'll mend, but he'll never be the same.'

'I'm sorry,' said Van der Sandt. 'Has he any family?'

'Divorced, two kids.'

'Make sure they're looked after. Nick, too. And I'll pick up all the bills, obviously.'

'Thank you.'

'Do you want a coffee?'

Bell shook his head. 'I'm good,' he said. He leant forward. 'How do you want to play this, Mr Van der Sandt?'

Van der Sandt frowned. 'What do you mean?'

'Are you still sure you want to go into the forest alone?'

'What are you saying? I should let you go in? If I did that, the whole exercise becomes pointless. I want those bastards dead and I want them to suffer, and I want to be the one to make them suffer. If I let you do it for me, we might as well have shot them in the house when we had them.' He sat back in his chair. 'I appreciate your concern, Colonel, but I have hunted and killed some of the most dangerous predators in the world. These men are scum. Worthless scum. And I'll hunt them down and kill them like the dogs they are.'

Bell smiled thinly. 'I understand,' he said. 'If it's all right with you, I'd like to stay here with a few men until Nick gets the all clear to leave the hospital.'

'Of course. You can stay in the staff cottages, though I'm afraid there won't be a maid service and you'll have to take care of yourself food-wise.' Van der Sandt had given all the regular staff extra paid vacation until he'd finished his hunt. He knew that

Bell and his men would stay tight-lipped about what had happened but he couldn't say the same about the legion of housekeeping staff and gardeners who took care of the mansion and its extensive grounds.

'That's not a problem, sir,' said Bell. 'And would you do one thing for me, sir, to keep my mind at rest?'

'If I can,' said Van der Sandt. He sipped his coffee.

'I'd like you to take a radio with you. That way you can at least stay in touch with me. And if anything goes wrong, I can come with the chopper and pick you up.'

'Nothing will go wrong, Colonel,' said Van der Sandt. 'But yes, I'll take a radio with me.'

The Colonel smiled. 'And I really think I should keep the full team here until everything is resolved.'

'That's not necessary, Colonel. You can stand some of your men down. Just keep the bare minimum on the estate. My own security team will be back with Neil Thomas in two days. As soon as I've been dropped in the clearing, most of your men can head for the airport.'

'Roger that,' said Bell. 'So when do you want to leave?'

Van der Sandt pushed back his chair and got to his feet. 'I'll get my gear and we'll be off,' he said. He picked up his plate and mug and headed inside.

CHAPTER 27

The first sign of dawn was a lightening of the patches of the sky that Raj could glimpse through the tree cover. Then there were streaks of red and the sound of birds overhead. He was sitting outside the shelter, his back to a tree. He had only slept for five or six hours. Sid had woken him up when he had accidentally jabbed him in the ribs while rolling over. Raj had tried to get back to sleep but Sid had started snoring and eventually Raj had rolled out of the shelter and sat by the tree. He was used to snatching sleep in short bursts; working at the short-staffed hospital meant he was on call pretty much any hour of the day or night. The temperature had dropped drastically during the night but Raj kept rubbing his hands for warmth, and once the sun made an appearance it began to get warmer.

He heard a cough from the second shelter, and then a rustling of leaves. Jaffar appeared. 'What time is it?' he asked Raj, blinking blearily.

Raj looked at his watch. 'Five forty-five,' he said.

'What are we going to do about food?' asked Jaffar, standing up and stretching.

'You might be able to find some berries,' said Raj. 'Hazelnuts maybe.'

'And what about water?'

'What about it?'

'How are we going to get some?' said Jaffar. 'You're the survival expert.'

'The priority is to get to safety,' said Raj. 'There's a nutter with a gun after us, remember?'

Jaffar walked over to Raj, then sat down and pulled his knees up to his chest. 'So what's the plan?' He gestured at the gun by Raj's side. 'You planning on shooting him?'

'My plan is to get as far away from here as possible,' said Raj.

'The quicker the better, right?'

'Right.'

Jaffar moved his head close to Raj's, and lowered his voice. 'Thing is, we'll move faster without Mo, and that's a fact.'

Raj frowned. 'I thought he was a friend of yours?'

Jaffar pulled a face. 'I'd never met him until we went to the training camp. Barely said a word to him. Bit of a twat, to be honest. Thing is, like you said we need to get the hell out of here, and carrying Mo is going to make that more difficult.'

'So we do what, leave him here?'

'Why not? Maybe light a fire or something to keep him warm.'

'So that the hunter can find him, you mean? That's harsh, Jaffar. That's really harsh.'

'It's survival of the fittest, innit?'

'And what if you were the one with the broken leg? Would you be happy if we left you behind?'

Jaffar shrugged. 'I'd understand,' he said. 'I wouldn't expect to be carried.'

'That's very noble of you,' said Raj. 'But we're not leaving a man behind.'

Jaffar sneered at him. 'That's just fucking crazy. It's bad enough the way Erol is limping but at least he can walk.'

'Erol is your mate, right? You're both from Bradford?'

'Yeah, we used to live next door to each other. We went to primary school together.'

'Would you leave him behind? If he couldn't walk?'

'That's different. He's a mate.'

'So you'd carry Erol but not Mo?'

Jaffar grimaced. 'When you say it like that, you make me sound like an arsehole.'

'If that cap fits,' said Raj.

'What the fuck does that mean?' snapped Jaffar.

'You know exactly what it means,' said Raj quietly. 'Look, if you want to take your chances out there on your own, be my guest. But I'm not leaving Mo.

If we do he'll either die of exposure or that guy will kill him. The only chance he has is if we stick with him. And I think you know that, otherwise you'd have left with the other two last night.'

'I just want to get out of here,' said Jaffar quietly.

'You and me both,' said Raj. He got to his feet, then reached down and picked up the carbine. He slung it over his shoulder and then went over to the smaller shelter where Erol was asleep on his side. Raj prodded him with his boot. 'Wakey, wakey,' he said.

Erol blinked and screwed up his eyes. 'What?'

'It's dawn,' said Raj. 'Time to move.'

Erol sat up and ran his hands through his hair. 'Have we got anything to drink?' he asked.

'Room service is closed,' said Raj. 'Wake Mo up.'

Raj went over to the larger shelter. Sid was already sitting up and rubbing his eyes. 'What time is it?' he asked.

'Time to start moving,' said Raj.

Sid shook his head. 'Salat al Fajr,' he said. 'Morning prayers.'

'There's a man with a gun who wants us all dead,' said Raj. 'We need to move now.'

Sid rolled out of the shelter and got to his feet. The Glock was still tucked into his belt. 'Good Muslims pray five times a day,' he said.

Raj took a deep breath. It was time to set the record straight. 'Mate, let's get one thing straight. I'm not a Muslim and I don't want your religion putting us in the firing line. We need to go, now.'

Sid's eyes narrowed. 'What do you mean, you're not a Muslim?'

'What do you think I mean? You see an Asian guy with a beard and you automatically assume he's a Muslim?'

'But you were out in Syria, helping Muslims in the hospital?'

'I was helping anyone who needed help.'

'So what are you then?'

'What am I? What sort of question is that? I'm British, mate.

If you want to define me by race then I'd accept British Asian. But so far as religion goes, I'm not interested. I go to the temple now and again but that's only to make my parents happy. I've seen too much evil in the world to believe in God. Any God.'

'Temple? So what are you, a Sikh?'

'No, I'm a Hindu if I'm anything. Are you happy now you can slap a label on me?'

Sid held up his hands. 'Bruv, there's no need to get pissed off. I was just asking.'

'The only good Hindu is a dead Hindu, that's what you're thinking. I'm a kafir so I'm lower than the shit on your shoes, is that what's going through your mind?' The carbine was swinging from its sling and Raj put a hand on it to keep it steady.

Sid's eyes widened. 'Hey, bruv, don't take me the wrong way!' he said quickly.

Raj let his hand fall away from the weapon. 'It's your religion that's got me into this mess, so just keep it to yourself and we'll get along fine.'

'I hear you, bruv, but the guys are going to want to pray,' Sid said. 'They're not going to take no for an answer.'

'Then pray,' said Raj. 'But it won't be Allah who gets us out of this hole.'

CHAPTER 28

Something buzzed by Sal's ear and he swatted it away. 'I fucking hate insects,' he muttered. 'What time is it do you think?'

Abdullah frowned. 'Six. Seven maybe? No way of knowing.'

Sal crawled out of their makeshift bed, keeping low to avoid the thicker tree roots, then winced as he straightened up. His knees cracked and his right arm had gone numb. He waved it around, trying to restore the circulation. Abdullah joined him, grunting. 'I'm fucking starving,' he said.

'I know,' said Sal. 'But what the fuck can we do?'

'There has to be something to eat, right? There are birds and animals so they must eat something.'

'Berries maybe,' said Sal, looking around. 'Insects.'

'Insects?'

'Flies. Spiders. Beetles. It's all protein.'

Abdullah laughed harshly. 'I'll be fucked if I'm gonna eat a bug. Anyway, are bugs halal?'

'An imam once told me that most insects are forbidden but that grasshoppers are halal.'

'Fuck me, I ain't gonna eat no grasshopper. What about potatoes and carrots and shit? They grow in the ground, right?'

'On farms, yeah, not in the forest.' Sal looked up through the trees. Dawn was breaking and there was a reddish tinge to the sky to their left. He pointed at the reddening sky. 'So the sun rises in the east, right? And sets in the west?'

'Sure.' Abdullah stood up, shivering. 'I am so fucking cold.'

Sal got to his feet. 'When they flew us here, did we fly north or south?'

'How the fuck would I know that?'

'We can work it out, can't we? It was afternoon so the sun was going down which means it would be going to the west. So if we could remember if it was on the right or the left of the helicopter then we'd know if they flew us north or south.'

'Why the fuck does that matter, bruv?'

'We need a plan, right? And the best plan as I see it is to get to a road or something. Then get help.'

'Help?' said Abdullah. 'Who's going to help us?'

'Anyone. Everyone. We haven't done anything wrong, have we? Not here. Not in this country. They've got cops here and the cops will help us.'

'And we tell them what? We're fucking ISIS fighters, bruv, they'll put us in Guantanamo Bay in orange jumpsuits.'

Sal shook his head. 'No, bruv. We tell them we were working for an NGO in Syria and we were kidnapped by that nutter. There's no way they can prove we were with ISIS.'

'Do you think?'

'He's hunting us like we're animals. He's the fucking criminal here and they'll see that. How the fuck else did we end up in the woods?'

Abdullah nodded. 'Yeah, okay, that makes sense.'

'Course it does. So we don't wanna be heading back towards the house because that's where the guy is. We need a road and we need to find someone with a phone.'

'I didn't see any roads when we flew here, did you?'

'No bruv, I didn't,' said Sal. He took the radio from his pocket and looked at it. There was a stubby flexible aerial and two knobs. One was an on–off and volume switch, the other was to change the frequency. 'I don't suppose you know what frequency the cops use do you?'

'It's nine-one-one, innit?'

'That's for the phone, bruv. These are frequencies.' He switched on the radio and turned the volume switch halfway. There was a button on the side. He squeezed it. 'Yeah, anybody there? Anybody listening?' He let go of the button. 'Nothing,' he said.

'Try another frequency.'

'There's hundreds,' said Sal.

'We've got nothing to lose.'

'No, but we'll drain the battery.'

'Just try a few.'

Sal began turning the frequency knob slowly. The first few clicks produced nothing but on the sixth they heard static. He pressed the side button again and asked if there was anyone there. There was only static. 'It's a piece of shit,' said Sal.

'Maybe there are too many trees,' said Abdullah.

'Trees?'

'Yeah, maybe they're blocking the signal. And we're in a valley. We need to be higher.' He gestured up the slope. 'If we go higher, we might get a signal.'

'It's not a fucking phone, bruv,' said Sal dismissively. 'It's a radio. They work differently.'

'Yeah, I get it, but they still have to transmit, right? And the more trees there are, the more interference. That's just obvious.'

Sal nodded. 'Okay, yeah, maybe.' He tried the radio again but there was still only static. 'Shall we go up, see if it works better?'

'We need to pray, bruv,' said Abdullah.

'I know. But which way is the qibla?'

Abdullah looked around. 'Which way did we come from?'

Sal pointed to the left.

'And which way is that?' asked Abdullah.

'How the fuck would I know?' said Sal. 'North, south, east, west, who the fuck knows which way is which?'

'But if we don't know the direction of the qibla, the prayers aren't valid. We have to bow towards Mecca. You know that, bruv.'

Sal shook his head. 'Nah, bruv you're wrong. I had an imam explain it to me. If a Muslim is in a place where he just doesn't know the direction of the qibla, then he has to pray in the direction he thinks it is. If the Muslim believes that he is praying in the right direction, then the prayers are valid.'

'You're sure?'

'What, you think I'm making it up? Fuck you. I'm just telling you what he told me.'

Abdullah raised his hands. 'I'm not arguing with you, bruv.'

'So which direction do you think?' asked Sal.

Abdullah frowned, then pointed towards the sun. 'If the sun rises in the east, it should be that way.'

'Yeah, I hear you. Okay, let's get this done,' said Sal. He knelt down and Abdullah joined him. They began to pray.

CHAPTER 29

'We're coming up to the drop zone,' said Bell, staring at the GPS unit in his hand. 'Two minutes.'

Van der Sandt took a deep breath and exhaled slowly. He had asked to be dropped at a clearing to the south-west of the area where they had dropped the jihadists the previous day. They had almost certainly moved on but now that they were armed it would be safer to approach them on the ground. Van der Sandt was sitting in the front row of the helicopter, next to Bell. Two of Bell's men were behind them, cradling their carbines. Van der Sandt was holding his Ambush between his legs. It held a five-round magazine and he had six spare magazines in his jacket. Seven magazines in total, thirty five rounds. More than enough. He had a transceiver clipped to his belt and a water bottle slung across his shoulder. There were half a dozen energy bars in his backpack, along with a small first aid kit, and other items he thought he might need. On his head was a floppy camouflage hat.

He looked out of the window at the tree cover as it flashed by. The forest was full of wildlife, most of it harmless. There were deer and elk, pine martens and raccoons. There were bobcats, but they usually kept well away from people. The wolves that he had introduced to the woods at Laura's behest also tended to steer clear of humans. The only real danger came from the black bears that called the forest home. An adult male could be seven feet tall and weigh up to three hundred kilos and could easily disembowel and kill with one slash of its massive claws. Its jaws were wide enough to clamp around a man's head and they could flip boulders weighing a hundred and fifty kilos or more. But Van der Sandt wasn't interested in bears. All he cared about were the men who had killed his family.

The helicopter banked to the left and through the window Van der Sandt saw the clearing. Rocks protruding from the ground had prevented trees and bushes from growing there over the years. The clearing was oval in shape and surrounded by towering redwoods.

'We're not going to be able to touch down, the ground is too uneven,' said the pilot in the left-hand seat. 'I'll get you as close as I can.'

The helicopter went into a hover over the centre of the clearing and then slowly began to descend. As they went down, the darkness of the forest seemed to swallow them. Bell pulled back the door. 'Good luck, sir,' he said, then moved to the side to give Van der Sandt room to get out. The skids of the helicopter were about a metre above the rocks.

'I can get a bit lower,' said the pilot.

As Van der Sandt looked out of the door, the helicopter dropped down until the skids were almost touching the rocks. Bell patted him on the shoulder. Van der Sandt gritted his teeth and stepped out of the doorway. The moment his feet were on the ground, the helicopter lifted off. Van der Sandt put his left hand on his hat to stop it blowing away and looked up. Bell was leaning out the doorway. He waved his hook at Van der Sandt and Van der Sandt waved back.

The helicopter reached the treetops and then it banked to the left and headed south. The roar of the twin turbines faded into the distance. Van der Sandt stood at the edge of the clearing, turning his head slowly from side to side, listening to the forest. The birds and insects had fallen silent when the helicopter had descended, but now that it had gone the sounds of the forest gradually returned. Van der Sandt gritted his teeth and walked into the trees. The damp sweet smell of the forest enveloped him. His boots crunched softly on the vegetation beneath his feet. The trees around him were second growth. Logging had started in the 1850s and new trees had grown in their place. Further north there were original growth forests, areas where no man had ever walked. But Van der Sandt wouldn't be going that far. The men he was hunting were only a few kilometres away.

CHAPTER 30

While the rest of the men knelt and prayed, Raj dismantled the two shelters and threw the branches, ferns and leaves into the undergrowth. He stopped when he heard the helicopter in the distance. He moved his head from side to side, trying to pinpoint the direction of the sound. It was getting louder. He took the knife from its scabbard and checked the compass. The sound was coming from the south-west. Raj couldn't tell how far away the helicopter was because the trees muffled most of the noise. If it was heading to the clearing where they had been dropped, it would have to fly north. He listened intently. The pitch of the sound changed. It was hovering, he realised, some distance away. He checked the compass again. The sound was definitely not coming from the clearing. He continued to turn his head from side to side, trying to work out how far away the helicopter was. The sound diminished. Was it flying away or was it descending? He peered off into the distance but all he could see were trees.

He checked the compass again. It was definitely south-west of their position. He was fairly sure that it was the same helicopter that he'd been on, the Airbus. If it was, then they were probably dropping off the man who wanted to kill them.

The engine noise started to get louder. The helicopter had descended and the forest had absorbed the sound, and now it was climbing again. The noise reached a peak and then there was a change in pitch and it began to move south. It was flying back to the house. They had dropped off the hunter. Raj rubbed the back of his neck. Just one hunter or more than one? There was no way of knowing. When the man had spoken to them in the hangar, he'd made it clear that he wanted personal revenge for the death of his family. But that was before he had learnt that his quarry were now armed. They had the Heckler and the Glock and the knife. Would that change his plans? Would he now come mob-handed? Were there now several armed men on their trail? If so, then his chances of survival were almost zero.

CHAPTER 31

The jihadists finished their prayers, oblivious to the helicopter in the distance. Sid and Jaffar got to their feet and helped Erol up. Mo hadn't been able to kneel for his prayers; he had bent at the waist as best he could. Raj was sitting by a massive redwood, cleaning his carbine. 'What's his problem?' asked Jaffar. 'Why isn't he praying with us?'

'He's not a Muslim,' said Sid.

'What the fuck? What is he?'

'Hindu.'

'He's a fucking Hindu? Fuck him, bruv.'

'Jaffar, he's our best hope of getting out of here. We've got to put our differences aside if we're going to get out of this alive.'

'Sid's right,' said Erol. 'The guy knows what he's doing. You saw the way that he handled that gun. He's a pro.'

'Hindus hate Muslims,' said Mo. 'They always have and they always will.'

'He's not religious, bruv,' said Sid.

'Religious or not, he's a fucking kafir,' sneered Jaffar.

'A kafir who might just save our lives,' said Sid. 'And the way things are, we need all the help we can get.' He lowered his voice to a whisper. 'Look, bruv, he didn't ask to be part of this. We grabbed him from his hospital and took him to our camp. Now he's stuck here with us. He could have taken that gun and gone off on his own. You heard what he said, he used to be a Marine. They're like the SAS, they train for all sorts of shit. He could have just looked after number one. He'd move a lot faster on his own.'

'He knew what to do with my leg,' said Mo. 'It still hurts, but at least I can move.'

Jaffar held up his hands. 'Fine,' he said, 'If you want to team up with a fucking kafir, so be it.'

'Keep your voice down, bruv,' whispered Sid. 'I don't want to piss him off.'

'Are you scared of him?' sneered Jaffar.

Sid's eyes hardened. 'Watch your mouth, Jaffar. I'm not scared of anyone.' His hand moved towards the Glock in his belt.

'You want to shoot me, bruv?' Jaffar tapped his chest above his heart. 'Go ahead and fucking shoot me.'

'You two guys need to chill,' said Erol. 'Fighting among ourselves isn't going to get us anywhere. There's a madman with a gun out there who wants us dead, and if we don't get our act together we're going to die in this forest. You hear me?'

Sid kept his eyes on Jaffar. 'He's right.'

Jaffar sighed. 'Okay. I'm cool.'

Sid moved his hand away from his gun. 'Let's just do what we have to do to get out of here.'

CHAPTER 32

Sal and Abdullah reached the top of the wooded hill. They were still surrounded by trees and even though they had reached the high point, they couldn't see more than fifty or sixty feet in any direction. Sal looked up at one of the towering redwoods. 'The only way we're going to be able to see where we are is if we climb,' he said.

'Fuck that, I'm no monkey,' said Abdullah. He dropped down and sat at the base of the tree, his arms wrapped around his knees. 'I'm gasping for a drink.'

'I don't see any water,' said Sal. He put his hands on his hips as he looked around. 'There's no streams or anything, how the fuck does anything drink? There are animals, right, and birds. There has to be water somewhere.'

Abdullah reached out and grabbed a handful of earth. 'The trees have to get water. Can't we dig down and get water that way?'

'Dig with what, bruv?' asked Sal. 'I don't see any spades around, do you? We need a stream or a lake or something.' He looked up through the branches. 'It doesn't look like it's going to rain, either.' He pulled the transceiver out of his pocket and switched it on. He began switching frequencies. Each time he heard static he stopped and pressed the transmit button to see if anyone could hear him.

'You're wasting your breath,' said Abdullah.

'If you don't try, you don't get. Do you have any bright ideas?'

'I just want to get the fuck out of here,' said Abdullah.

Sal clicked the frequency switch and there was a burst of static. He put the transceiver to his face and pressed the transmit button.

'Is there anyone there?' He released the transmit button and listened but there was only static. He pressed the button again. 'Hello? Is there anyone there?' He released the button and took the transceiver away from his face, scowling.

'Just throw it the fuck away,' said Abdullah. 'What time do you think it is?'

'I don't know. He shaded his eyes with his left hand. 'It's hard to see where the fucking sun is.'

The transceiver crackled. 'Hello? Are you receiving me?'

Sal jumped and the transceiver fell from his hand and hit the ground. 'Shit!' he shouted. He bent down and picked it up, and held it to his ear. 'Hello?' he said. 'Hello? Hello?' He realised he wasn't pressing the transmit button and he cursed as he pressed it again. 'Yes, hi, who is this?' he said. There was only static. Abdullah got to his feet and walked over to him. 'Hello?' repeated Sal. 'Hello? Hello?'

'You've got to take your finger off the button to hear them,' said Abdullah.

'I'm not fucking retarded, bruv,' snapped Sal.

He released his grip on the transmit button. There was a burst of static and then a man's voice. 'This is Chris Schnapp of the US Forest Service. Do you have a problem, sir?'

'Yeah, we have a major problem,' said Sal. 'There's a guy with a gun trying to kill us.'

'I'm sorry, sir. What was that?'

'There's a guy. With a gun. Trying to kill us.'

'What is your name, sir?'

'Sal. My name's Sal.'

'Your full name, sir.'

'What does it matter what my name is?' snapped Sal. 'You need to come and get us before this maniac shoots us.'

'It's for our records, sir. I'll need your name.'

'Okay, fine. My name's Salmaan Yousif.'

'And who else is with you, sir?'

'My friend. Abdullah Rarmoul.'

'So there's just the two of you?'

'Yeah. Now can you come and get us?'

'What is your location, sir?'

'I don't know. We're in a forest. All I can see are trees.'

'That doesn't help me, sir. There are hundreds of thousands of acres of forest. You could be anywhere.'

'Yeah, but what is the range of your radio?'

'My radio, sir? Twenty kilometres on a good day.'

'Right, so you must be twenty kilometres away or closer? That's not too far, is it?'

'Sir, a twenty kilometre radius would mean you could be anywhere within twelve hundred square kilometres.'

Sid cursed under his breath. 'Look officer, my friend and I have no food or water, no shelter, no nothing, and there's a madman with a gun trying to kill us. Can't you track my signal or something?'

'On a phone that might work, but you can't track a radio signal, sir. Do you have a gun?'

'A gun? Why?'

'Because if you fire your weapon the sound might carry and I might hear it.'

'I don't have a weapon,' said Sal.

'Could you light a fire?'

'I don't have a lighter.'

'If you could light a fire and make smoke, I would possibly be able to see that.'

'Okay,' said Sal. 'We'll try.'

'And are there any identifying features where you are, sir? Any rocks, a clearing, a lake, flowing water?'

'Just fucking trees,' said Sal.

'Is the ground flat? Are you in a valley, on a hill?'

'On a hill,' said Sal. 'Does that help?'

'Not really, sir, there are plenty of hills in the area. Look, your best bet would be to light a fire and make smoke. If that fails, head down the hill and look for water. If you find water follow the stream in the direction it flows and with any luck that will take you to a lake.'

'There's a lake?'

'There are several lakes in the area, sir. As soon as you make your way to one, call me on this frequency. But as I said, a fire is your best bet.'

'We'll try,' said Sal. He switched off the transceiver and shoved it back into his pocket.

'So there's a lake,' said Abdullah. 'We need to find it, bruv.'

'How the fuck do we find a lake?' said Sal.

'He said we find a stream.'

'Yeah, well there was no stream on the hill on the way up. And there's no stream here.'

'So we head down the other side.'

Sid shook his head. 'I think the fire's the best idea.'

'A fire? Unless you've got a Zippo stuffed up your arse that's not going to happen.'

'I saw that Bear Grylls light a fire with sticks.'

'Nah, bruv, he fakes all his stuff. It's all done off camera.'

'He did it for real. He took a stick and sharpened one end and then used string to make it twist real fast into another piece of wood. Then when it got hot he dropped on wood shavings or something and then he blew on it and that burst into flames.'

'Bruv, we don't have anything to sharpen a stick, or string, or wood shavings.' Abdullah threw up his hands. 'We're fucked.'

'We're not fucked, bruv. All we've got to do is get to the park ranger or whatever he is.' He pointed at Abdullah's belt. 'You've got a belt with a buckle.'

'So?'

'So maybe we can use a rock and your buckle to make a spark.'

'Come on, bruv.' Abdullah shook his head contemptuously.

'Just give it a try,' said Sal. 'What have we got to lose?'

Abdullah sighed and took off his belt.

CHAPTER 33

Van der Sandt slotted the transceiver back into the pocket of his vest. 'Morons,' he muttered to himself. The range of the transceiver was only about ten kilometres in the heavily wooded terrain, and they were definitely somewhere ahead of him. There were two of them, which meant that the group had split. That at least would make it more of a hunt.

Abdullah and Sal were the Somalians. It was one of the few parts of Africa that Van der Sandt hadn't visited. There was nothing of value to hunt in Somalia and most of the country was a war zone. He took a drink from his water bottle and started walking, heading north-west.

It had been more than a year since he had been in the woods and that had been closer to his house. Laura had been seeing friends in New York and the children were at boarding school near Boston, so he had gone out to replenish the kitchen's meat stocks. He had bagged a blacktail, a buck that judging from its antlers must have been five or six years old. Blacktails were the ghosts of the forest. Their defence strategy was simple enough – at the first sign of danger they would simply vanish into the undergrowth. They usually only appeared in the last few minutes of light to graze and would return to their lairs as soon as the sun came up. They did have their weaknesses though. They tended to graze within an area of just a few square kilometres and during the winter months that area was very specific. They needed enough old-growth tree canopy to trap the snow but with enough spaces between the leaves and branches to allow sunlight through to give life to the grasses, lichens and shrubs that they ate. Once they found an area that satisfied their needs, they tended to stay put. Their colouring was also a weakness. In the summer they were reddish brown and in the winter they changed to greyish brown, but either colour made them stand out against the green background of ferns and mosses.

Blacktail deer could live up to ten years in the wild, but there were so many predators – including black bears, wolves and coyotes – that they rarely made it beyond six. The one that Van der Sandt had killed probably only had a year or so left. He had approached it from downwind, slowly but surely, taking the best part of an hour to cover a hundred metres. Then he had killed it with a single shot from his VO Vapen rifle. It was one of his favourite rifles, handmade by master Swedish gunsmith Viggo Olsson and his son Ulf. Van der Sandt had made several visits to their small factory in the grounds of Trolle-Ljungby Castle in the south of Sweden. The stock was made of walnut root that had been air dried for six years and the engraving alone had taken three months. It had taken eighteen months from start to finish and had cost him close to three hundred thousand dollars. Even that was cheap compared with what Olsson's other customers paid. The likes of the Crown Prince of Dubai, the Sultan of Oman and the Crown Prince of Abu Dhabi paid hundreds of thousands of dollars for hunting rifles inlaid with gold and precious jewels. They were for show, of course. Van der Sandt had never met an Arab who could shoot to save his life.

The VO Vapen rifle was in his gunroom. It was far too good a weapon to kill the seven men in the forest ahead of him. Besides, he wanted to get up close and personal when he killed them. He wanted to see the fear in their eyes and he wanted to see the bullets rip through their flesh and the blood spurt from their wounds and he wanted to be the last thing they saw as their miserable lives ebbed away.

CHAPTER 34

The jihadists walked over to Raj, who was sitting with his back to a redwood, cleaning his gun. 'Okay, we're good to go,' Sid said. Jaffar helped Mo over. Every step was clearly painful, but Mo gritted his teeth defiantly. Erol was able to walk on his own, but he was still using his makeshift crutch. 'What's the plan, Raj?'

'We need to get to the house,' said Raj, getting to his feet. 'If nothing else there'll be a phone there and we can call for help. But if there's no phone there'll be transport. We covered three kilometres last night, but we went east – not south, towards the house. It's six now and last night the sun set just after nine. If we can average three kilometres an hour we should make it to the house before dark.'

Mo grimaced. 'I'm not sure I can walk for fifteen hours.'

'We can take breaks. I think it's doable.'

Mo forced a smile. 'I wish I had your optimism.'

'Do the best you can. We'll take it in turns to help you. You're going to have to walk, Mo. I don't see that we can carry you.'

'I'll walk,' said Mo.

Raj looked at Erol. 'What about you?'

'I'll be okay,' he said. 'You did a good job of binding it.'

'Good man,' said Raj. He took his knife from its scabbard and used the compass to check which way was east. 'Right,' he said, sliding the knife back into place. 'I think we should keep going east for another three kilometres, then we'll head south. I'll take point, Erol you stick behind me and Sid can help Mo. We'll rotate every kilometre – me, Jaffar and Sid. Okay?'

The four men nodded. Raj forced a smile. 'We'll get through this,' he said. 'As we move, try to keep any noise down to a minimum. The route we're taking should keep us out of trouble, but better safe than sorry.' He turned east and began walking, counting the paces in his head.

CHAPTER 35

Van der Sandt looked down at the tracks. There were only two sets of prints. Both men were wearing sandals. He took a drink from his water bottle, then took a small GPS unit from his backpack and switched it on. He was about six kilometres from the clearing where Bell had dropped the men. He switched the unit off and took another drink. Sal, the one he had spoken to on the radio, had said that there were just two of them, and the tracks did seem to confirm that. He decided to make sure, and started walking around in a widening spiral, his eyes on the ground. After five minutes of searching, he had still only seen the two sets of prints. So the group had split up then. Two had gone one way and the other five had taken another route. He put his water bottle away. He'd take care of the two close by, then head to the clearing to pick up the tracks of the rest. He could feel his pulse quicken in anticipation of the killing that was to come.

CHAPTER 36

Raj transferred the stone to his pocket and raised his hand to signal that they should all stop. They had covered three kilometres and it was now 7.15 a.m. After one kilometre, Jaffar had taken over from Sid to assist Mo. Sid and Erol were now bringing up the rear. They had stopped in a small clearing.

'I need to rest,' gasped Mo. 'Sorry.'

'It's okay, mate,' said Raj. 'Sit down for a bit.' Jaffar helped lower Mo to the ground and then walked over to join Raj.

'He's struggling,' said Jaffar, lowering his voice.

'I know,' said Raj.

'Why don't we leave him here, cover him up so he can't be seen, and go for help? We can move twice as fast. We've got forty kilometres or more to cover, we could do it in what, ten hours? We could be back here with help first thing tomorrow morning.'

Sid walked over. 'What's up?' he asked. Erol sat down next to Mo.

Raj gestured at Jaffar. 'Your pal here still wants to leave Mo behind.'

'I'm just saying, he can lie low here, maybe with Erol, and we can make double time to get help,' said Jaffar. 'That's got to be less stressful for the two of them, right?'

'We're not leaving anyone behind,' said Sid.

'The rate we're going, it's going to be two days, maybe three, before we get to the house. And that's three days without food or water. What state are we going to be in by the time we get to the house?'

'It'll be two days, max,' said Raj. 'And if we push on, we can still make it by tonight.'

Jaffar pointed at Mo. 'Look at the state of him. He's struggling.'

'If it was you, bruv, would you want us to leave you?' asked Sid.

'For the greater good,' said Jaffar with a shrug.

'Bollocks,' sneered Sid. 'You'd be begging us to take you with us and you know it.'

'Jaffar, if you want to head off on your own, no one's stopping you,' said Raj.

'I haven't got a gun,' said Jaffar.

'Well you're not having mine,' said Sid.

Jaffar looked at Raj, who shook his head. 'Don't even think about it.'

'Look, I'm not saying I want to go off on my own,' said Jaffar. 'I just thought we'd be quicker if just the three of us went. If you want to stay together, that's cool.'

'Three of us?' said Sid. 'So you want to leave Erol behind as well?'

'Like I said before, survival of the fittest, innit?'

Raj stared at him for several seconds. Jaffar clearly only cared about himself and that meant he wouldn't be an asset if they found themselves in a dangerous situation. Survival in combat was all about teamwork – you fought as a team and if you were lucky you survived as a team. But if the team fell apart and it was every man for himself, survival was that much harder. 'You need to decide now what it is you want,' said Raj. 'No one is holding you here against your will. If you want to go it alone, now's the time to go.'

Jaffar put up his hands. 'I'm cool,' he said. 'I won't mention it again.'

Raj nodded. 'We can rest for five minutes.' He pointed at the crest of a hill. 'Once we reach the top there we'll start heading down so that'll be easier. I'll support Mo this time.' He looked around. They could go without food for several days but it would lift their spirits if they could find something – anything – to eat. He walked to the edge of the clearing and peered into the undergrowth.

Sid joined him. 'You looking for something?'

'Berries,' said Raj. He walked through the undergrowth, scanning left and right.

Sid followed him. 'What sort of berries?'

'The sort we can eat.' Raj grinned as he spotted a cluster of bushes. 'There you go.' He walked over. The bushes were dotted with purple berries. He plucked one and popped it into his mouth. He bit into it and the sweetness exploded.

'Blueberries?' said Sid.

'Huckleberries,' said Raj. 'Bears love them.'

'You think there are bears in these woods?'

'If this is the States, then yes. Wolves, too. And coyotes.' He began pulling away berries and popping them into his mouth. Sid followed his example. The berries were small but they were sugar rich and tasted good. Twenty or so made a decent mouthful, and after five minutes of frantic picking, Sid grinned. 'Not bad,' he said.

'They're good to eat but the sugar rush will be temporary,' said Raj. 'We need protein but we haven't got time to go hunting. And if we did we'd need a fire to cook whatever we kill.' He picked another handful of berries and threw them into his mouth. 'We should take some back for the others.'

They ripped some large leaves off a plant growing at the base of a redwood tree and used them as a makeshift basket. Sid held it while Raj picked several handfuls of berries, then they took them back to the clearing. 'We come bearing gifts,' said Sid.

Jaffar hurried over. 'What are they?'

'Huckleberries,' said Sid.

'They're safe to eat, right?'

'Raj and I have tucked in and we're okay,' said Sid. He held out his hands and Jaffar scooped some out and ate them greedily. He reached for a second helping but Sid moved them out of reach. 'Share and share alike,' he said. He went over to Mo and Erol and gave them both berries.

Jaffar followed him and took what was left. 'Can we get more?' he asked.

'We need to go,' said Raj. 'We can look for more next time we get a break.' He bent down and helped Mo up. 'You good to go?'

Mo put his left arm around Raj's shoulder. 'Okay,' he said.

Raj pulled his knife from its scabbard and checked the compass. 'Right, we need to change direction and start heading south,' he said. He pointed ahead. 'That way, okay Sid?'

'No problem,' said Sid. He headed off. Raj moved forward but he realised within a few steps that helping Mo was throwing out his pacing. He stopped and called Sid over. 'Take these,' he said, handing him the nine stones. 'Use them to keep track of how far we've gone. Count off a hundred and thirty-five steps – that should be about a hundred metres – and transfer one stone to your pocket. Once you have transferred nine, the final hundred metres takes you to one kilometre. Got it?'

Sid grinned. 'It ain't rocket science, bruv,' he said, taking the stones.

Sid took the lead, followed by Jaffar. Erol brought up the rear.

'I'm sorry about this,' said Mo.

'Don't worry about it,' said Raj.

'I heard what Jaffar said. If it was up to him . . .'

'Yeah, well it isn't,' said Raj. 'And I'm not leaving you behind.'

Mo yelped in pain as he stepped on a rock that twisted his ankle. All his weight fell against Raj and they staggered to the side before they regained their balance. Raj realised he had been optimistic about reaching the house before nightfall.

CHAPTER 37

Sal hit the belt buckle against the rock and gritted his teeth in frustration. It was his tenth attempt and so far he hadn't even managed to get a spark.

'You're wasting your time,' said Abdullah. He was sitting with his back against a tree.

Sal glared at him. 'Do you have a better idea?'

'I don't have any fucking ideas. I'm just saying, you're wasting your time.'

Sal sat back on his heels. He didn't like Abdullah's attitude, but the guy was right. He hadn't managed to produce a spark and even if he did the pile of leaves he was using as tinder was damp. He cursed and tossed the belt to Abdullah. 'Let's go,' he said.

'Why not try the radio again?'

'Because we're no further on than the last time we spoke to that ranger,' said Sal. 'What are we gonna say? We tried to light a fire but couldn't? Then he'll ask us where we are and we have the same fucking conversation we had last time. We need to find some sort of landmark.'

'We could try shouting,' said Abdullah.

'What?'

'He didn't know where we were because we were using the radio. He wanted you to shoot a gun but we don't have a gun. But we could try shouting.' He waved away Sal's look of contempt. 'You asked if I had a better idea, and that's what I've got.'

Sal exhaled. Maybe it was better than nothing. 'Okay, let's try. What do we shout?'

'"Help" is always a good start.'

'Okay,' said Sal. He took a deep breath and then bellowed 'Help!' at the top of his voice. Abdullah joined in. The two men screamed in unison for the best part of thirty seconds, then they stopped and listened. There was only silence. Even the birds had gone quiet.

Abdullah opened his mouth to start shouting again but Sal put a hand on his shoulder. 'There's no point, bruv.'

Abdullah nodded grimly. 'Yeah, you're right.'

'Let's head down the hill, see if we can find a stream or something. The ranger said there'd be water. If we can find a stream maybe we can find a lake, then we'll radio him.'

'Water would be good,' said Abdullah. 'I'm so thirsty.'

'Yeah, me too,' said Sal.

The two men started down the slope. They had to weave their way through the trees which was easy enough, but the bushes that blocked their way were harder to negotiate. Some had wicked thorns that tore at their clothes and scratched their skin. Even though they were heading down it was tough going and within half an hour they were both bathed in sweat and breathing heavily.

They reached a clearing and Sal stopped to catch his breath. Abdullah joined him. A thorn had scratched his right cheek and there was a trickle of blood dripping down to his chin. 'You're bleeding, bruv,' said Sal, gesturing at Abdullah's cheek.

Abdullah lifted his hand but before he could touch his face it exploded into a bloody pulp. Abdullah dropped to the ground and blood splattered across the grass. Sal threw himself down and as he moved he felt a second shot whizz above his head and thwack into the tree behind him. He looked up but there was no sign of the shooter. He hadn't heard a gun being fired, but then he remembered that Raj had told them the man's gun had a silencer fitted on it. He took a quick look down and he grimaced when he saw that Abdullah was definitely dead. Most of his face had been blown away and there was brain matter mixed in with the blood spatter. Sal was hyperventilating. He had to move – the hunter knew where he was and was clearly a marksman.

As Sal straightened up a third shot missed him by inches,

passing so close to his face that he felt the air flick against his skin. Again there was no sound from the gun. Sal bent double and started to run. As he reached the nearest tree, another bullet thwacked onto the bark sending splinters flying. He ducked behind the tree and looked around, panting for breath. He knew he had to keep the tree between him and the shooter, but that meant he'd have to fight his way through a thicket of bushes that were almost as tall as he was. He realised he didn't have a choice; if he tried to go around the bushes he'd be exposing his back to the shooter. He grunted, pushed himself away from the tree, and ran towards the bush. He crashed into it and began to fight his way through.

CHAPTER 38

'That's a kilometre,' said Sid, coming to a halt. He turned to look at Raj. 'Do you want to rest or not?'

Raj wanted to press on, but it was clear that Mo was struggling. For the last few hundred metres, Mo had been leaning heavily on Raj and he was grunting with every step. 'We can take a breather,' he said, and lowered Mo to the ground. Erol used his makeshift crutch to sit down next to him. Raj looked at his watch. The last kilometre had taken the best part of half an hour. The ground was uneven and they could only go as fast as the slowest member of the team, and that was Mo.

'I'll take Mo from here,' said Sid. He took the stones from his pocket and gave them to Raj. 'That's a neat trick. They teach you that in the Marines?'

'It was an American Ranger who showed me,' said Raj. 'I did a three-month exchange with the Rangers and they sent me to their HQ in Fort Benning. The Navy sent three Marines to Fort Benning and three Rangers went to our HQ in Plymouth. The idea was we'd learn from each other.' He held up the stones. 'This is one of the things I learnt. The Rangers use a string of beads in two sections. Nine beads and four beads. That means you can count up to five kilometres.' He put the stones in his pocket and then tilted his head on one side. 'Can you hear something?'

Sid frowned. 'Like what?'

'Water,' said Raj.

The men all listened intently. 'I hear it,' said Erol. He pointed off to the left. 'It's coming from over there.'

Raj and Sid headed in the direction of the sound. They threaded their way through towering redwoods, through bushes and shrubs, then broke through into a rocky ravine, a dozen or so feet deep, at the bottom of which was a babbling stream.

'Water!' said Sid. 'Do you think it's drinkable?'

'Moving water is always a good bet,' said Raj. 'But it's not guaranteed to be pure. There could be all sorts of parasites and bacteria in it.'

'But we can boil it, right?'

'We've got nothing to boil it in. And like I said before, we don't want to light a fire because it'll give away our position.'

'I really need a drink, bruv,' said Sid.

'I hear you.'

'So what are the odds?'

'Of getting sick from the water?' Raj shrugged. 'Impossible to say. Like I said, running water is generally safe but we don't know what's going on upstream. An animal could shit in the water or even die in it, and that obviously wouldn't be good news.'

'But we could follow it upstream to where it starts, right?'

Raj nodded thoughtfully. 'You could. It's not rain run-off because it hasn't been raining so it must be coming out of the ground. If you could find the source, that should be pure. But we don't know how far away it is.'

'Come on, let's give it a go.'

'We don't have time.'

'A couple of minutes. Come on.' Sid started heading up the ravine. Raj stared after him and then he sighed and started to follow.

'What's happening?' shouted Jaffar.

'We found a stream, we're checking it out,' shouted Sid.

'Wait for me!' Jaffar rushed over and whooped when he saw the water.

'Don't touch it until we're sure it's safe,' said Raj. 'We'll check out the source, you stay with Erol and Mo.'

Raj followed Sid as he went up the ravine. It got deeper the further uphill they went. 'I see the source,' said Sid excitedly. He began to clamber into the ravine.

'Be careful,' said Raj. He didn't want Sid breaking his leg or twisting his ankle.

Sid reached the bottom of the ravine and pointed at a spout of water gushing from the rocks. 'There it is,' he said. He scrambled across the rocks to where the water was emerging from the ground, knelt down and used his hands to scoop water into his mouth. He sat back on his heels, grinning. 'That tastes good,' he said.

Raj carefully climbed into the ravine and knelt down next to Sid. He scooped some water into his mouth too. It was ice cold and he gulped it down. Sid started drinking again, then threw handfuls of the water over his face.

Eventually the two men had drunk as much as they could and they stood up, laughing. 'I fucking needed that, bruv,' said Sid.

'Yeah, it hit the spot, didn't it?' said Raj. 'Let's give the good news to the guys.'

They climbed out of the ravine and walked back to the clearing, where Jaffar was waiting for them anxiously. 'I thought something had happened to you,' he said.

'We're good,' said Sid. 'We were just checking the water. It's good.'

'We can drink it?'

'It's clean,' he said.

Jaffar grinned and hurried towards the stream. Sid helped Erol to his feet, then gave him his branch. As Erol hobbled over to the stream, Sid and Raj pulled Mo up. 'We can't bring you the water, we've got nothing to carry it in,' said Raj. 'But we can get you close to the stream and you can help yourself.'

Mo nodded and the two men helped him through the undergrowth and over to the water. Erol was already there, kneeling and drinking.

Jaffar was lying on the bank, his face in the water.

Raj and Sid took Mo over to the edge of the stream and helped him sit down. Mo cupped his right hand and began drinking.

Jaffar lifted his head from the water, roared with pleasure, then submerged it again.

Raj waited until they had all drunk their fill, then told them it was time to start walking again. 'I'll take Mo,' said Sid.

Jaffar got to his feet and shook his soaking wet hair. 'I'll help you, bruv,' he said.

The two men lifted Mo to his feet and took an arm each. Raj checked the compass in his knife. 'This way,' he said. Erol grabbed his stick and used it to push himself up, and together they headed down the slope.

CHAPTER 39

Van der Sandt walked purposefully towards the clearing, his rifle pressed against his chest. The man he'd shot had taken the round in the face so he was as dead as dead could be. The suppressor had cut down most of the noise, but the birds had gone quiet. Van der Sandt stopped and listened. The birds were beginning to regain their confidence. Off to his left he heard the *ps-seet, ps-seet, ps-seet* of the Pacific-slope flycatcher and to his right it was answered by the rapid twittering of a Wilson's warbler. He had one bullet left but he ejected the magazine and slotted in a fresh one.

The second jihadist had disappeared behind a massive redwood and Van der Sandt had heard the sound of breaking twigs and rustling leaves. Now there was only silence.

Van der Sandt started walking again, his gun at the ready, his finger on the trigger. He reached the body of the man he'd shot. The subsonic 220-grain round had ripped through the face leaving it a red pulpy mass, and the back of the skull had been blown away. It had been a good kill, an almost perfect one, but he had been too quick with his follow-up shots. He wouldn't make that mistake again.

The man he was hunting had made a good call keeping the tree between his body and the gun, but that limited his options when it came to running away. He pretty much had to run in a straight line. Van der Sandt brought the gun to his shoulder and stepped to the side, widening his view around the tree. In the distance, a hundred metres away, maybe more, he saw a figure moving through the bushes. He sighted on the man's back, but then slid his finger off the trigger. He didn't want to miss again.

He ran to the edge of the clearing. He looked left and right and decided that heading right would be easiest. There were bushes there but they weren't thick and they were free of thorns. Van der Sandt held his rifle high as he pushed through. The jihadist disappeared into the trees but he was moving slowly now, clearly exhausted.

Van der Sandt emerged from the bushes. The trees were closer together and the lack of light meant there were fewer plants. He walked quickly, his gun still at the ready. Walking at a fast pace was more efficient than running, and made less noise.

He was mainly looking ahead, but kept scanning left and right, giving his peripheral vision the maximum opportunity to spot movement. He was breathing slowly and evenly and he knew without checking that his palms were dry.

He saw a flash of movement off to his left and almost immediately he realised it was a bird. A woodpecker.

He moved to the right, scanning the trees ahead.

The woodpecker landed on a branch and began to tap at the trunk. A large flying insect buzzed by Van der Sandt's ear but he ignored it.

Something moved between the trees – a flash of brown, lighter than the trunks, clearly visible against the green of the ferns. Van der Sandt took aim but then smiled when he realised it was a deer. A female blacktail deer, just two or three years old. He lowered his gun. 'Not today, girl,' he whispered. 'You go in peace.'

He moved through the trees, his feet crunching on small twigs that popped like corn in a microwave. He stopped and listened but all he could hear was the sound of the forest. Had his quarry stopped to rest?

Van der Sandt reached a redwood with a trunk that was almost four metres across. He headed right, raising his rifle to his shoulder again. He moved slowly. The man he was hunting didn't have a gun but he could have picked up a branch or a rock, and at close range either could be deadly. He gave the tree a wide berth as he went around it. It was clear. He kept the rifle up as he scanned the trees ahead of him.

The undergrowth was sparser now. Van der Sandt picked up the pace, keeping his distance from the trees as much as he could. If he had been the quarry he would have done one of two things – he'd have run as fast as he could, or he'd have picked up a rock and hidden behind a tree and waited. Van der Sandt didn't know the man well enough to know which option he would choose. He'd started running as soon as Van der Sandt had killed his friend, but that didn't mean he wasn't now waiting to attack.

He stopped and listened again. More birds. The buzzing of insects. Van der Sandt slowed his breathing. Over the years he had developed something like a sixth sense – the ability to know if there was prey nearby. Often he would know his quarry was close without seeing it or hearing it. Just a sense. A tightening of the stomach and a shiver down his spine. He was feeling that now. He approached a large redwood and instinctively knew to go left. He kept his rifle up and kept well away from the tree as he went around. He stopped and listened. Something scraped against the bark. Something soft. He tightened his finger against the trigger and then slowly backed away, a few inches at a time.

The birds had fallen silent as if they were anticipating what was going to happen. He moved his right foot back and a twig snapped. He froze. There was the scraping sound again. Softer this time. It was the sound of a man leaning against the tree and changing his position. Van der Sandt started to back away again. Slowly. When he was about three metres from the tree he started to move left again, keeping his rifle aimed at where the prey would appear. He could feel his heart pounding now, but his breathing was still slow and even. It wasn't fear or trepidation that he was feeling, it was anticipation. The anticipation of a kill.

He took a step to the left. Then another. And another. His foot touched a twig and he lifted it and took a wider step. He was five metres from the tree now. There was another, thinner tree to his left, and he didn't want to go around it so he took a step forward. As his right foot touched the ground the man appeared from behind the tree, roaring with rage. His right hand was up and he held a fist-sized rock but before he could throw it Van der Sandt put a round in his throat. The man staggered back as blood gushed down his chest, his eyes wide and panicking. Van der Sandt held his rifle against his chest as he watched the man struggle to breathe. The rock fell to the ground and the man's hands clutched at his throat.

Van der Sandt moved closer to him. He could see frothy blood bubbling from the wound and the spreading stain on his shirt. Van der Sandt snarled. 'How does it feel?' he asked.

The man fell down onto his knees. His eyes were still open and his mouth was working soundlessly.

Van der Sandt walked up and stood looking down at him.

'You're shit,' said Van der Sandt. 'You're worse than shit. Fuck you and fuck your religion. Did your god lift a finger to help you? There is no Allah, your whole life has been a waste of time.' He raised his rifle and brought the stock down hard, smashing the man's face to a pulp.

The man fell back. His chest was still moving as the lungs tried to claw in air. His whole body went into spasm for a couple of seconds and then went still. Van der Sandt stared down at the dead man, still sneering. 'I hope you burn in hell,' he said. He took his GPS unit from his rucksack and checked it, then started walking again.

CHAPTER 40

Raj transferred the ninth stone to his pocket and then began counting off the next hundred metres. He had to move to the left to get around a massive redwood tree ahead of them. They were constantly having to weave in and out of the trees which would throw off his calculations but there was nothing he could do about that. He took his knife from its scabbard and checked the compass. It was easy to lose track of their bearings as there were no landmarks to aim for, just trees and bushes.

'Everything okay, Raj?' asked Erol behind him. Erol was managing to keep up with Raj, though he was breathing heavily and limping.

'Another ninety metres and then we can take a break,' said Raj. He looked at his watch. It was taking them close to half an hour to cover a kilometre and they had just over thirty kilometres still to travel. At their current pace that equated to fifteen hours, which meant they would have to spend the night in the forest again.

At some point they would have to head west but Raj planned to leave that until they were closer to their destination. Hopefully their hunter would take the most direct route to the clearing so they would be some distance away from him. That was assuming that the hunter would first go to the clearing where the helicopter had dropped them off. Raj couldn't see that the man would have any choice. There hadn't been any helicopters or drones overhead in the past few hours, which meant the hunter had decided to track them the old fashioned way, by following their trail. That they were leaving a trail was beyond doubt. Five able-bodied men could perhaps move through the forest without leaving tracks, but Erol and his crutch would be unmissable, and they'd also been dragging Mo through the undergrowth. Once the man reached the clearing he wouldn't have any trouble spotting their trail. The question was, how quickly could the hunter move through the forest? Three kilometres an hour? Four out in the open maybe, but with the undergrowth, bushes and trees three would be as fast as a man could go.

Mo yelped and Raj looked over his shoulder. His splint had raked across a stone and from the look on his face he was in agony. Raj turned and held up his hands. 'Okay, we can rest here.'

Mo continued to moan as Sid and Jaffar lowered him to the ground. Raj went over and examined the splint. It had loosened and the wood was rubbing against the ankle. He pulled out his knife and used it to cut a piece of material from the sleeve of Mo's shirt, which he wound around the wood. 'I'm sorry about the pain,' said Raj. 'There's nothing I can do, I'm afraid. You're just going to have to grin and bear it.'

'I'm okay,' said Mo, but it was clear to Raj that he wasn't.

Raj stood up. Sid came over. 'He's not getting better, is he?'

'It's tough going,' said Raj.

'Do you want us to try carrying him?'

Raj grimaced. 'Better he tries to walk for as long as possible,' he said. 'I can build a stretcher but carrying him all the way will really slow us down.'

'I can walk,' said Mo.

Sid leant down and patted him on the shoulder. 'I know you can, bruv, but you're in a lot of pain.'

'Give me a few minutes, Sid,' said Raj. 'Let me have a look around.' He walked away to a clump of waist-high bushes. The forest was made up mainly of redwoods but there were other trees around, some of which he recognised and many of which he didn't. He found a huckleberry bush and picked off a few berries as he walked by. He wasn't looking for food – he wanted a specific tree, a willow. The leaves and bark of willows could be used for medicinal purposes. The faster-growing varieties, such as the black willow and white willow, were the ones most often used but in the situation he found himself in, beggars couldn't be choosers. He grinned when he spotted a multi-trunked Scouler's willow close to the edge of a clearing. The branches were dark brown and smooth and the newer twigs were velvety. It had the typical willow leaves, long and narrow, widest in the middle and tapering to a point on both ends. The leaves were bright green on the upper side and pale green underneath, and it was the combination of shades that gave the tree its silvery appearance.

Raj pulled his knife from its scabbard and used it to hack off several low-hanging young branches. He took them back to the group, who were now all sitting on the ground. Sid frowned at the branches that Raj was carrying. 'What are they for? The stretcher?'

'Pain relief,' said Raj. He sat down next to Mo and began stripping the outer bark off one of the branches with the knife. When he had revealed the creamy-coloured inner bark, he stripped off small sections and handed them to Mo. 'Chew on these,' he said.

'Seriously?' said Mo. 'How does chewing a tree help?' He took the strips of bark and sniffed them suspiciously.

'The inner bark contains a chemical called salicin which your body turns into salicylic acid,' said Raj. 'That's an anti-inflammatory and works as a painkiller.' He grinned. 'It doesn't taste great, unfortunately. Salicylic acid is a precursor to aspirin, which is pretty much what the willow bark tastes like.' He nodded at Mo. 'Go on, give it a go.'

'Do I have to swallow it?'

Raj shook his head. 'Chew the strips and swallow the juice, then spit out what's left,' he said. 'You should feel the benefits in about half an hour.'

Mo put the creamy strips in his mouth and then grimaced. He started to chew, with a look of disgust on his face.

'Give me some for Erol,' said Sid.

Raj took another branch and cut off four two-inch strips of bark. Sid took them over to Erol who popped them into his mouth. He shuddered and his stomach heaved but he managed to stop himself from throwing up.

Raj cut the inner bark from the rest of the branches and gave them to Mo. 'Keep them in your pocket. If the pain gets bad again you can chew on a few more of the strips.' He got to his feet and put the knife back in its scabbard, brushing the bits of bark from his trousers.

'We can rest here,' Raj said to Jaffar. He pointed into the trees. 'There are some huckleberry bushes out there and I think I saw some wild raspberries. Grab yourself some if you want.'

'Hell, yeah,' said Jaffar and he headed off. Sid went with him. Raj sat down and lay on his back, staring up through the tree canopy. The sky above was a clear blue with not a cloud to be seen. Birds were singing, and the occasional insect buzzed by. He was dog tired and within seconds he was asleep.

CHAPTER 41

Van der Sandt raised his rifle to his shoulder as he approached the clearing. There was always a chance that the remaining jihadists had stayed put. The only tracks he had seen belonged to the two men he'd killed, which meant the others had either gone in a different direction or not moved. He moved slowly as his eyes swept the clearing. It was a couple of hundred metres across at its widest point, an area that was too rocky for trees to ever get hold. There were a few dozen bushes that had managed to get a foothold between the rocks but they were too small to provide any cover. It took him only a few seconds to confirm that there was no one hiding in the clearing, but that didn't mean they weren't seeking cover among the trees around it. He skirted the south of the clearing, keeping his gun at the ready, placing his feet carefully to keep any noise to a minimum.

There was a fluttering of wings above his head and he caught a flash of blue out of the corner of his eye. It was a Steller's jay, one of the most common birds in the forest, and he had been hearing its *wek-wek-wek* call for the past few minutes.

He had traversed all of the southern perimeter and half the eastern side when he came across the tracks. He smiled to himself when he saw the marks in the dirt. Five men. So they were sticking together as a team. One of the men was wearing boots with a distinctive tread. When the men had been in the house, none of them had boots on, so they must have been taken from Nick. Another of the men had clearly been injured; his feet were scuffing the ground and he was being supported as he walked. And another was taking small steps accompanied by a round hole, which could only have come from a branch being used as a walking stick. Two of the men weren't wearing shoes or sandals but seemed to have bound their feet with cloth. So, five men, two of them injured, one badly, all heading east. He frowned. Why east? The ground was sloping to the east so it would be easier for the injured men. But it was taking them in the wrong direction. He cradled his gun in his arms as he studied the footprints and tried to put himself in the mind of his quarry. There was nothing to the east, just hundreds of kilometres of forest. And they wouldn't know the geography of the area. Had they chosen the direction at random, assuming that they would eventually reach a road or even a town? If that was the case, they were wrong. He frowned, then tucked his weapon under his arm and took a drink from his water bottle.

Maybe they were heading down the slope because that was the best chance of finding water. Or maybe they wanted to move away from a direct route between the house and the clearing, figuring that he would be coming for them on foot. Van der Sandt screwed the top back on his water bottle and put it in its holster on his belt. It didn't matter why they had chosen the route they'd taken. All that mattered was that he was on their trail. He started walking, following the tracks the men had left. They hadn't made any effort to conceal their progress, but Van der Sandt was a good enough tracker that it wouldn't have made any difference if they had.

CHAPTER 42

There were six of them in the back of the Mastiff, sweating from the heat as it bumped along the pot-holed road. The Mastiff was capable of ninety kilometres an hour, but it was going much slower – the road had been mined in the past so the two-man crew were driving on full alert. The six-wheeled Mastiff was festooned with armour plates and equipped with a 7.62 mm general purpose machine gun and a 40 mm grenade launcher. The dual air conditioners did their best to keep the temperature down, but Raj was still sweating. He was on patrol with B Company, 40 Commando, on his second tour of Afghanistan. They were based at Patrol Base One in the Nahri Saraj district of Helmand Province, in the south of the strife-torn country. The group had been tasked with training the local police in the village of Char Kutsa. The police had already undergone training at the base but the top brass had decided that they would benefit from extra training on their home turf.

Raj had been in the country for a month, and morale had fallen since his first tour, mainly because the troops knew that the fight had been lost and that they would be abandoning the country sooner rather than later. What they were doing was the equivalent of rearranging the deckchairs on the *Titanic* and everyone knew it. The Afghans they were instructing knew it too, and went through the training half-heartedly at best.

Raj had his SA80 assault rifle between his legs. Bob 'Bugsy' Malone, who was sitting next to him, had one of the new Sharpshooter rifles that had just been issued to 40 Commando. The new weapons were in short supply and were jealously guarded by those who had them. They fired a 7.62 mm round and were accurate up to eight hundred metres, perfect for longer-range firefights, which is how the enemy in Afghanistan tended to work. The Afghans weren't great at fighting up close and personal; they preferred remotely operated IEDs or to fire from a distance behind cover. Raj wasn't a fan of the new gun; the heavier round meant that it did more damage, but Raj was able to carry three of his Nato 5.56 rounds for every one that Bugsy had in his packs.

The only other member of the team with a Sharpshooter was their sergeant, Pete Kershaw, a big Geordie with a shaved head and a scar on his cheek that he'd picked up in Iraq ten years earlier. He claimed it was the result of fighting a Taliban warrior hand-to-hand, but Raj had heard from another medic that he'd tripped during a game of badminton and fallen against an ammo box. Kershaw had been transferred to Raj's unit after the previous sergeant had been struck down with appendicitis and he had hit the ground running. He'd made it clear from the start that he didn't like Raj, but as Raj was a surgeon lieutenant there wasn't much he could do to show his disapproval other than to throw him the odd scornful look. Raj did know that Kershaw had been bad-mouthing him around the base, saying that doctors were no use in combat and should never be allowed out on patrol. Truth be told, it wasn't a point of view that Raj could argue with. When it came to combat, his rank meant nothing. Kershaw had far more experience and the times they had come under fire, Raj had allowed the sergeant to call the shots.

The rest of the unit were carrying SA80s except for the youngest member, Mike Cross, a Liverpudlian with an almost childlike sense of humour, who had been issued with a combat shotgun. Cross was sitting next to Raj, and he too was sweating profusely.

They had been sitting in the Mastiff for the best part of forty minutes, and the further they had got from the base the slower they went. The Mastiff was covered with slat armour, a rigid slatted metal grid that was effective against RPG attacks, and the vehicle itself was sturdy enough to shrug off small arms fire and

Kalashnikov rounds. It was also well protected against IEDs, but a large enough bomb planted under the road could overturn it, so the driving crew were keeping their eyes peeled.

'Approaching the police station now, Sarge,' shouted the driver, a stocky Scot called Alistair Turner who at some point in his military career had acquired the nickname Kevin because of his fondness for bacon.

The Mastiff came to a halt and Kershaw opened the rear door. 'Right, everyone out,' he said.

The men piled out of the vehicle. The sky was clear of clouds and the sun was close to its zenith. The police station had been built by an American construction company. It contained an office, an armoury, and half a dozen cells, most of which were usually occupied by Afghan cops napping between shifts. It had a flat roof with a communications mast and a satellite dish, and Raj had been told that the American Government had paid the contractors just over five million dollars for the work. It looked to Raj as if a team of half-competent builders could have thrown it up in about a week. Around it were old mud houses and new ones built from concrete breeze blocks. Women in full burkas shepherded their children inside while old men in dishdasha robes stood and stared at the soldiers with undisguised hostility.

The captain in charge of the Char Kutsa police was in his early thirties, dark-skinned and bearded. He was serious about his job and applied himself well, but his men were a motley crew, ill-disciplined and with a tendency to slope off for a sneaky cigarette given half the chance. There were eight of them and the captain was trying to get them lined up and at attention in front of their two black Ford Ranger pick-up trucks, also provided by the US Government. The men carried Hungarian-made AMD-65 Kalashnikov copies and had Russian-made 9 mm Makarov pistols in holsters on their hips. They were reasonable shots on the range but despite several weeks of training they were still a danger to themselves when taking on moving targets that could fire back. They had run numerous exercises at the camp, but the Marines had never felt confident enough to let the Afghans use live ammunition. It didn't matter how many hours the cops spent practising, when confronted with a live target the Afghans reverted to 'pray and spray' and were more concerned about their own safety than taking out the hostiles. They had rehearsed clearing rooms and again their discipline was so bad that more often than not they'd end up shooting one of their own.

The captain came over, grinning. He was the only cop who could speak any English, and his language skills were rudimentary at best. Pretty much all communication was through the unit's interpreter, a former schoolteacher called Ahmad. Ahmad's school had been destroyed in a drone strike that had been aimed at a high-ranking Taliban fighter. Luckily there had been no children in the school at the time of the attack, but whereas there had been funds available to build the police station, no money had been found to rebuild the school. Ahmad had a wife and four children to feed so had asked for and been given a job with the British forces as an interpreter. The interpreters were regarded as prime targets by the jihadists who saw them as traitors to Islam.

Ahmad translated for the captain. The men were ready and eager to start their training. The plan was to carry out a few house-to-house searches and later in the day to set up a roadblock on the main highway. 'Tell him they don't look ready,' growled Kershaw. 'Get them lined up properly and tell them to have their weapons ready for inspection.'

Strictly speaking it was supposed to be Raj who issued orders, but he was enough of a realist to know that operational matters were best left to the sergeants. Kershaw did at least look at Raj and give him a nod. Raj nodded back.

'We've got company, Sarge,' said Jimmy Belcher, who was manning the machine gun on the roof of the Mastiff. He pointed off to the south. Three sand-coloured pick-up trucks were heading their way. They were flying black, green and red Afghan flags and the men in the back were wearing Afghan Army uniforms. Two of the pick-up trucks had machine guns mounted at the rear.

Raj had a pair of binoculars on his belt and he used them to check out the vehicles as they sped along the road towards them. They were heading from the direction of an Afghan Army base, but ISIS often attacked under false colours. There were three men in the back of each of the trucks with machine guns, and half a dozen in the back of the third truck, which was bringing up the rear of the convoy. The vehicles looked legitimate and had the Afghan Army insignia on the side. The uniforms also looked right, as did the weapons the men were toting. Then Raj stiffened as he spotted an RPG in the hands of one of the men in the final truck.

'They kosher?' asked Kershaw.

'I see an RPG,' said Raj.

'That's not good.'

It wasn't good at all. Rocket-propelled grenades were used against armoured vehicles or fortified defences, neither of which were used by ISIS, so it wasn't the sort of weaponry carried by a regular Afghan Army patrol. Raj lowered his binoculars and turned towards Ahmad. Ahmad was monitoring Taliban radio frequencies and listening for any talk of ambush or attack. He shook his head. 'No chatter,' he said.

'Tell the guys to . . .' Raj was cut off by a hail of bullets from the lead truck that thwacked against the protective screen around Belcher. One of the rounds smacked into Belcher's helmet and knocked him back. A second burst of fire hit the screen again and Belcher was hit in the throat. Blood spurted over his gun as he fell back, arms flailing.

'Take cover and return fire!' shouted Kershaw, crouching by the rear of the Mastiff. He started shooting at the approaching pick-up trucks.

Ahmad had ducked down and turned to face the Afghan cops, who were already scattering, most of them heading into the police station.

'Tell the fuckers to return fire!' shouted Kershaw.

Raj took up position at the front of the Mastiff, next to Cross. Cross moved to the side to give Raj room, knowing there was little point in firing his shotgun. The three pick-ups had fanned out, with the one in the centre heading straight for them, its machine gun firing full on. Raj took aim at the offside tyre and started firing single shots. Behind him, Ahmad began to shout at the cops. Malone joined Raj at the front of the Mastiff and began firing.

There was a whooshing sound from one of the trucks, and a puff of grey smoke. 'RPG!' shouted Raj. As the missile sped away from the truck, Raj realised it wasn't heading towards the Mastiff – the police station was the target. He opened his mouth to shout a warning but there was no time. The warhead slammed into the side of the building, close to the door. Two of the Afghans who had been fighting to get inside the station were blown apart, and three others fell to the ground screaming in agony.

Raj looked back at the approaching vehicles. They were continuing to fan out and bullets from the machine guns were thudding into the Mastiff or whizzing overhead.

Two of the remaining cops had run around behind their pick-up trucks and were returning fire but they were doing it haphazardly, more concerned about their own safety than hitting the target. One was holding his gun up but keeping his head down below the side of the vehicle as he fired, unable to see where his shots were going. Another of the cops scrambled inside what was left of the police station.

Fire was starting to come in from the sides now that the pick-up trucks were further apart, and it wouldn't be long before the jihadists would be able to shoot around the Mastiff.

Raj switched his aim to the truck on the left. So did Malone. Another Marine joined them – Billy McKee, a red-haired Scotsman on his third tour of Afghanistan. He grinned at Raj. 'All go, eh Sir?'

All three Marines continued to fire at the pick-up truck, Raj aiming for the front wheel with three-shot bursts while McKee and Malone aimed single shots at the men in the back. Cross pulled out his Glock and joined in the shooting.

Raj heard shouting to his left and he turned to see the police captain standing by the shattered wall of the building, screaming as he fired his Kalashnikov from the hip, like the star of some second-rate action movie. In his panic he'd clearly forgotten everything he'd been taught about firing from cover. 'Ahmad, tell him to get down!' Raj shouted.

Ahmad started to yell at the captain but the moment he opened his mouth the officer was cut down in a hail of machine gun fire that practically ripped him in half. He staggered back and fell into the doorway of the station. The three cops who had been injured in the blast had all stopped screaming and their uniforms were glistening with blood.

Raj fired another short burst at the front tyre of the pick-up on the left. The rubber disintegrated and the pick-up began to veer from side to side.

'Nice one, Sir,' said McKee.

The pick-up flipped over and rolled twice before it came to a stop, white smoke pouring from under the bonnet. Two of the men in the back lay still on the ground but when the third got to his feet McKee picked him off with a single shot.

Raj switched his attention to the pick-up truck on the right, which was now heading directly for the Mastiff. He and McKee both aimed their carbines at the vehicle, but Kershaw beat them to it, firing three-shot bursts at the driver. There was another puff of smoke and a whooshing sound as a second RPG warhead roared through the air. 'Down!' shouted Raj and they all ducked. The warhead hit the Mastiff dead centre but the slat armour did its job and it exploded without penetrating the vehicle. The Mastiff shuddered and the noise was deafening, but within seconds the Marines were back up and shooting.

Two of the Marines had set up behind one of the police trucks and were firing at the truck to their left. They came under heavy return fire from the machine gun mounted in the back and they ducked down. Kershaw fired at the truck's gunner, taking single shots, and the fourth hit the man in the head, blowing away the top of his skull. As the man fell back he kept a grip on the machine gun and the barrel swung up, the bullets heading skywards. The two Marines behind the police truck were immediately up, firing again.

Raj and McKee continued shooting at the truck that had fired the RPG. McKee took out one of the men in the rear of the truck, then Malone killed a second. Raj aimed at the front wheels and pulled the trigger but cursed when he realised he was out of ammunition. He ejected the magazine and slapped in a new one. His first burst hit the passenger door but his second hit the target and the tyre exploded. The truck slowed and Raj switched his attention to the passenger side window. The window disintegrated and after the second burst the truck came to a shuddering halt. There were only two ISIS fighters still alive in the back and McKee picked them off with two quick shots.

The third truck had come to a halt and two fighters jumped down, firing Kalashnikovs. McKee, Malone and Raj ducked as bullets came their way, then bobbed back up and fired off quick shots. Raj caught one of the fighters in the leg and the man fell to the ground. The driver and the front passenger got out and took cover behind their truck, then started firing at Kershaw. The sergeant moved back behind the Mastiff to avoid the bullets. Raj moved to the side to get a better angle but realised he'd immediately exposed himself to the fighter running towards them. The man's Kalashnikov moved towards Raj but before he could pull the trigger McKee brought him down with two quick shots to the chest. 'You're welcome, Sir,' said McKee.

Raj aimed his carbine at the closest of two jihadists who were firing at Kershaw but Malone beat him to it, putting three shots in the man's chest. Cross got the second man, two rounds from his Glock hitting the fighter in the stomach. Then there was silence, broken only by the hissing of the radiator of the overturned truck.

Raj, McKee and Malone walked around the Mastiff, keeping their guns at the ready. Kershaw joined them from the rear. The two Marines who had taken cover behind the police vehicles stepped out, carbines at the ready. Ahmad climbed up to check on Belcher, though there was no doubt he was dead. Cross put his Glock back in his holster. 'We were set up,' said Cross. 'They knew we were coming.'

'It could be they were attacking the police station,' said Raj. 'We might just have been in the wrong place at the wrong time.'

'Lieutenant's right,' said Kershaw. 'They would have come mob-handed if they'd known we were here.' He looked down at the dead cops. 'They panicked,' he said. 'Fucking Darwinian selection at work.'

The cop who had sought sanctuary in the police station appeared in the doorway. He was covered in dust but didn't seem to be harmed. Kershaw sneered at him in disgust.

'Call this in, Dave,' Raj said to the Mastiff driver. 'Everybody okay? Anybody hurt?'

'Only Jimmy,' said Kershaw.

Raj walked over to look at the dead jihadists. Two bullets thudded into the ground close to his feet. 'Contact!' shouted Kershaw.

A jihadist had appeared from behind the overturned truck and was running towards them, his gun blazing. Bullets thwacked into the Mastiff and Raj ducked. Kershaw brought up his carbine and put two shots in the jihadist's chest. The man fell face first to the ground.

'Cross, McKee – go and check there are no more surprises in store!' shouted the sergeant. Kershaw looked over at Raj and nodded and Raj smiled thinly. He should have given the order and the sergeant knew it.

He walked over to the jihadists who had run from the middle of the three trucks. The first two were clearly dead but the third one was still alive, blood pouring from a leg wound and a hole in his shoulder. Raj reached for his medical pack and pulled out a technical tourniquet, emergency trauma bandages and wound-packing gauze. He pulled his knife from its scabbard and cut away the man's shirt and the material around the injured leg.

'What are you doing, Lieutenant?'

Raj looked up to see Kershaw standing over at him.

'This one's not dead,' said Raj. 'I need to get a tourniquet on the leg and pack the wound. Can you call for a medevac?'

'Are you shitting me? Are you fucking shitting me?'

'We need to get this man to a hospital, now,' said Raj. He ripped open a pack of gauze and slapped it onto the shoulder wound. 'And I mean now.'

'Raj! RAJ!'

Raj frowned. Who was calling him?

'RAJ!'

Raj woke up, his face bathed in sweat. Sid was looking down at him, a look of concern on his face. 'You all right, bruv?' he asked.

Raj wiped his mouth with his hand and sat up. 'Yeah. I'm good.'

Sid bent down and patted him on the shoulder. 'Sounded like you were having a nightmare.'

Raj looked at his watch. He had only been asleep for eight or nine minutes. He got to his feet and blinked his eyes. 'Did you get any berries?'

Sid nodded. 'Found what looks like hazelnuts, too.' He held out his hand to reveal a dozen or so nuts.

'Nice,' said Raj.

'Take a few,' said Sid.

Raj took four of the nuts, peeled one and chewed on it.

'There's plenty more, I wasn't sure how long we should stay here.'

'Let's gather some more, we can eat them on the move,' said Raj.

CHAPTER 43

Van der Sandt stopped and looked around, taking everything in. There were footprints everywhere, moving in every direction, many of them overlapping. They had thrown the remains of their shelters into the undergrowth but that wasn't a serious attempt to cover their tracks. It was the man in the boots who had destroyed the shelters, and Van der Sandt was fairly sure that he was the one who had built them in the first place. Boots had established himself as the alpha male and he spent most of the time leading the group as they moved through the forest. Some distance away from where the shelters had been was an area where four of the men, including the two who were injured, had knelt. They had prayed, Van der Sandt realised. Prayed to their god. Van der Sandt smiled to himself. God wasn't going to help them. That's not what gods did. In the whole history of human conflict, praying never stopped anything bad from happening. They could kneel and bow to Allah as many times as they wanted, it wouldn't change the end result.

What interested Van der Sandt was that Boots hadn't prayed. Why would that be? They were jihadists, they killed for their sick twisted religion, so why hadn't Boots prayed with the others? If he had time, at the end, Van der Sandt would ask him the answer to that riddle.

Van der Sandt found the tracks of the men leaving the campsite and followed them for a while. Boots was leading the way again. The one with the crutch was walking alone and the others were supporting the one with an injured leg. After three kilometres, they had changed direction and begun to head due south. They had been walking due east, and Van der Sandt had wondered if they had chosen the direction at random. But the change of direction, and the fact that they had changed to due south, suggested they had a compass. If they carried on walking due south they would miss the house, so at some point they would probably move west.

After following the tracks for another few kilometres, Van der Sandt took off his backpack and switched on his GPS. Once he had established his position he switched it off and ripped open one of his energy bars. He chewed it as he looked around. The men had rested in a small clearing. Boots had walked into the forest and cut branches off a Scouler's willow tree. The man clearly knew his trees. The inner bark of all willow varieties was a natural painkiller. That meant at least one of the injured men was having trouble.

He finished his energy bar and shoved the wrapper in his trouser pocket. Boots clearly had first-class survival skills. The shelter, the willow, the ability to navigate without GPS – it all suggested he had been very well trained, training that went above and beyond what Van der Sandt would have expected from an ISIS terrorist. They lived and fought in the desert, a totally different environment to the redwood forest.

He took his water bottle from his belt and took a couple of sips. The men hadn't been born in Syria, of course. They were Europeans, so who knew what they had done before joining ISIS in Syria. He could never understand the ease with which Muslims born in the West could so easily turn against their home countries. It seemed to happen across Europe – the UK, Germany, Spain, France – countries that had opened their borders to asylum seekers were then betrayed by the children of the people they had rescued. It was something that Van der Sandt had struggled to understand ever since he had buried his wife and children. The killers who had taken the lives of his family hadn't lived in poverty or hardship, they hadn't had to struggle against oppression or fight for their homelands. They had lived in safe countries with first-class education and health systems, countries where they were free to grow and develop their interests, to become productive citizens. Instead they had chosen to join a group of terrorists who thought it acceptable to throw homosexuals off rooftops and to burn their enemies alive. What they had done in Cyprus was unforgivable. Van der Sandt could understand if they had attacked military or police targets, if they had assassinated government officials or politicians, but these animals had attacked holidaymakers, shooting dead men, women and children who were absolutely no threat to them.

Van der Sandt had often faced criticism for his hunting, but when he had killed he had never killed juveniles. Every animal he had ever killed had been an adult. And when he had killed, he had killed a single animal. A trophy animal. He had never, ever, killed indiscriminately.

A hunting friend of his, an English lord who was related to the Queen, had once asked Van der Sandt to go pheasant shooting with him. He had an estate in Scotland – a fraction of the size of Van der Sandt's land – where birds were raised to be shot. Van der Sandt liked the man but he had always turned the invitations down. Shooting animals indiscriminately wasn't sport; it wasn't even hunting. There was no skill in shooting birds that could barely fly, birds that had to be startled by beaters to even get them into the air. Bird hunters used the excuse that they always ate what they shot, but that wasn't true. On a single day's shoot hundreds of birds would be shot and most of them were given away to the people in the nearby village. Maybe they ate the birds, maybe they didn't, but they weren't being shot for food, they were being shot because the shooters got a thrill from mass killing.

What had happened in Cyprus was like a bird shoot. The men had turned up with big guns and had shot everything that moved. Men, women, and children. Like the birds they would have been startled and tried to flee for their lives. But it wasn't possible to outrun a bullet. One by one the holidaymakers would have been shot, most of them in the back. What sort of person would do that? They had killed without caring who they were killing. For all they knew, there could have been Muslims on the beach and in the hotel. They would have been killing their own. Van der Sandt shuddered. He tried not to think about the last moments of his wife and children. How scared they would have been. How the children would have called out to their mother for help. Maybe they had called out for him. He felt tears prick his eyes and he blinked them away. He put his water bottle back on his belt and started walking again. It wouldn't be long now.

CHAPTER 44

Raj looked up through the branches of the redwoods around him. The trees were less dense than they had been and he was able to get a good view of the sky. There were clouds high overhead but they were white and wispy and didn't appear to be threatening rain. He wiped his forehead with his sleeve. He really wanted a drink but there had been neither sight nor sound of running water since the stream they had found a few hours ago.

'Can we forage for food for a while?' asked Sid.

Raj wanted them to keep up the pace, but he knew that the lack of nutrition was sapping their energy. 'Okay, but let's not take too long.'

Raj took Sid into the undergrowth. Jaffar followed them. Raj scanned the smaller trees that were managing to grow among the redwoods and pointed at one. 'There you go,' he said. 'Hazelnuts.' The two men went over to the tree. It was a good size and the branches were dotted with clumps of nuts. Jaffar reached and pulled away a handful. He peeled one, chewed on it, and nodded. 'Good,' he said. He began ripping nuts off the tree.

Raj and Sid pushed their way through the bushes, looking for berries. They came across a redwood that had rotted and died, and fallen on its side. The bark was dotted with large snails. Raj picked one off and showed it to Sid, but Sid backed away, his hands up. 'No way,' he said. 'I'm not that hungry.'

Raj laughed. 'It's okay, you wouldn't want to eat one raw,' he said. 'But boil them for a few minutes in some wild garlic and they're quite tasty.' He put the snail back. 'The woods are full of beetles and worms and termites that you can eat.'

'Thanks Raj but I'm gonna stick to berries and nuts,' said Sid.

Raj grinned. 'If you're hungry enough you'll eat anything,' he said.

Sid looked up through the tree canopy. The sky was a pale blue with only a few wisps of cloud. He sighed. 'What the fuck is going to happen to us, Raj?'

'We're going to get out of here and get back to our lives,' said Raj.

'But that bastard wants to kill us. He's out there somewhere with that fucking gun.'

'I know. But we've got guns, too. He hadn't planned that. He didn't expect us to be able to fight back.'

'Do you think he might have changed his plan? Do you think he might leave us alone?'

Raj shook his head. 'You killed his family. He's not going to forgive you for that. I wouldn't. Would you?'

'What do you mean?'

'If someone killed your family, you'd want revenge. Anyone would. It's the most natural reaction in the world.'

'I didn't kill his family.'

'Yeah, you said that back at the house. I didn't get what you meant. You were at the beach, right?'

Sid sighed. 'Yes, I was at the fucking beach. And yes I was shooting. But I wasn't shooting women and kids. I just couldn't.'

'Sid, that makes no sense at all.'

'I joined ISIS because I wanted to fight for Islam. I wanted to be a warrior. I thought I'd be fighting troops. Shooting at soldiers. I thought it would be war.'

'You must have known what they were planning.'

'I don't know what I thought. But when I got off the jet ski all I could see was women and kids. I fired high, I shot men, but I didn't shoot any of the women or kids.'

'You took part in a terrorist attack.'

'I know, I know. I'm not saying I'm not a fucking terrorist, I'm just saying I didn't kill his family.'

'And he says he's holding you all responsible.' Raj wiped his forehead with his sleeve. 'You weren't born a Muslim, right?'

'Nah. My dad's Church of England. My mum's a lapsed Catholic.'

'So what happened?'

Sid laughed harshly. 'What happened? I guess skunk happened.'

'Skunk?'

'Cannabis. Ganja. My dealers were a couple of Pakistani guys. At first I was just a customer and then eventually I started hanging out with them. They took me to their mosque and that was pretty much it.'

'It's a bloody big jump from buying cannabis to massacring tourists,' said Raj.

'They opened my eyes to the way the world is,' said Sid. 'Their imam is a really smart guy. He explained things to me. I did classes in the Koran and started to learn Arabic.'

'And he's the one who arranged for you to get trained?'

'Yeah, he explained that all good Muslims have to fight for Islam. It's our duty.'

'You were groomed, mate,' said Raj. 'They spotted you and they groomed you. You're the perfect weapon for them because of your colour.'

'Nah, that's bollocks. Islam isn't about race, it's about faith.'

'And you believe? In Islam?'

Sid frowned. 'Of course.'

'But now you're having doubts, obviously. Or reservations.'

'I'm starting to think that maybe Allah's word is being polluted. I tried raising it with the imams at the camp but . . .' He shrugged. 'They didn't want to discuss it. They said that it would be best if I just listened to what they said and didn't start trying to interpret the Koran myself.' He sighed. 'And now I'm fucked. Well fucked.'

'Yeah. True that.'

'This guy's a fucking nutter,' said Sid.

'I don't know about that,' said Raj. 'You can't fault his logic. You murdered his family and he wants revenge. What he's doing makes more sense than what you did.'

'Yeah, well we're going to have to agree to differ on that,' said Sid. 'But I'm sorry you got dragged into this. It's not your fault.'

'You can say that again.' Despite the precariousness of his position, Raj couldn't help but smile. 'But at the end of the day I'm a kafir, right? Of less value than a dog.'

'Bruv, you might be a kafir but you're the best chance I've got of getting out of here in one piece. Seriously, bruv, you've nothing to fear from me. We're on the same side.'

Raj stared at him for several seconds and then nodded. 'We need each other,' he said. 'No doubt about that.'

'So we put our differences aside?'

Raj nodded. 'Yeah.'

'Thank fuck for that,' said Sid. He began to scratch his stomach vigorously. 'You've done survival stuff like this before? With the Marines?'

'Not exactly like this, no. But then this is a one-off, isn't it?'

Sid smiled ruefully. 'Yeah, I guess. But you've been trained with weapons and stuff, obviously.'

'Sure. I'm a doctor but I'm a commando, too. Or I was, anyway.'

'So you shoot people and then you patch them up? How fucked up is that?'

'That isn't how it works,' said Raj. 'My job was to take care of our guys. I wasn't usually used in an attacking role, I was there to take care of our casualties, and to deal with medical issues on base.'

'And all this jungle stuff? You learnt it from the Rangers?'

Raj smiled thinly. 'This isn't jungle, mate. This is forest. But yeah, I did several survival courses in different parts of the world as part of my training.'

'So why did you pack it in?'

'Long story,' said Raj. He pointed off to the left where there was a collection of shrubs, more than two metres tall. 'There you go,' he said. 'Thimbleberries.'

'You're making that up,' said Sid.

'Nah, mate, they're similar to raspberries.' He went over and picked a bright red berry and tossed it to Sid, then picked a couple more and ate them.

Sid chewed his and flashed him a thumbs up. 'Sweet,' he said.

Raj pulled out his shirt and used it to hold the berries he picked. Sid copied him and after ten minutes of quick picking they each had more than a pound of berries. They carried them back to Jaffar who had gathered several handfuls of hazelnuts and placed them on a large leaf. They took the fruit and berries back to the others and divided them up. The men wolfed them down, but Raj ate his slowly, chewing each berry thoroughly before swallowing.

'They taste better than that willow bark shit,' laughed Mo.

'How are you feeling?' asked Raj.

'A bit better. I'm sorry about this.'

'It's not your fault,' said Raj. 'They could have thrown any one of us out of the chopper. You were just unlucky.' He looked around. 'We should start moving,' he said.

'I need a leak,' said Erol, and he hobbled off into the undergrowth.

'I need a piss, too,' said Mo. Sid helped him over to a tree, then walked away as Mo unzipped his trousers.

'Hey, come and look at this!' shouted Erol, off in the distance. Raj looked over, seized his gun and hurried towards Erol. Sid followed him. Raj moved cautiously, sweeping his eyes left and right as he pushed his way through the ferns and bushes.

Erol was standing at the base of a large redwood, more than four metres across. He pointed up at the branches above his head. 'Look at that!' he shouted.

Raj looked up. There were two black bear cubs in the tree; one clinging to the trunk, the other out in a branch.

'Can you see them?' shouted Erol, pointing at the cubs with his stick.

'What is it? asked Jaffar, coming up behind them.

'Get back,' said Raj urgently. 'You too, Sid.' He waved at Erol. 'Get over here, now!'

'What's wrong?' asked Jaffar. 'They're only pups, they're not gonna hurt anyone.'

'They're cubs, and that's the problem,' said Raj. 'If they're here the mother won't be far away. She won't be anywhere near as cute and cuddly. Just very quietly back away.'

Erol grinned and waved his stick. 'You worry too much, bruv. They're as happy as Larry.'

'Yeah, but Mum might not see it that way,' said Raj. He patted Sid on the shoulder. 'Let's go.'

'What's happening?'' shouted Mo, who was hobbling across the clearing towards them.

'Stay where you are, Mo,' said Raj. 'We're coming out.'

Erol still hadn't moved so Raj waved at him impatiently. Erol shook his head contemptuously and turned away from the tree. Together they pushed their way through the bushes. As they entered the clearing, Raj heard a growl and the thud of something heavy pounding on the grass. He took a step to the side and saw a fully grown black bear charging towards them. 'Mo, get down!' shouted Raj. Mo turned but the bear smashed into him. Mo fell back and the bear was immediately on him, clawing at the splint and ripping it off his leg. Mo screamed in pain and lashed out with his hands. The bear must have been three times Mo's weight and when it batted him with one paw it moved him a couple of feet across the grass. 'Help me!' he screamed.

'Play dead!' shouted Raj.

Mo continued to scream in terror and the bear slashed his chest with his right paw, ripping his shirt.

Sid pulled his Glock from his belt and pointed it at the bear.

'Don't shoot, you'll give away our position!' shouted Raj. He grabbed his knife and ran towards the bear. Raj held the knife with both hands, raised it above his head, and brought it down into the back of the bear's neck. It only went a couple of inches through the fur and the bear didn't seem to notice. Raj pulled the blade out and raised it again. He roared as he brought it down with all his might and this time it went in deeper.

The bear released her grip on Mo's head and shuffled backwards. 'Leave him alone!' shouted Raj, waving his arms frantically.

The bear turned to look at Raj, snarling.

'Go on, fuck off!' yelled Erol, prodding at the bear with his stick.

'Careful, Erol!' shouted Sid.

Erol ignored him. 'Get the fuck away!' he shouted, jabbing the stick at the bear's jaws.

The bear was still snarling at Raj. Raj backed away, knowing there was little he could do with the knife to fend off a full frontal attack.

Erol prodded the bear again and this time the end of the stick caught the animal's ear. The bear reared up on its hind legs and roared in anger. It was a good seven feet tall and its massive muscles rippled under its glossy black fur.

Raj lashed out with the knife, though he realised immediately that it was futile. The knife was tiny compared to the bear's massive paws. Raj bent down and picked up a rock and threw it as hard as he could. It hit the bear in the ear but didn't appear to do any damage. Raj bent down to grab another rock but as he did the bear dropped down onto all fours and charged towards him. Raj leapt to the side and hit the ground. The bear's paws scrabbled on the grass as it tried to turn around. Raj was on his back and he kicked out with his legs. He was close enough to feel the warmth of the animal's breath.

A rock thudded against the bear's head, then another. Jaffar was throwing them at the animal, trying to take it down. The bear reared up onto her back legs again, then she dropped down and charged towards Jaffar. Jaffar screamed in terror and turned to run.

'Don't run!' shouted Raj, but it was too late. The bear bounded across the grass and sideswiped Jaffar's leg with its claws. Jaffar screamed in pain as he fell to the side, blood pouring from his wounds. He rolled onto his side and tried to get up.

Sid still had the Glock in his hands and he fired. The bullet hit the bear in the shoulder but it didn't react. Sid pulled the trigger again, and this time caught the bear in the leg. The bear changed direction and began to charge at Sid. Sid held his ground and continued to pull the trigger. The bullets were having no effect on the bear, and it opened its jaws, ready to bite. Raj reached for his carbine and swung it up. Now that shots had been fired he might as well use the more powerful 5.56 rounds.

Sid was shuffling backwards as he fired. His left foot caught on a rock and he fell back. The bear reared up to throw herself at him and Sid got off two quick shots that hit her in the chest. Blood was glistening on the bear's fur but the shots weren't slowing her down.

Raj put the carbine to his shoulder, sighted on the bear's neck and fired. The round hit its target and the bear's head shuddered. It dropped down on all fours and snarled at Sid, who was struggling to get to his feet. Raj fired again, this time hitting the bear in the shoulder. The round hit with enough force to knock the shoulder back but the bear still didn't go down.

Raj aimed between the bear's eyes but before he could pull the trigger she turned and ran into the undergrowth, heading towards the cubs. Raj lowered the carbine. Sid fired another shot but Raj shook his head. 'Leave it, mate, she's not a threat any more.' He hurried over to Jaffar who was lying on his side, curled up and moaning softly. 'Are you okay?' asked Raj.

Jaffar grunted but didn't answer. Erol hobbled over. 'Check on Mo, will you?' asked Raj. He patted Jaffar on the shoulder. 'Roll over on your back, I need to check your leg.' Jaffar continued to moan in pain and Raj had to move him to get a better look at the wound. There were two deep cuts and a shallow one. All three were bleeding profusely but there was no pulsing blood, so it didn't look as if any major arteries had been severed. Raj pulled out his knife, sawed off a long piece of cloth from the bottom of Jaffar's shirt and then used it as a tourniquet at the top of his thigh.

Sid and Erol came over. 'Mo's okay,' said Sid. 'His chest was scratched and the bear fucked up his splint but he's okay.' He knelt down and looked at the cuts on Jaffar's leg. 'That's bad.'

'It's worse than it looks,' said Raj. 'I can patch him up but we need to get away from here first. The hunter will have heard the shots.'

'I can't walk,' said Jaffar.

'We'll carry you,' said Raj.

'Carry him?' said Sid. 'You're having a laugh.'

'Just to get him away from here,' said Raj. 'I'll put him over my shoulders, and when I get tired you can take over. Help me get him up.'

Sid and Raj got Jaffar to his feet, then Raj bent at the knees, put the man over his shoulder and straightened up. Jaffar probably weighed eighty kilograms but it was doable. He nodded at Sid. 'Okay, you and Erol help Mo.' He headed south while Sid and Erol went to pick up Mo.

CHAPTER 45

Van der Sandt emerged into the clearing, his gun cradled across his chest. His eyes scanned the ground, looking for anything out of the ordinary. It had taken him almost forty-five minutes to reach the clearing after he had heard the shots. There were no hunters for at least fifty miles so he figured his quarry had fired at something, probably wildlife. He alternated between checking the ground and scanning the surrounding trees, looking for movement. He stiffened as he saw bits of broken branch and strips of bloody cloth scattered around. They were the remains of a splint, he realised. It must have belonged to the man they had been dragging. Something had ripped off his splint and it had almost certainly been a bear.

He heard a sigh to his left and he whirled around, his rifle at the ready. There was another sigh, and a whimpering sound. Van der Sandt walked towards the noise, his finger tightening on the trigger. He reached the edge of the clearing and stared into the undergrowth. Something had forced its way through the bushes, smearing blood across the leaves. He knelt down and examined the forest floor. There were paw prints in the soil. Big prints. Van der Sandt put his hand down over one of the tracks and splayed his fingers. The bear's print was three times the size of his hand. There were two sets of smaller prints, too. Cubs following the adult. So the big bear was almost certainly female – the males didn't bother raising their offspring, they were off at the first opportunity. A bit like Van der Sandt's own father, who had walked out on his mother when he was still a toddler.

As he straightened up he heard another sigh that morphed into a whimper. He pushed through the bushes, looking left and right. An injured bear could be deadly, especially a mother wanting to protect her cubs.

He emerged from the clump of bushes and walked around a massive redwood, then stopped when he saw the source of the sounds. A large female bear lay on her side, her black fur glistening with blood. Her chest was slowly rising and falling. Next to her were two cubs, oblivious to Van der Sandt's arrival. He walked slowly towards them, his boots crunching softly on the ground.

One of the cubs looked around and saw Van der Sandt, but then turned back to the mother, nudging her and making snuffling sounds. Van der Sandt looked down at the bear. She was dying and was clearly in a lot of pain. Her cubs snuggled against her. Cubs usually stayed with their mothers until they were between eighteen months and two years old. The cubs were born in the winter and the mother would nurse them until spring when they would all emerge from their den. The mother would then teach her young how to feed on fish, insects, fruit, leaves and nuts. The two cubs looked to be about eighteen months old, and were almost ready to leave their mother and fend for themselves.

The bear shuddered and then moaned softly. Van der Sandt wasn't a vet but he could see there was nothing that could be done to help her. From the look of it she had been shot in half a dozen places, by someone who clearly didn't know what they were doing. One of the rounds had hit the bear in the shoulder, two had hit her chest and two had struck the head. The bear's right front paw was also bleeding. The shooter was probably panicking and firing at random.

The bear's chest was slowly rising and falling and there was a bloody froth oozing from one of the chest wounds. The lung had been penetrated and was filling with blood. Van der Sandt could see the confusion in the bear's eyes. She didn't understand what was happening but she knew it wasn't good. The bear opened her mouth and groaned in pain.

The two cubs were butting their heads against their mother, clearly distressed.

Van Der Sandt pointed the suppressor at the base of the animal's left ear. He took no pleasure in taking the life of the bear. It wasn't killing that he enjoyed, it was hunting, but the animal was in pain and the only decent thing to do was to put her out of her misery. He grimaced and pulled the trigger. The gun kicked in his hands and the bear twitched once then went still. Blood trickled from the ear. The two cubs both flinched at the muffled sound of the shot, then backed away as if they weren't sure what had happened.

'Off you go,' he said. 'Time to start your new life.'

The cubs looked at each other then turned and scampered off into the undergrowth. Van der Sandt doubted that they would stay together for long. Juvenile males sought out their own ranges and lived solitary lives until it became time to find a mate.

He turned and pushed his way back through the bushes to the clearing, and made his way over to the remains of the splint. He walked around slowly looking at the crushed grass and prints in the ground, trying to work out what had happened. The bear had obviously come out of the undergrowth, presumably to protect her cubs. For some reason it had attacked the injured man and the others had tried to shoot the bear. He saw the glint of brass in the grass and bent down to pick up a shell. It was a 9 mm. He looked around and found another five cartridges, all the same calibre. Six shots. All fired from the Glock.

He continued to scan the ground and spotted a longer cartridge, a 5.56 Nato round. As he picked it up he saw another. So two shots from the Heckler. And it was clear from the tracks that Boots had the carbine. The bear had taken eight shots before it had run off into the undergrowth. He walked away from the body, looking for the footsteps leading away. He found them quickly, heading south. There were three sets of prints. Boots, the injured man who needed a stick, and the guy in sandals. He frowned. There had been five of them before the bear had attacked. But there were only three sets of tracks leaving the clearing. He bent down and peered at the footprints. He smiled as he realised they were much deeper than they had been before.

Boots was carrying one of the men. The other two sets of prints suggested they were carrying the fifth man in the group. So now two of the group were badly hurt. He continued to check the grass until he found where the second man had been injured. There was more blood and crushed grass. So the bear had attacked two of the men before the shots had driven it away. Then they had picked up the injured men and were carrying them. Van der Sandt looked at his watch. It had now been an hour since he had heard the shots so they could only be a couple of kilometres ahead of him. He hurried after them, his heart racing.

CHAPTER 46

Raj was breathing heavily and was starting to stagger under Jaffar's weight. Luckily the terrain was reasonably flat but even so it was tough going. They reached a clearing and Raj called a halt. He lowered Jaffar to the ground as Erol and Sid placed Mo next to a tree. Raj knelt down and examined Jaffar's wounds through his ripped trousers. Fresh blood was still oozing out. Jaffar was groggy but conscious.

'I'm going to have to take your trousers off,' said Raj. Jaffar grunted but didn't say anything. Raj took the tourniquet off the thigh and then unbuttoned Jaffar's trousers and gently pulled them off. Sid and Erol peered down. 'Is he going to be okay?' asked Sid.

'It could have been worse,' said Raj. 'I think she was only toying with him.'

'That's not funny, bruv,' said Jaffar through gritted teeth.

'Seriously mate, she just swiped you, she could have taken the leg off if she'd wanted to.' Raj prodded the top wound and fresh blood appeared. 'I'm going to have to stitch this,' he said. He looked over at Mo who was leaning against a tree, his eyes closed. 'How is he?'

'Not good,' said Sid. 'His leg is a mess.'

Raj pulled the knife from its sheath, unscrewed the compass and slid out the plastic container. He opened it and took out the fishing hook and the nylon line.

'You're fucking joking,' said Sid.

'It's not how I'd choose to sew up a wound, but it'll have to do.'

Jaffar squinted at the hook. 'No fucking way.'

'It's just a curved needle, mate,' said Raj. He threaded the line through the eye of the hook. 'It's going to hurt, but you're a big boy.' He looked up at Erol. 'Have you got any of the willow left?'

'Yeah,' said Erol. He took some of the bark from his pocket and handed it down to Jaffar. Jaffar thrust it between his lips and chewed.

'Do you want to bite on something?' asked Raj.

Jaffar shook his head. 'Just do it,' he said. He closed his eyes and turned his head to the side.

Raj pushed the tip of the hook into the skin and pushed it through. He grabbed the point and eased the line after it. Then he pushed it through the other side of the wound and pulled the line. He smiled grimly when he saw that it was working. He tied the line, pulling the two sides of the flesh together, then cut it with the knife. 'Nice one, bruv,' said Sid.

'Are you done?' asked Jaffar, his eyes still closed.

'That's the first stitch, there's a few more to do,' said Raj. He looked up at Sid. 'We're going to need to replace Mo's splint,' he said. 'Can you and Erol grab some branches? You know the sort, an inch or so thick and straight as you can get.'

Sid patted Erol on the back. 'Come on. And I could do with some more berries.'

'Remember, we need to move quickly,' said Raj. 'The hunter can't be too far away.'

As the two men went into the forest, Raj threaded the hook again and used it to insert a second stitch. The top wound was just over six centimetres long and Raj managed to close it with five stitches. He worked as quickly as he could. Jaffar kept his head turned to the side and grunted occasionally.

The wound below it was deeper and longer, almost ten centimetres, and took eight stitches to close. The final wound was less deep and took just four. Eventually Raj sat back on his heels and admired his handiwork. Considering he had been using a fish hook and not a needle, the stitches weren't bad at all. He wound up the surplus line.

'Is that it?' asked Jaffar.

'All done,' said Raj.

Jaffar turned his head and opened his eyes.

'The bleeding will stop soon,' said Raj. He put the hook and the remains of the line back into the handle of the knife, then stood up. 'Stay where you are, I'm going to see if I can find something to help.'

He walked to the edge of the clearing and looked around. He saw Sid in the distance pulling a branch off a tree and walked over to him. 'What are you looking for?' asked Sid. 'More willow?'

Raj shook his head. 'The willow bark's a painkiller. I want something to act as an antiseptic to stop the wound getting infected.'

Raj moved slowly through the undergrowth looking at the smaller bushes. He pushed his way through a clump of large spreading ferns, then walked around a giant redwood that had died and fallen over, exposing rotting roots. The roots were covered with lichen and moss. Some varieties of moss had medicinal qualities but they could also be poisonous, and Raj wasn't knowledgeable enough to take the risk.

There were more ferns beyond the dead tree, and a cluster of evergreen shrubs. Raj smiled when he saw a bush dotted with white flowers. He grabbed a handful of its fern-like leaves and crushed them. When he held the leaves to his nose he caught the distinctive bitter aroma that let him know he was right – it was a yarrow plant. He grabbed several handfuls of leaves and took them back to the clearing. Sid was still pulling branches off the tree and Erol was gathering berries. Raj left them to it.

He reached the clearing and sat down next to Jaffar who frowned at the leaves. 'Do I have to eat that?'

'Nah, mate. We'll use it like a poultice. I just need something to keep it in place.'

'What does it do?'

'The leaves contain chamazulene, which is good for staunching bleeding and making sure infection doesn't take hold,' said Raj. 'Native Americans have been using it for centuries.'

He put the leaves on the ground and then used the knife to

cut two strips of cloth from the bottom of Jaffar's shirt. Then he crushed the leaves, pressed them against the wound and used the cloth to tie them into place.

'It hurts like fuck, bruv,' said Jaffar.

'I know. There's nothing I can do about that, I'm afraid. But the willow bark should take the edge off it. Let's get your trousers back on.'

Raj helped Jaffar pull his trousers back up, then looked at his watch. It was just after 4 p.m. There were about five hours before the sun went down. He frowned. They had run out of time. There was no way they could reach the house before dark. Jaffar was going to have real trouble walking and the more he put pressure on the leg, the greater the chance that the wounds would reopen.

Sid and Erol returned. Sid was carrying eight small branches and Erol had used two large leaves as a makeshift tray to hold several handfuls of berries. He shared them out and tossed the leaves away. 'Will he be okay?' Sid asked, gesturing at Jaffar.

'If he was in hospital, sure,' said Raj. 'But we're in the middle of a forest.' He straightened up. 'We need to talk.' He looked across at Erol and waved him over. Erol limped towards them with his crutch. 'We need a rethink,' said Raj. 'We've just over twenty-five kilometres to go and it'll be dark in about five hours. We'll need an hour to get a shelter together, so whichever way you cut it, we're not going to beat the dark. And assuming the hunter heard those shots, he'll be heading in our direction.'

'So what do you want to do?' asked Jaffar. 'You want to dump me and Mo, don't you? So that you three can go off on your own.'

'You need time to heal, Jaffar. Even if we carry you, those wounds are going to reopen and you'll bleed to death. And Mo, you really are on your last legs, no pun intended.' Raj pointed west. 'Assuming the helicopter dropped the hunter over there this morning, he probably headed to the clearing. At that point he would have picked up our tracks, and Sal and Abdullah's too. We don't know if he went after them or us first, but he's either to the west or the north of us. We can keep heading towards the house, but eventually he's going to catch up. And if our tail-end Charlie is having to look at the rear all the time, we'll make even slower progress.'

'Just spit it out, Raj,' said Sid. 'Tell us what you want to do.'

'Whatever we do, we have to be in agreement,' said Raj. 'All I'm doing is discussing options.'

'So tell us the options,' said Jaffar.

'Okay, so option one is we continue as we are, going as quickly as we can. Even though we know we won't be moving quick enough.'

'And option two?' asked Erol.

Raj sighed. 'We fix up a hide for Jaffar and Mo and we leave them here with a gun. We three move on, leaving a trail that he can't miss. Then one of two things will happen: either the hunter passes close to Jaffar and Mo and they can shoot him, or he passes them by and follows us.'

'And then what?' asked Sid.

'We'll be moving faster without Mo and Jaffar, so with any luck he won't catch us.'

'So then we get to the house, which is presumably chock-a-block with all those fucking Americans we saw.'

'Yeah, but they won't be expecting us. Sid, one way or another we'll be getting to the house. Let's not go crossing bridges until we get to them. I'm not happy about leaving anyone behind, but with the injuries that Jaffar and Mo have got, we're going to be moving far too slowly. If we put them in a hide, we can move at a decent pace and come back for them later.'

Sid looked over at Erol. 'What do you think, bruv?'

'I dunno,' said Erol. 'I don't like the idea of leaving them behind, but on the other hand they're sitting fucking ducks anyway.'

'We'll leave them with one of the guns,' said Raj.

Erol nodded. 'I like the sound of that.' He looked down at Jaffar. 'What about you?'

Jaffar waved at his injured leg. 'Best will in the world, I'm going to be crawling along,' he said. 'I'd need help and that means I'd be tying up the two of you. And like Erol says, if he catches up with us, we're sitting ducks.' He sighed. 'I'm not fucking happy but I don't see we've got any choice.'

Raj nodded in agreement. 'That's how I feel,' he said. 'The odds are better if you two dig in and Sid, Erol and I move on.'

'You're sure about this, Jaffar?' asked Sid. 'We're not going to do this unless you and Mo agree.'

Jaffar shrugged. 'I'm okay if Mo's okay.'

Sid looked over at Raj. 'We need to go and ask Mo, but looks like we do it,' he said. 'What's your plan for the hide?'

Raj looked around. There was an area of large ferns to the left and beyond it a row of thick bushes. 'If we dig a pit over there, you can stay hidden and he's not likely to come up behind you. If he misses this area completely you'll be fine, but if he does follow our trail you should get a decent view of him as he goes by.'

'And you'll give us a gun?' asked Jaffar.

Raj wasn't happy about surrendering one of the weapons, but he didn't see that he had a choice. There was no way he could leave the two men behind with no way of defending themselves. 'Sure, yeah.'

'The Heckler?' asked Jaffar, nodding at the carbine on Raj's back.

'The Glock's a better bet,' said Raj. 'Easier to use from cover.'

'I'm not giving up my gun,' said Sid quickly.

'We can't leave them unarmed,' said Raj.

'They'll be hidden, you said.'

'Yeah, but if he passes close by, they could get a shot off and end it right there. If they don't have a gun, what can they do?'

Sid scowled but didn't press the point. Jaffar held out his hand and Sid sighed and gave him the Glock. 'Just don't shoot yourself,' Sid said to Jaffar, sourly.

'Bruv, I know what I'm doing.' He ejected the clip, checked how many rounds he had, and then slotted it back in place.

Raj pointed at the ferns. 'Let's get started on the hide.' Erol turned towards the ferns but Raj called him back. 'Best bet is to walk south a bit, then move into the undergrowth and work our way back. I don't know how good a tracker this guy is but there's no point in making it easy for him. But let's make sure Mo is on board.'

Raj, Sid and Erol went over to Mo, who had been watching them as he snacked on the berries and nuts that he had been given. 'You're leaving us, aren't you?' he said.

'Bruv, it's the best . . .' began Sid, but Mo held up a hand to silence him. 'I get it,' he said. 'What's the plan?'

Sid explained what they were going to do while Raj made a new splint and fixed it to Mo's injured leg.

'It makes sense,' said Mo. 'Just make sure you come back for us.'

'You can bank on it, bruv,' said Sid.

Once the splint was in place, Raj took Sid and Erol to the area where he figured they should build the hide, taking care not to leave any tracks. He picked up a fallen branch and used it to mark out a two-metre-by-two-metre square in the soil at the edge of a patch of ferns. 'Okay, so you need to get some flat stones and use them to dig out a trench, about a foot deep here and two feet at the far end. Dump the soil among the bushes. If the two of you work together, it shouldn't take too long.'

'What are you going to be doing?' asked Erol.

'I'll cut the branches to build a canopy over the pit,' said Raj. As the two men picked up stones and began hacking at the soil, Raj went off in search of a tree with suitable branches. He found a clump of red alders, with whiteish bark and long, straight branches. He used his knife to hack away eight branches, then stripped off any twigs and leaves before carrying them back to where the others had made a good start on the pit.

Raj dropped the branches on the ground, then pushed his way through the ferns until he was a hundred metres or so from the pit. He began gathering large armfuls of ferns. When he had a couple of dozen, he went back to the pit and dropped them next to the branches. He found a flat stone and used it to help the others dig away at the soil.

It took them almost half an hour to get the pit deep enough to hold the two men. Once it was ready, Raj asked Sid to collect some more ferns, to line the pit.

As Sid gathered ferns, Raj had Erol help him construct a simple frame with the branches. He used the knife to cut off his left sleeve below the elbow and then cut it into strips, which he used to tie the branches together. Once he had tied the branches in place, he threaded through ferns to fill in the gaps between them. He was putting the finishing touches to it all when Sid returned with an armful of ferns. Raj and Sid spread them out across the bottom of the pit, then went to fetch Mo. They carried him to the pit, then brought Jaffar.

'Right guys, if you need to pee or anything, now's the time to do it, because once you're in there you're going to have to stay put,' said Raj.

'I'm good,' said Jaffar. He stepped gingerly into the pit. He knelt down and then lay on his stomach. Raj and Sid helped Mo into the pit and together they lowered the frame over the two men.

Raj went around the edge of the frame kicking dirt and leaves over it, then stood back to admire his handiwork. 'Looks all right, doesn't it?' he asked Sid and Erol.

The two men nodded their approval. 'It blends in okay, you'd really have to be looking for it to see it,' said Sid.

'What about you guys, can you see all right?' asked Raj.

'Just about,' said Jaffar. 'But I'd be happier with the Heckler.'

'That's not going to happen,' said Raj. 'Do you think you can get a shot off if he walks by?'

'Yeah,' growled Jaffar.

'Sid, you and Erol go back to where we were and see what it looks like from there. Take the long way round and try not to break any ferns or branches. Softly softly.'

Sid nodded, then he and Erol threaded their way through the ferns. When they reached the trail, Sid flashed Raj a thumbs up. 'Can't see a thing, bruv!' he called.

Raj bent down to look at Jaffar and Mo. All he could see was their eyes. 'Okay, we'll leave you to it,' he said.

'You are coming back, right?' said Jaffar.

'Of course,' said Raj.

'You fucking better, bruv,' said Jaffar.

Raj nodded. There was nothing else he could say. He'd do everything in his power to keep his word, but he knew that there were armed men waiting for him in the house and a hunter with a rifle on their trail. He was between a rock and a hard place, and all he had was the Heckler and its remaining rounds. He headed through the ferns, slowly and carefully to minimise any damage, and rejoined Sid and Erol. Sid was right: the hide was totally invisible from a distance. He checked the compass in his knife and pointed south. 'That's the way,' he said. 'We need to move as quickly as possible.'

'We're not going to reach the house before dark, are we?' said Erol.

'It'll be touch and go,' said Raj. 'But if we can get to within sight of the house we might be able to approach it in darkness.'

'Then what? We've got one gun and how many of them are there? Ten? Twelve?'

'Mate, all we can do is take it one step at a time.' He patted Erol on the back. 'Come on. I know your ankle is still hurting, but we need to quicken the pace.'

Erol nodded and gritted his teeth in frustration. The three men headed through the trees.

CHAPTER 47

Van der Sandt stopped when he saw the dried blood on the grass. There had been regular blood drops after the bear attack but this was different, and the grass had been pressed flat. He looked at the footprints, knowing that they would tell the story. Boots had knelt by the injured man, and gone to and fro. There were leaves that didn't belong in the area – they had clearly been stripped from bushes nearby. He picked up one of the crushed leaves and sniffed it. It was yarrow. The plant could be used as an antiseptic and a blood coagulant. They had obviously rested here after they had escaped the bear and Boots had treated the wound.

He took a few steps back and looked around. The wound had been bleeding badly but once they started moving again, the blood had stopped. Whatever Boots had done had obviously worked, but the injured man still needed help to walk.

He followed the tracks to a stony area where there were fewer footprints. They were still heading south, towards the house. Van der Sandt slowed, looking for tracks among the rocks and stones. Eventually he was walking on grass again but he realised immediately that something was wrong. There were still three sets of tracks but the points weren't as deep and the strides were greater, so they were no longer carrying the two injured men. He frowned, stopped, and looked around. There was no mistake. Boots had passed that way, and so had the guy wearing sandals. And the guy who was using a stick was still there. That meant they had left the two injured men behind. He turned and walked back to the rocky area. That must have been where the other two had taken a different direction. His frown deepened. Why would they be travelling separately? Had they argued? Or had Boots decided that they would be able to move faster without the injured men holding them back? And how had the injured men been able to move without help? He scratched the back of his neck, trying to work out what was going on.

CHAPTER 48

Mo nudged Jaffar in the ribs. Jaffar glared at him. 'I see him, bruv,' he whispered. 'Leave me the fuck alone.'

The man was about thirty metres away, walking slowly as his eyes scrutinised the ground. He was holding his rifle in both hands. He was dressed pretty much as he had been in the house, though he now had a floppy hat on his head.

'Are you going to shoot or not?' hissed Mo.

Jaffar had the Glock in both hands but he wasn't aiming it.

'You've got to take the shot,' whispered Mo.

'If I shoot and I miss then he'll shoot back,' said Jaffar.

'He can't see us,' said Mo. 'That's the point of us lying up here.'

'I'm not sure I can hit him from here.'

'Then give the fucking gun to me. I'll do it.'

Mo reached for the Glock but Jaffar moved it away. 'I'm a better shot than you and you know it.'

'Then take the fucking shot,' said Mo. 'If you don't, he'll catch up the others.'

'Yeah, well Raj kept the big gun for himself, didn't he?'

The hunter had stopped and was looking down at the ground.

'Come on, shoot him,' hissed Mo.

Jaffar sighted the Glock and tightened his finger on the trigger as he aimed at the centre of the hunter's body. He took a breath, let half of it out, steadied himself, and pulled the trigger.

CHAPTER 49

Van der Sandt heard a muffled bang off to his right and then the crack of a bullet as it whizzed past the back of his skull. For a second he froze, not realising what had happened, then he ducked down and ran forward. A second shot rang out but the bullet must have gone wide because he didn't hear it zip by. He veered to the left and ran behind a huge redwood, then stopped and listened, turning his head from side to side. The birds had fallen silent and he couldn't hear anyone in pursuit. It had been an ambush rather than an attack. They were lying low. Van der Sandt wasn't used to being on the receiving end of gunfire but he was pretty sure that it had been a handgun. Two shots. It had been an amateur move; a handgun wasn't generally accurate beyond twenty metres or so, even in the hands of a professional. If they'd had the Heckler they'd probably have used it, which reinforced his belief that the group had split into two. He continued to listen but heard nothing. They were hiding somewhere. Van der Sandt smiled to himself. It was time to go stalking. Often he took as much pleasure from the stalking and the hunt as he did from the kill itself, and this time would be no exception.

A bird began to call high overhead. He looked up but it was hidden in the foliage. The *cuk-cuk-cuk* call, rising and falling in pitch, was distinctive to the pileated woodpecker. He heard a rustling to his left and he whirled around, bringing up the rifle. The rustling continued but it was moving away from his position, and whatever was causing the noise was clearly small – a chipmunk perhaps, foraging for food.

Van der Sandt slipped his finger off the rifle's trigger. He had a pretty good idea where the shot had come from.

CHAPTER 50

Mo narrowed his eyes as he looked left and right. 'I don't see him,' he whispered. 'What about you?'

'Maybe he's gone,' whispered Jaffar.

'Why would he go? We shot at him. He knows we're here.'

'Yeah, but he knows we've got a gun.'

'What, you think we've scared him off? He wants to kill us, he's not going to just leave, is he?'

Jaffar gestured with his chin. 'He went that way, right? And he's not come back.'

'How long ago, do you think? Five minutes?'

'More than that. Closer to ten.'

'What do we do?' asked Mo.

'What can we do? You want to get out and go looking for him?'

'Maybe we hit him. Maybe he's lying out there bleeding to death.'

'No way did I hit him, bruv,' said Jaffar. 'This gun's a piece of shit.'

'Give it to me, then.'

'That won't make no odds. The sights are off. Keep looking, bruv, he's going to come back, I'm sure of it.'

'I wish we had a fucking watch, I've no idea how long we've been here.'

'Yeah, well Raj has the watch and the knife and the only decent gun. He's not one for sharing.'

'He's okay. He stopped you from dying.'

'Yeah? And then he left us here as bait.'

'Come on. You know it was the right call.'

Jaffar opened his mouth to argue, but before he could speak there was a popping sound and Mo's whole body jerked.

'What happened?' asked Jaffar.

There was a second dull pop and Mo twitched again. Blood began to seep from between his lips.

'Fuck!' screamed Jaffar.

Mo's head imploded into a bloody pulp and Jaffar cried out in terror. He pushed himself up onto his knees. Ferns and branches cascaded around him. His eyes scanned the trail but there was no sign of the hunter. He held the gun out in front of him, but even with both hands on the weapon he was trembling. He heard a twig snap over to his left and he pointed the gun at the source of the sound but saw nothing. He looked down at Mo. The back of his head had been blown away and blood was spreading across the ferns.

Jaffar heard a soft chuckle behind him and he whirled around. The hunter was standing about twenty feet away, an amused smile on his face. The rifle was pointing at Jaffar's chest. Jaffar opened his mouth to roar at the man, to scream his defiance as he brought up the Glock, but before the sound left his lips the rifle had fired and he felt as if he'd been punched in the chest. The gun felt heavy in his hands and he tried to breathe but he couldn't get any air into his lungs.

He tried to talk but there was something blocking his throat and he tasted blood. The gun fell from his hands and there was a dull thud as it hit the ground. The hunter was saying something but the words didn't seem to be reaching Jaffar's ears.

The hunter lifted his rifle to his shoulder and pulled the trigger again. Jaffar fell backwards. He saw branches and leaves and sky, and then everything went black.

CHAPTER 51

Raj heard the sound of running water off to his right and motioned for Sid and Erol to stop. 'Hear that?' he said, and Sid nodded. They pushed their way through some waist-high bushes and found a small creek, just a couple of feet across. The water was moving quite quickly and seemed clean.

'Do you think we can drink it?' asked Sid.

'It looks okay, and we don't have time to find the source,' said Raj. He knelt down, cupped his hand and scooped water into his mouth. It was cold and refreshing – he hadn't realised how thirsty he was. Sid and Erol followed his example.

When he'd drunk enough, Raj stopped and pulled out his knife, checked the compass and gestured at the two men. 'You okay to keep moving?' he asked.

Sid nodded.

So did Erol. 'How much longer?' he asked.

Raj looked at the pebbles in his hand. 'We've covered just over ten kilometres since we left Mo and Jaffar,' he said. 'So by my reckoning we have another sixteen kilometres to go.' He looked at his watch. 'It'll be dark in two hours.'

'Can we cover sixteen kilometres in two hours?'

'No way, not over terrain like this.'

'So we're fucked.'

'Not necessarily.'

'We can't move through the forest at night, can we?'

'We should be able to cover ten kilometres if we can keep up the pace,' said Raj. 'By then we might well be in sight of the house. If the trees thin out, there might be enough moonlight to see by. And approaching at night might give us an advantage.'

'Or they might have night vision gear, in which case we'll be well fucked.'

'Maybe not,' said Raj. 'There'll be lights on, presumably. And there are no trees close to the house so if there's any moonlight we should have some vision. What we need to do is to get as close as we can before night falls then we'll see where we stand.' He straightened up and forced a smile. 'I know it's not much of a plan, but it's all we've got.' He looked over his shoulder. He hadn't heard any shots from Mo and Jaffar. It could have been that the forest had absorbed the sound, or the hunter had bypassed them and they hadn't had the opportunity to shoot. Either way, he had to assume that the hunter was still on the trail he, Erol and Sid were leaving.

CHAPTER 52

Van der Sandt stopped and took a drink from his water bottle. He shrugged off his backpack and unzipped it. He sat down with his back to a redwood and looked at his GPS. The three men must be making good time – they were probably going to continue moving after dark.

He took the transceiver from its holster and switched it on. He put it to his mouth and pressed the talk button. 'This is Victor Sierra for Charlie Bravo. Over.'

Colin Bell replied almost immediately. 'Charlie Bravo here. Over.'

'There are three targets heading your way, and one of them is armed. Can you send some of your people out with a view to intercepting them? Over.'

'Not a problem. Do you have a location? Over.'

'I'll leave my GPS on so you'll be able to see my position from now on. It looks as if they're heading straight to you. Over.'

'Give me a second and I'll check your location.' Van der Sandt looked around as he waited for Bell. Eventually he came back on the radio. 'Right, yes, I can see where you are,' he said. 'Can you confirm what action you need my men to take, over?'

'Just turn them away from the house,' said Van der Sandt. 'They have one gun between them, the Heckler that they took from Nick. I'm not far behind them. Over.'

'I'm on it,' said Bell. 'Over and out.'

CHAPTER 53

Colin Bell strode into the kitchen. Two of his team were sitting at the table, drinking coffee. They stood up as he walked in. Keith Emmett and Rick Holland were both former Delta Force with extensive experience in Afghanistan and Iraq. Emmett had worked with Bell for almost three years and Holland was a more recent recruit. Emmett was the taller of the two, just over six feet with a lanky stride that stood him in good stead on long marches. Holland was shorter and stockier. He had a shaved head and usually sported a pair of wraparound sunglasses, no matter what the conditions.

'Right, I need you out in the woods,' Bell said. 'Mr Van der Sandt is heading this way, following three of the targets, one of whom has Nick's Heckler. We're tasked with making sure they don't reach the house. Remember this is the client's operation so we don't want to take the wind out of his sails. Our mission is to send them packing but not to wound or kill. Understood?'

The two men nodded.

'These guys aren't professional soldiers but they have been trained by ISIS and they were among the group that massacred the tourists in Cyprus, so we can assume they'll have no qualms about shooting at us. We can obviously return fire if necessary, but the client wants them alive.'

'So he can kill them himself?' said Emmett.

'The client is paying our wages, so he gets to call the shots – literally,' said Bell. He took out his GPS and showed it to them. There was a small blue dot showing Van der Sandt's position. 'This is where the client is. The targets are somewhere between him and the house. I need you on the way, stat.'

'Our gear's in the cottages,' said Emmett, taking the GPS unit from the Colonel. 'We'll pick it up and head straight out.'

The two men left at the double. Bell made himself a mug of strong coffee. He had stood most of his team down at Van der Sandt's request, so other than Emmett and Holland, there were only four more men left at the estate: Andy Isom, who was manning the guardhouse at the main gate, Dean Parrott who was on patrol in the gardens, Billy-Joe Maxwell who was standing guard outside the house and Gerry Lineham, the helicopter pilot, who'd returned after taking Nick to the hospital. There was another man at the hospital monitoring Nick's progress but Bell didn't want to bring him back. There was no need. Only one of the men that Van der Sandt was pursuing was armed and Bell's men had been trained by the best.

CHAPTER 54

Raj transferred the ninth stone into his pocket. Sid saw him do it and smiled. 'Nine hundred metres?'

'Yeah. I know it looks crazy but you'd be surprised how easy it is to lose track. Your mind can start playing tricks on you, but the stones don't lie.'

They were on a relatively flat section of the forest, but they could see a hill ahead of them. Erol was a short distance behind them. His ankle was holding up well and on the flat he barely needed the stick for support. 'Are we resting for a bit?' he asked when he reached them.

'Let's keep going,' said Raj. He gestured at the hill ahead of them. 'I'd prefer to be up there looking down rather than down here looking up.'

'A drink would be nice,' said Sid.

'Yeah, and a burger and chips would go down a treat too,' said Raj.

'First thing I'm doing when we're out of this is getting a curry,' said Erol.

'How do we get out of this, Raj?' asked Sid. 'What's the plan? We get to the house and then what?'

'We call for help,' said Raj. 'There has to be a phone there. We call the cops. Or we steal a car and drive to the nearest town. To be honest, I don't know for sure yet. We just have to take it one step at a time.'

'If we do call the cops, how do we explain what we're doing here?'

'That's easy enough. We're being hunted by a madman.'

'I don't mean that. I mean, if we tell them we were brought

from an ISIS camp in Syria, they'll send us to Guantanamo Bay and waterboard the fuck out of us.'

'He's got a point,' said Erol.

'Like I said, one step at a time,' said Raj.

'I heard you,' said Sid. 'But what will you tell them, about us?'

Raj wiped this forehead with the back of his hand. 'What's on your mind, Sid?'

'Okay, assume we get back to the house. And assume we get a car or a phone and get to the cops or the FBI or whoever. Are you going to grass us up? Are you going to tell them who we are?'

'Sid, mate, I just want to go home.'

'And if we say we were working for an NGO when we were kidnapped, what will you tell them?'

'I won't tell them a blind thing. You tell them whatever you want.'

Sid nodded slowly. 'Okay.' He looked at Erol. 'You okay with that?'

'I don't see we've got any choice,' said Erol.

'We really don't have time for this,' said Raj. 'Come on.' He started walking again. Sid and Erol hurried after him.

CHAPTER 55

Emmett and Holland had been assigned adjoining staff cottages. There were a dozen in all and theirs were at the far right-hand side. 'Two minutes and we're out of here,' said Emmett.

'Roger that,' said Holland.

Emmett's cottage contained two single beds and he had set his equipment out on the one closest to the door. He stashed his radio into one of the pockets of his Kevlar vest, along with two magazines for his carbine. Van der Sandt wanted the men turned away from the house and not killed, but that didn't mean that he wasn't going to return fire if he was attacked. He put two bottles of water and a couple of energy bars into the backpack, along with a first aid kit, a trauma kit and the GPS unit. His thermal vision goggles were charging on his bedside table. They were a special batch of dual system goggles – infrared and thermal imaging – being tested by Delta Force. All of Bell's team had been issued with them. They were too expensive to be issued to all American troops but Delta Force were hoping they would become standard special forces issue. The IR system was fine for general night-time use, but it wouldn't work in fog, dust storms or places where there was zero ambient light, such as caves. The thermal imaging system sensed changes in temperature and so could be used anywhere day or night, and was perfect for spotting snipers – their thermal footprints could be detected no matter what the light conditions. They weren't quite good enough to see through walls but they would pick up enemy troops at night or hidden in the jungle or forest. Emmett unplugged them and put them in the backpack.

He paid a quick visit to the bathroom, then shouldered the backpack, picked up his carbine and put on his Kevlar helmet.

Holland was already outside, grinning. Like Emmett he was wearing a helmet and had his backpack on. He had ditched his trademark sunglasses as night was closing in. 'You said two minutes.'

'Fuck me, bro, is everything with you a race?' laughed Emmett.

'The quick and the dead, man,' said Holland. 'I know which I'd rather be.'

They hurried over to the west gate where Bell was already waiting for them. It was a black-painted barred gate set into the high stone wall. Bell unlocked it for them and wished them well.

Emmett checked the GPS unit, showed it to Holland, and then pointed west. The two men entered the undergrowth and moved apart. Their camouflage fatigues helped them blend into the undergrowth and within a few minutes Emmett had lost sight of Holland, though the occasional snap of a twig let him know that he was still close by.

CHAPTER 56

Raj and Sid stopped and waited for Erol to catch up with them again. The sun was dropping low in the sky but the tree cover was so thick it wasn't making much of a difference. They were heading down a long slope and ahead of them was a steeper hill dotted with boulders. 'I need to take a dump,' said Sid.

'Sure, go ahead,' said Raj.

Sid went behind a large redwood as Raj scanned the area. The trees were tall but the widest was only a couple of feet across, which suggested that it was secondary forest, replacing the original trees that had been chopped down to satisfy the country's never-ending appetite for building materials.

'How much further?' asked Erol.

'A few kilometres,' said Raj.

In the distance a bird flapped into the air and headed for the treetops. Raj stiffened as he saw movement on the slope ahead of them, appearing from behind a tree. A man, in camouflage fatigues, cradling a carbine. As the man stepped around the tree, another bird broke cover and flew skywards. The man was short and stocky and wearing a Kevlar helmet.

'Get down,' said Raj, pushing Erol to the ground. He looked over at the tree that Sid was hiding behind. 'Sid!' hissed Raj, but there was no reply.

The man was working his way down the slope opposite where Raj was, some three hundred metres away.

'Sid!'

There was no response. Raj narrowed his eyes as he scrutinised the slope. He doubted that the man would be out alone. 'Can you see anyone else?' he whispered to Erol.

They scanned the undergrowth. It took Raj almost a minute to spot another man, to the left of the first one. He was further up the slope and moving slowly. Raj's jaw tightened as he recognised the man. He was one of the team who had been in the helicopter when they had been dropped in the clearing.

'What do we do?' whispered Erol.

Raj pressed his finger to his lips and shook his head. Erol nodded. 'Sid!' hissed Raj. Still no answer. Raj cursed under his breath. If Sid walked out from behind the tree, there was a good chance he'd be seen. He put his Heckler to his shoulder and aimed at the first man he'd spotted.

'Sid, can you hear me?' hissed Raj again. The two men were about two hundred metres away now. He could see them clearly despite the camouflage gear so he was sure that if Sid started moving they would see him.

He heard a rustling sound to his left and he whirled around, his carbine at the ready. The sound continued but there was no movement. It was probably a rat, he realised. He switched his attention back again to the two men coming down the slope. They were heading right for him. It was either a coincidence or somehow they had worked out his heading. The bush he was crouching behind was a little over three feet tall. If he stood up they'd see him immediately.

'Sid!' He heard a twig snap behind the redwood, and the sound of a zip being pulled up. 'Sid! Stay where you are!' he hissed. There was a crunching sound, then Sid appeared from behind the tree, wiping his hands on his pants. 'Get down!' whispered Raj.

'What?' said Sid, but before Raj could reply bullets ripped through the branches overhead.

'Fuck!' shouted Sid and he threw himself to the ground. There was a tree to Raj's left and he crawled towards it. He knew he was in an impossible position, facing two different fields of fire; all the attackers had to do was to move apart and he'd have nowhere to hide.

Erol had curled up under a bush, but Raj knew it would provide absolutely zero cover.

A second burst of fire ripped through the bushes to Raj's right. He looked over his shoulder. Sid was lying face down, his hands over his head.

Raj scrambled to the tree, knelt down and brought up his gun. He knew he'd only be able to get off a couple of shots before they spotted his position so he had to make them count. He was fairly sure they hadn't seen him; they had only started shooting when Sid walked around the tree.

There was a third burst of fire, three quick shots, then a fourth. Raj could fire around the left or the right side of the tree. The right would be more comfortable as the carbine was up against his right shoulder, so he slipped his finger over the trigger and leant around the tree. The man on the right was taking aim again and Raj sighted on his chest and squeezed the trigger. The carbine kicked against his shoulder and almost immediately the man jerked back and his weapon fell from his arms. Raj was already moving, rolling against the trunk to get to the other side of the tree. He dropped down to the ground and crawled back to Sid. 'Stay where you are, mate,' he whispered.

'I'm not fucking going anywhere,' said Sid. 'Is Erol all right?'

'Scared shitless but he's okay.' Raj crawled past him and reached the tree that Sid had been using for cover. He crawled around it and got up. He was now fifteen metres or so from his original position, still in the remaining man's line of sight but hopefully far enough away that he would be able to get off the first shot. He took a deep breath, steadied himself, then stood up and moved around the tree. He scanned the slope ahead of him but there was no sign of his target. Then a bullet thudded into the tree and a second whizzed by his head, so close that he felt the wind against his cheek. He ducked back and pressed himself against the trunk. The man was firing from cover and Raj hadn't had time to pinpoint his position.

'Sid!' he hissed. 'You gotta help me.'

'I don't have a fucking gun,' replied Sid.

'I know, I know,' said Raj. 'I need you to get up and run to the tree I was at before.'

'Fuck that,' said Sid.

'He won't have time to get a bead on you, trust me,' said Raj. 'You need to keep low, then sprint. By the time he's got you in his sights, you'll be at the tree.'

'You're not using me as bait,' said Sid.

'Not bait, a decoy. He'll have to reveal himself to make a shot and his attention will be focused on you.'

'He'll be shooting at me, bruv. Fuck that. Get Erol to stand up.'

'Erol can't move as quick as you. Look, you'll be a moving target. At that range, with you moving fast, he won't stand a chance of hitting you.'

'Easy for you to say.'

'It's true. At the range he's at, he'd be lucky to hit you if you were standing still.'

'Don't fucking lie to me, bruv.'

'I'm not lying, Sid. Look, mate, we don't have a choice. The hunter is still out here and if he comes up behind us, we're dead in the water.'

Sid didn't reply. Raj peered over. He was still lying on his front, hands over his head.

'Sid?'

'Okay, okay, I'll fucking do it,' said Sid.

'You can call it,' said Raj. 'Count down from three. On one, you go and I'll come out. You don't look, you just run, full pelt, for the tree.'

'Don't let me down, bruv.'

'I won't, Sid.' He clicked the fire selector switch so that pulling the trigger once would fire three quick shots.

'Okay. Okay.' There was silence for a few seconds, then Sid started to count. 'Three, two . . .' As he got to one he pushed himself to his feet. Raj began to move, swinging his gun up to his shoulder and stepping around the tree.

He heard Sid crashing through the undergrowth but he concentrated on the slope ahead of him, sweeping the Heckler smoothly, his finger tight on the trigger. He registered movement to the left at the same time as he heard a shot. The man had stepped around a redwood tree but the trunk was blocking most of Raj's view – all he could see was the gun. There was no way Raj could get a decent shot from where he was. He needed to move, so he started to run as he heard the man fire again, this time two shots in quick succession.

Sid began to scream in terror. Raj continued to run, trying to get a decent view of the shooter. The man's hand came into view holding the gun, and then Raj could see his face and the top of his helmet. Raj slowed and brought up his carbine, but then his foot caught on a root and he pitched forward, off balance. His finger jerked on the trigger and the gun went off, the round burying itself in the ground. Raj continued to stumble forward. He had to keep hold of the Heckler, which made it harder to maintain his balance, and he realised that he was going to fall. He went with it, hitting the ground with his right shoulder and rolling over. He heard the triple crack of the Heckler in the distance but couldn't tell if he or Sid was the target.

He came up on one knee and he could see the man now, leaning against the tree for stability. He was aiming at Raj. The gun fired again, another three-round burst, and the rounds whizzed by Raj's left cheek. Raj aimed and pulled the trigger. The three bangs were almost a single sound – *crack-crack-crack* – and they hit the target almost instantaneously: one in the chest, one in the throat, and one in the face. The man fell back and Raj got to his feet, panting. He looked over to his left. Sid had reached the tree and was standing with his back to the trunk, trying to catch his breath.

Raj flinched as a bullet whizzed by his shoulder. He whirled around, bringing up his carbine. The first man he'd shot was back on his feet and aiming his gun at Raj. Raj frantically tried to get his Heckler up but he was too slow and the man fired again. Raj's head jerked back and everything went black.

CHAPTER 57

Sid stared in horror at Raj. He had heard the two shots but hadn't seen Raj get hit. By the time he'd realised what was happening, Raj was on the ground, blood glistening on his hair. Sid cursed. He listened intently. The shooter was heading down the slope, pushing his way through ferns and bushes. Sid couldn't stay where he was, he was a sitting target. He could run, but he'd only be prolonging the inevitable. He had to fight back.

He looked over at Erol, who was curled up under a bush with his hands over his ears. He didn't appear to have been shot but he was clearly in no state to help. He dropped down onto his hands and knees and crawled slowly towards Raj. Every few metres he stopped and listened. The shooter was still moving. It sounded as if he was heading towards the tree where Sid had been hiding, but he wasn't sure and couldn't risk sneaking a look. He crawled the rest of the way to where Raj lay and picked up the gun. He checked the fire selector. It had been set to fire a three-shot burst. He moved the selector to the fully automatic position. He figured he was only going to get one chance.

Sid listened again. There was only the sound of the birds overhead. He turned his head from side to side, frowning as he concentrated. Eventually he heard a rustling from somewhere down the slope. The man was heading up, towards him. Sid's heart was pounding and he took several slow, deep breaths to calm himself. The rustling stopped, then after a few seconds it started again. Sid took another deep breath, then jumped to his feet. His eyes scanned the slope in front of him. The man was off to his left, in a crouch, his Heckler moving from side to side. As Sid stood up, the man turned to look in his direction. His eyes widened in surprise and he began to swing his gun around but Sid was already pulling the trigger. The gun kicked in his hands and he had to fight to keep it from pulling to the right. The first rounds ripped through the ferns next to the man but then he managed to get the bullets on target and several shots smacked into his chest and face. Sid kept his finger on the trigger until the magazine was empty and the man was falling backwards in a shower of blood.

CHAPTER 58

Van der Sandt stood with his rifle against his chest, frowning. He had heard sporadic shooting from the south. It wasn't possible to tell how many guns were firing but there must have been twenty-five or thirty shots. He took his transceiver from its holster and put it to his mouth. He pressed the transmit button. 'Charlie Bravo are you receiving?' There was no reply. 'Charlie Bravo, this is Victor Sierra, talk to me.'

'Charlie Bravo here,' said Bell.

'I've just heard shots. It sounds like your men made contact. Can you find out what's happening?'

'Give me a minute. Charlie Bravo out.'

Van der Sandt stared at the undergrowth ahead of him. The shots had sounded close. He checked his GPS and could see that Bell's men were around a kilometre away.

The radio crackled and Bell was back on. 'My men are out of contact,' he said.

'That's not good.'

'They could be operating under radio silence; they could be having problems with the equipment.'

'Or they could be dead,' said Van der Sandt.

'I think that's unlikely, sir.'

'A lot that has happened today has been unlikely,' said Van der Sandt sourly.

'Do you want me to come and get you, Victor Sierra?' asked Bell.

'No, I'll handle it,' said Van der Sandt. He turned off the radio and put it back in its holster.

CHAPTER 59

Raj heard a voice in the blackness. 'Raj! Raj!' He was being shaken, hard. He groaned and opened his eyes. 'Fuck me, you're okay!' said Sid.

Raj blinked several times. 'What the hell happened?' Sid and Erol were looking down at him.

'You were shot, bruv. I thought you were fucking dead. Fuck me, that was close.'

Raj put his hands up to his right temple and winced as he touched a wound. 'How bad is it?' he asked.

'It's bleeding but I can't see bone or anything. You were lucky, bruv.'

Sid pulled the knife from the scabbard on Raj's thigh and used it to hack off a piece of his own shirt. He pressed it against the wound on Raj's head.

'Help me up,' said Raj, holding out his left hand. Sid helped him to his feet. He looked over at the slope opposite and saw the body of the second man he'd shot. Then he spotted the one he'd shot first, some fifty metres away from where they were standing. He frowned. 'I shot him. In the chest.'

'They're wearing vests,' said Erol.

Raj forced a smile. 'Well that's not a mistake I'll make again.'

Sid bent down and picked up the carbine. He handed it to Raj. 'It's empty,' he said.

'We can get ammo off them,' said Raj, nodding at the bodies. 'And the vests might be a good idea, too.'

They headed down the slope to the man that Sid had shot. He was short and stocky with a dagger tattoo on one arm. The man had a backpack and Raj pulled it off him. He went through it as

Sid undid the man's ballistic vest. There were two energy bars in the backpack and he tossed one to Sid and the other to Erol. Erol ripped the wrapper off his bar and devoured it. Sid did the same and then went back to removing the vest. There was a bottle of water in the pack. Raj took a long drink and then passed the bottle to Sid. Sid took a drink and then gave it to Erol.

There were three magazines for the man's Heckler, a first aid kit, an emergency foil blanket, a torch, a set of night vision goggles and a battery pack. Raj opened the first aid kit and took out a large plaster. 'Do me a favour mate and stick this on my wound, will you?' he asked Erol.

Erol checked the wound. 'It looks like it's stopping bleeding already.'

Raj handed him a tube of antiseptic cream. 'Slap some of this on it, too.' Erol applied some of the cream to the wound and then ripped the back off the plaster and fixed it in place. There was a strip of paracetamol tablets in the first aid kit and Raj swallowed a couple and washed them down with water. He picked up the dead man's Heckler and handed it to Sid. There were still ten rounds in the magazine.

Sid finished taking the vest off the corpse and began pulling it on over his shirt. 'Sid, how about you put on all his gear: fatigues, boots, everything,' said Raj.

Sid frowned. 'Why?'

'It might give us an edge when we get closer to the house.'

'Because I'm white?'

'Yeah, if they see a white guy in full combat gear they're less likely to shoot.'

'Okay,' said Sid. He knelt down by the body and started to unfasten the boots.

Raj took one of the magazines from the backpack, ejected the old one from his Heckler and slapped in the replacement.

Raj and Erol went over to the second body. Raj removed the backpack from the corpse. It was different to the first one, and made of Kevlar. Heavier and bulletproof. Raj opened it. The contents were similar to the first backpack. He tossed Erol another energy bar and a bottle of water, then he pulled out the goggles and examined them. They seemed to be a dual-system pair, using infrared and thermal imaging. He spotted what looked like a transceiver, but when he pulled it out he realised it was a hand-held GPS unit.

'What is it?' asked Erol, unfastening the man's Kevlar vest and picking up his carbine.

'GPS,' said Raj. He showed the screen to him. 'And see that blue dot? I'm pretty sure that's the guy on our tail.'

'So we can find him?'

Raj nodded. 'He's about a kilometre away.' He paused. 'We've got a decision to make. We can press on to the house, or we can double back and get him.'

'If we head to the house, he'll be coming up behind us,' said Erol. He put on the dead man's vest and fastened it. 'That feels more dangerous to me.'

Raj nodded. 'That's what I think.' He held up the GPS unit. 'We can go straight to him. You okay with that?'

'Sure.'

'What about you, Sid?' asked Raj.

'Sure. Why not? All three of us are armed now, we've got the advantage.'

Raj took the dead man's holstered Glock and strapped it to his thigh. 'How's the head?' asked Erol.

'Hurts like hell still, but I'll live. Okay, let's go.' He put on the backpack.

Erol nodded at the GPS unit. 'If we can see his position, he'll be able to see us, right?'

Raj checked the screen, noted the position of the hunter, and switched off the unit. 'Only when it's on,' he said. 'We'll check again in a few hundred metres. For the moment he's still moving south, towards us.'

Sid stood up and jogged on the spot to test his boots, then bent down and picked up the remaining Kevlar vest. Raj helped him fasten it. 'At least now we've got him outgunned.' He put on the Kevlar helmet. 'How do I look?' he asked.

'Still butt ugly,' said Erol. 'But yeah, you look just like the bastards that grabbed us.'

'So we're good?' said Raj. 'We head north towards the guy?'

'Sounds like a plan,' said Sid.

The three men set off north, back the way they'd come. They walked for ten minutes and then Raj stopped and switched on the GPS. The hunter had moved south-west and was now just over two hundred metres away. Raj switched off the unit and nodded at Sid and Erol. 'We're getting close,' he said.

'What's the plan?' asked Sid.

'We'll try to come up behind him,' said Raj. He pointed ahead and off to the right. 'We can cut across that way for about three hundred metres to move a bit further away from him, then we cut back and circle round behind him once we're past him. We need to be quiet from here on. Erol, how's your ankle?'

'It hurts but I can live with it.'

'Are you okay to drop the stick so that you can keep both hands on your weapon?'

Erol nodded. 'Sure.'

'Good man,' said Raj, and he patted him on the back. They moved through the trees, keeping low and taking care not to step on any twigs. Raj's eyes were constantly moving, sweeping the area ahead of them. It was definitely getting dark now; the vibrant greens were becoming greyer and there were no beams of light shafting through the branches overhead. Raj counted off his steps until he reached three hundred metres, then he cut left and slightly back on himself to head west. The redwoods were thinner now and further apart, and other trees had managed to stake their claim. There were willows, oaks and Jeffrey pines, interspersed with bushes and shrubs. Sid stayed to Raj's left and Erol was on his right.

Raj heard a rustling sound off to their left and he signalled for Sid and Erol to stop. They had their carbines at the ready as they surveyed the area, but whatever was making the noise was small and moving away from them. They started moving again, skirting a cluster of rhododendron bushes and then wading through a patch of waist-high ferns.

Raj stopped at the edge of another clump of ferns and took out the GPS unit. He switched it on. The blue dot was two hundred metres away, to their left. He pointed at the dot, then pointed in the direction they were to go. Sid flashed him an 'okay' sign and Erol gave a thumbs up, and they all turned to face their target. Raj gestured for Erol to move further to the right and Sid to the left. Raj looked at the screen. 'Looks like he's stopped,' he whispered. He switched off the unit, then put out his hand and pulled Sid's Heckler towards him so that he could get a better look at the fire selector. 'You don't want to have it on fully automatic,' he whispered. 'Once you get beyond three shots it'll start pulling away and you'll be firing wildly. Set it to a three-shot burst. You can fire as many three-shot bursts as you want and you'll stay on target.'

Sid nodded and flicked the fire selector switch.

'Just remember, he's probably only got the rifle he was carrying back at the hangar, so it's harder for him to take down a moving target,' whispered Raj. He looked over at Erol to make sure he was listening. 'If you come under fire, get to cover if you can, but if you can't you need to move fast and low, zig-zag as much as you can. And if I draw fire, you need to lay down covering fire. The gun he had looked like it was a variant of the M4. A lot of states in the US restrict the number of rounds that hunting guns can carry and the one he was using looked like a five-round magazine. So if he's got the same weapon, he's going to have to change his magazine after every five shots which means we've got the advantage in terms of fire power.'

'I hear you, bruv,' said Erol.

'Let's do it,' said Sid.

'Okay, here we go,' said Raj. He patted Sid on the back, then straightened up and moved forward. Sid moved to the left. Erol moved right.

CHAPTER 60

Van der Sandt smiled as he watched the man walking slowly through a patch of ferns. They were so stupid, these people. That went without saying because anyone who truly believed that killing innocent civilians was somehow going to enable them to live in heaven with seventy-two sloe-eyed virgins was clearly borderline retarded. Did they seriously think he would have kept the GPS unit with him once he realised that they had killed Bell's men? And did they think that he would be fooled by them turning off their unit? He chuckled quietly. 'Fucking morons,' he muttered to himself.

He had placed his GPS unit under a bush and set up behind a fallen log some fifty metres away. From his vantage point he could only see the one man, but he was sure that the others were nearby. The man was wearing a vest that he must have taken off one of Bell's team. Van der Sandt would have preferred a body shot at that distance but he was more than capable of hitting him in the head. The downside of the headshot was that the man wouldn't know what had happened. One second he would be alive, creeping through the undergrowth, the next he would be dead. It would be as quick as flicking a switch. Alive. Dead. Game over. There would be no time for the man to realise that he had been shot, that the man whose family he had killed had taken his revenge. He sighted on the man's head and tightened his finger on the trigger. He had to fight the urge to shout to get the man's attention, so that he would look in Van der Sandt's direction. Part of him wanted to see the look of panic on the man's face as he realised that he was about to die, but there were two other men out there and Van der Sandt only had eyes on one. Drawing attention to himself would be a fatal mistake.

The man stopped and looked over to his left. Presumably looking towards his companions. Then he slowly looked forward again. Van der Sandt's stomach tightened as he realised that the man was looking straight at him. He smiled and gently squeezed the trigger. The man's face imploded and he fell backwards, crashing into the ferns. Van der Sandt's smile widened. One down, two to go.

CHAPTER 61

Raj heard the dull pop off to his right and then the crash of something falling into the ferns. He frowned. The last position on the GPS had been some fifty metres ahead of him, not off to the right. 'Erol,' he whispered. 'Erol!' There was no reply. Raj looked around, his carbine at the ready. It was a muffled gunshot he'd heard, he was sure of that. There had been a suppressor on the gun back in the hangar which would muffle the sound but not kill it completely. If the hunter was off to the right that meant he'd dumped the GPS and then taken up a firing position. Raj gritted his teeth in frustration. He had clearly underestimated the man. If he was dug in he probably wouldn't move; he'd stay put until he got a shot at Raj and Sid. Raj knelt down, using the ferns as cover. He took off his backpack and took out two fresh magazines and shoved them in the back pockets of his trousers. He took a swig of water before shouldering the backpack again. He was going to have to move at some point, and the sooner the better. He looked to his left. There was no sign of Sid and Raj had no way of knowing if Sid had heard the shot.

He kept low until he was behind a redwood, then stood up. He peered over in the direction where Erol had been walking but he couldn't see him. There had only been one shot which meant the hunter had been sure of his kill. Erol must be dead. Or so badly injured that a second shot wasn't necessary. Raj peered slowly around the tree, just enough to see with his right eye. There was no sign of the hunter. Just trees and bushes and ferns. He moved back, then checked the other side of the tree. Still nothing. Erol had been about fifty metres away from Raj. The hunter's gun was accurate up to a couple of hundred metres but most shooters would be happier with half that distance. So the hunter was somewhere between a hundred and fifty and two hundred metres away. It had been a few years since Raj had trained with a Heckler and that was too far to be sure he'd hit his target.

Raj rested his back against the trunk as he considered his options. He could try waiting the hunter out, stay put and see if he'd reveal himself eventually. Or he could try to get back to the house and call for help from there. Or he could go on the attack. The Heckler could fire off far more rounds than the hunter's gun. And there were thirty rounds in the Heckler's clip and another sixty in the two magazines in his back pockets. But firepower wasn't the problem. The problem was that Raj had no idea where the hunter was holed up.

He heard a rustling to his left and he swung up the Heckler with his finger on the trigger. He relaxed when he saw it was Sid. 'What's wrong?' Sid whispered.

'I think he got Erol.'

'Fuck,' said Sid. 'Fuck, fuck, fuck.'

'He must have ditched the GPS. It was a trap. I should have seen it coming.' Raj shook his head. 'This guy is a cunning bastard,' he said. 'And I can't see where he is so we're pretty much stuck here.'

Just then, an idea suddenly struck him. He leant his carbine against the tree and shrugged off his backpack. He crouched down and took out the night vision goggles.

'We're going to wait until it's fully dark, is that the plan?' asked Sid.

Raj shook his head. 'Nah, these goggles are special. They've also got a thermal imaging system, which means we'll be able to see the hunter's heat signature. Get yours out and I'll show you what I mean.'

Sid took the goggles from his backpack. Raj showed him the on–off switch and another switch that toggled between the two functions, infrared and thermal imaging. 'The infrared system works in the dark, but the thermal imaging system can be used any time,' whispered Raj. He set the goggles to thermal, and switched them on. There was a faint buzzing sound as they booted up, but it soon stopped and Raj put them on. Sid did the same. Everything was green, even the darkening sky. As he looked up through the dark green branches of the trees overhead Raj could see two small blobs of a lighter green. Birds. He looked straight ahead. All he could see was a wall of ferns.

'These are awesome,' whispered Sid.

'Okay, so what we have to do is to get down low and creep, as slowly as we can, through the ferns,' said Raj. 'We should be able to pick up his thermal image. As soon as you see anything, let me know.'

'Okay,' said Sid.

The both got down onto their hands and knees, and they lay flat on the ground. They began to slowly crawl around the tree and towards where they figured the hunter was hiding. Raj felt as if he was moving in slow motion but he knew that to move any faster would risk giving away his position. Left arm. Right leg. Right arm. Left leg. Check. Still just a wall of green. He inched forward, trying to disturb the ferns as little as possible. It took him almost five minutes to cover twenty metres. Sid was slightly behind him. Eventually Raj could see the end of the patch of ferns, and through it, a clearing. Beyond the clearing, redwoods and smaller trees. Pines and oaks. Raj stopped. His face was bathed in sweat and his muscles were aching, from the tension as much as the physical exertion.

He motioned for Sid to join him. Sid crawled slowly through the ferns until he was at Raj's side. Raj raised his head to just below the tops of the ferns and slowly looked around. The heat signature of the trees was pretty much the same but he could make out the different shapes. High up in the branches he could see the brighter shapes of birds and the occasional blotch of a squirrel or chipmunk.

He scanned left and right at ground level. The resolution was good enough to pick out the different plants and bushes that had grown up between the redwoods. Here and there were small brighter patches, some almost white. Rats or mice, probably. Raj continued to check out the forest around him. There was nothing larger than a small rodent or a bird. Had the hunter already left? Maybe his plan had always been to hit one target and then pull back. It made sense. He could have moved to another ambush point, somewhere closer to the house. Or he could be still holed up in his vantage point, waiting. Raj had no way of knowing which option he was facing. The only way to know for sure would be to stand up and see what happened.

His mouth had gone dry. He slipped off his backpack and drank from the water bottle. His head was throbbing so he swallowed two paracetamol tablets and washed them down with more water. He gave the bottle to Sid who drank and then returned it. Raj put the bottle back in the backpack and lifted his head again. He looked around cautiously. He could hear a woodpecker high overhead, attacking a trunk. Two rats were about fifty metres away, scuttling around a redwood. An insect buzzed by his ear.

He stiffened when he saw a white smudge above a fallen tree. Just a smudge, not much bigger than the rats, but it wasn't moving. Raj focused his attention on the patch. Could he make out an eye? Maybe. And a dark patch where the other eye should have been. The gun? Raj stared at the image but it was hard to be sure.

He tapped on Sid's shoulder and pointed to where he'd seen the smudge. Sid peered through his goggles and shrugged. 'Maybe,' he said.

Raj figured he'd be able to get a better look if he moved to the right. He hugged the ground and began to inch his way slowly through the ferns. After he'd crawled ten metres he stopped and lifted his head. He was looking at the white blur from the side now, and this time he could make out the barrel of the gun. He'd found the hunter. He sighed and rolled over onto his back as he considered his options. The man was about eighty metres away – a reasonable enough distance for a kill shot with the Heckler if he was on a shooting range, but if he fired from the ground through ferns, it could be touch and go. He could fire from a kneeling position but as soon as he moved, the hunter would probably spot him. The best bet would be to fire as he moved, laying down a hail of bullets as he ran, but running while wearing night vision goggles was a recipe for disaster. It was impossible to look down and see the ground, which meant it was a simple matter to trip and fall, especially when moving at speed.

He waved for Sid to join him and waited as the man crawled slowly towards him. 'It's definitely him,' Raj whispered. 'But we need to stand to see him. We need to move apart and then start firing together. With two angles of fire we should be able to pin him down and then we can move towards him.'

'Okay,' said Sid, hesitantly.

Raj patted him on the shoulder. 'It'll be okay. We'll catch him by surprise. But we'll need to take the goggles off, it's hard to run wearing them.'

They both pulled off the goggles, rolled over onto their fronts, and raised their heads cautiously. It was easy enough to see the fallen tree but the hunter was well camouflaged and it was only after several seconds of staring that Raj was able to spot him. He had taken up position next to a branch that provided cover above his head and had placed ferns and branches all around himself. The barrel of the gun was resting on the trunk, pointing towards where Erol had fallen. Even from his changed position, all Raj could see was the man's left cheek, and that appeared to have been rubbed with dirt.

'See him?' he whispered.

'I think so.'

'Okay, so you crawl ten metres or so that way so that we can get converging lines of fire on him. When you're in position, watch for my signal. We go on three.'

'Got it,' said Sid.

Raj waited as Sid crawled through the ferns. He breathed slowly and deeply as he stared at his target. He checked the carbine again, patted the two magazines in his back pockets as if to reassure himself they were still there, and prepared himself.

He looked over at Sid who was now in position. Raj took two deep breaths, then held up one finger and nodded. Then two. He flashed three fingers and then pushed himself up onto one knee. He fired a three-shot burst at the junction of the branch, then got to his feet and fired a second burst. Leaves and pieces of fern flew into the air. He fired again and this time his shots hit low, thudding into the bark of the trunk.

Sid was also up and shooting, his bullets ripping across the fallen tree.

A round whizzed by Raj's ear and he flinched, then he fired another three-shot burst and started running. A second shot cracked through the air but it didn't feel as close as the first one. He fired again and more leaves flew up into the air. Sid ran alongside him, still firing.

Raj veered to the right to avoid a bush and fired two quick bursts towards the fallen tree. It was impossible to aim with any accuracy but keeping up a hail of fire meant that the hunter would be forced to keep his head down. Sid fired two three-shot bursts as Raj rounded the bush and fired again and all three rounds thudded into the trunk.

Raj went right, pulled the trigger, and then went left and fired again. Both bursts went high. He had been counting on automatic pilot and knew that he had three rounds left in the magazine so he fired another burst, ejected the magazine and shoved in a replacement. Sid was still running and firing, crashing through the ferns.

Raj veered right, fired two bursts and then went left, firing several times again. He was just twenty metres from the trunk and his eyes were stinging from the cordite. He blinked away tears as he tried to focus, firing another two bursts and then moving to the right. His ears were ringing from the shots and he couldn't tell if he was coming under fire. He fired the final three shots in his magazine as he reached the trunk. Sid was also out of ammunition. Raj started to roar as he ejected the magazine and slapped in the last one but as he prepared to pull the trigger he realised that there was no one behind the tree trunk. He kept the carbine at his shoulder as he checked left and right, then he slowly walked around the trunk. There were marks in the soil where the hunter had been standing, and the smell of urine where he'd relieved himself at some point.

'Has he gone?' asked Sid.

'Looks like it,' said Raj. He gestured with his carbine at footprints showing that the hunter had run off south-west. Raj crouched down and put on the thermal goggles. When he was satisfied that the hunter wasn't hiding nearby he took off the goggles and put them into the backpack.

'There's blood here,' said Sid. He pointed at drops of blood on the ground and a red smear on the trunk.

'At least one of our shots hit home,' said Raj. 'That's something. What about you? Are you okay?'

'A few rounds went by me, but I'm fine.' He grinned. 'That was a fucking rush, wasn't it?'

'That's one way of describing it,' said Raj. He looked at the blood trail. The hunter obviously wasn't mortally injured because he'd been able to run away. If he was heading south-west, he was probably retreating to the house. Raj smiled thinly. Now their positions had been reversed – the hunter had become the hunted.

CHAPTER 62

Van der Sandt had his gun in his left hand and had his right pressed against his shoulder as he hurried between the trees. He was fairly sure the bullet had just grazed him but he was still bleeding copiously. The sudden attack had caught him by surprise. One of the rounds in the third or fourth burst had clipped his shoulder and at that point Van der Sandt had turned and ran.

The ground sloped down and Van der Sandt picked up the pace. He no longer had the GPS but he was familiar with the area and knew exactly where he was. He still had feeling in his left arm so there wasn't too much damage. He felt a bit queasy but he didn't think he'd lost enough blood for it to be life-threatening.

He reached a large redwood tree and stopped behind it. He listened intently but didn't hear anyone following him. He waited a full two minutes until he was satisfied that he wasn't being pursued, then put down his gun and took off his backpack. He opened the first aid kit and placed a field dressing and a tube of antiseptic on the ground, then took off his shirt. He flexed his hand and wiggled his fingers. Everything seemed to be okay. He put a large dollop of antiseptic cream over the wound and applied the dressing.

As he was pulling on his shirt, he heard movement behind him and he grabbed his gun and whirled around. A large female wolf was staring at him, its head down and tail up. As he stared at the animal he realised there were another two smaller wolves some distance away. Her cubs. And then he spotted another off to the right. The mother was almost certainly one of the animals he'd introduced to the area; her cubs must have been born in the wild. He lowered his gun. Wolves rarely attacked humans. She was probably only standing there because her cubs were close by. She was being a good mother, protecting her young. His smile tightened as a vision of what had happened in Cyprus came to him. He could imagine Laura and the children on the beach when the killers turned up on their jet skis. Maybe Laura had watched the killers arrive in the same way that the wolf was studying him, assuming that there was no threat to her or her offspring. Maybe she'd seen their guns and wondered what was happening, and then finally the penny had dropped and she'd shouted for the kids to get out of the way. She'd have tried to protect them, Van der Sandt was sure of that. She'd have stepped in front of the children, put herself between them and the killers, but to no avail. Tears pricked his eyes and he blinked them away. The wolf tensed as if she sensed his unease. He smiled at her. 'Don't worry, baby,' he whispered. 'I don't kill mothers and their children, that's not my style. But the cowardly bastards that do, well they're fair game.' He looked back the way he'd come. 'There's only two of them left, and they'll be dead soon. You have my word on that.' The wolf continued to stare at him with unblinking eyes.

Van der Sandt pulled on his backpack and headed towards the house.

CHAPTER 63

Raj and Sid pushed their way through a clump of bushes then headed up a gentle slope. Before they'd set off in pursuit of the hunter, they'd gone to check on Erol. They'd found his body slumped in the ferns, his face destroyed by a single bullet. Raj had taken Erol's bulletproof vest and Sid the magazine from the Heckler, and they'd set off again.

They had cut slightly to the south to make sure they kept well away from the hunter, but were now heading straight towards the house again. It was almost fully dark, but Raj wanted to put off wearing the goggles until as late as possible. They reached the top of the slope and he stopped and listened. They heard only wildlife. Raj took the GPS unit from his pocket and switched it on. The house was now at the top of the screen. According to the scale, they were just two kilometres away from it. Raj put the unit away and they started to jog, cradling their Hecklers as they ran.

CHAPTER 64

Van der Sandt's house was surrounded by a twelve foot-high wall. It was more to keep out wildlife than anything, but his security people had installed motion sensors and CCTV cameras so that every inch was covered and monitored in the gatehouse at the main entrance to the house. That entrance, to the south, was where Van der Sandt headed – he wasn't sure if the side gates would be manned now that Bell had let most of his team go.

As he approached the main gate, he was blinded by an LED torch. The light overload shocked him and he took a step back as if he'd been punched. 'Identify yourself!' shouted a voice.

Van der Sandt held his rifle above his head to show that he wasn't a threat.

'Drop the weapon or I will shoot!' shouted the guard.

'It's me, Jon Van der Sandt!'

The light went out and the gate opened. 'I'm sorry, sir. I was told to challenge all visitors.'

'Not a problem, son,' said Van der Sandt. 'Where is Colonel Bell?'

'In the kitchen, sir.' He opened the gate wider and Van der Sandt walked through. 'Keep your eyes peeled,' he said. 'There are two bad guys still out there.'

'Yes sir, roger that,' said the guard.

Van der Sandt walked down the driveway to the house. One of Bell's men was standing at the front door with his carbine across his chest. He nodded at Van der Sandt and stood to attention. Van der Sandt threw him a mock salute and then headed down the side of the house to the kitchen.

Colonel Bell was sitting at the oak table with a mug of coffee, two radios in front of him and a Glock in his holster. On the other side of the table was Gerry Lineham, the helicopter pilot. Bell's eyes widened when he saw Van der Sandt at the kitchen door and jumped to his feet.

'Sir, is everything . . .'

Van der Sandt interrupted him with a shake of the head. 'I'm pretty sure the two guys you sent into the woods are dead,' he said. 'Two of the targets are still out there, and they came after me.' He placed his rifle on the table and showed Bell the dressing on his shoulder. 'They got me with a lucky shot.'

'Do you want me to get you to the hospital? Gerry can fly us.'

'It's a flesh wound, nothing more.'

'You're sure?'

'I'm sure.' Van der Sandt took off his backpack and placed it on the table, then picked up his rifle. 'The two still out there – they'll be heading this way.'

'I'll take care of them, sir. There's no way they can get onto the estate. All the gates are locked, the CCTV and alarm system is working just fine, and I've got one of my best guys in the gatehouse. As soon as we see them, we'll be on them like flies on shit.'

Van der Sandt nodded. He wanted to do it himself but the shoulder wound made that impossible. There was no way he could aim and fire the weapon with any degree of accuracy. 'I'll be in my study,' he said. He headed upstairs.

'Billy-Joe is outside,' said Bell. 'Just to be on the safe side I'll send him up to you.' Van der Sandt was already out of earshot and Bell wasn't sure if he'd heard or not.

'Do you need me, Colonel?' asked Lineham.

'Can the chopper fly at short notice?'

'Sure. All fuelled up and ready to go. Just give me the word.'

'Let's see how we get on tonight.' Bell pulled his Glock from its holster, checked the action, and slotted it back before heading down the hallway to the front door. He grabbed one of the radios as he went.

Billy-Joe Maxwell was standing outside, his carbine across his front. He was a big man with a barrel-like chest and a square jaw who had done three tours in Afghanistan with Delta Force before joining the private sector. 'Go upstairs and keep an eye on Mr Van der Sandt,' said Bell. 'But don't disturb him.'

'Roger that, sir.' Maxwell went inside and headed up the stairs.

Bell looked up at the night sky. It was totally clear of clouds and there was so little light pollution in the area that there were millions of stars to be seen. He shuddered as a breeze blew across the lawn. He fished a pack of Marlboro from his fatigues and lit one.

CHAPTER 65

Raj lay on his stomach under a bush, studying the wall through his night vision goggles. He had them set to infrared and they gave him a near-perfect, albeit greenish view of his surroundings. There were CCTV camera housings every hundred yards or so, but no barbed wire. If they did climb the wall there was no doubt that they'd be spotted. There was a barred gate midway along the perimeter – he couldn't see a guard but the gate was covered by one of the cameras.

Sid crawled up next to him. 'What's the story?' he asked.

Raj removed his goggles. 'I don't see any guards but they've got CCTV everywhere. I could put together a ladder and we could get over without too many problems, but there's no way we could do it without being seen.'

He saw movement at one of the upstairs windows. A man was standing there, looking out. Instinctively, Raj knew it was the hunter. Raj sighted on the figure and eased his finger onto the trigger, but he knew it would be pointless to shoot – the man was well out of range.

'So what are we going to do?' asked Sid. 'We can't stay out here all night.'

'I've got a plan,' said Raj.

He turned and crawled back into the forest. Sid followed him.

CHAPTER 66

Andy Isom popped a fresh stick of gum into his mouth as he scanned the CCTV screens in front of him. The feeds from the cameras around the perimeter, grounds and house were shown on three large monitors, each showing nine views on a rotating basis. There was a fourth screen on the wall above them which could be used to see any individual views that were of particular interest. He spotted two figures on one of the displays and he clicked on it. The image transferred to the main screen.

Isom stood up and leant towards the display. An Asian man, dark-skinned and bearded, was walking towards the main gate, his hands on his head. Behind him was one of Bell's men, pointing his Heckler at the captive's back.

Isom pulled his Glock from its holster and headed out. The main gate was opened using a switch in the gatehouse but there was a smaller pedestrian gate to the side that was unlocked with a security card that Isom had on a chain clipped to his belt.

The men were about twenty feet away from the gate as Isom approached. The floodlights covering the area cast giant shadows over the ground. The captive's skin was glistening under the harsh light and Isom could see his eyes flicking nervously left and right.

'He give you any problems?' asked Isom.

'Nah,' said the guy with the gun. It must have been either Emmett or Holland – whichever one it was had their helmet pulled low over their face, so from a few metres away he couldn't tell.

The two men came to a halt and stood just inches from the gate. There was a holster on the captive's hip, but there was no gun in it.

'Everything okay?' Isom asked, looking down and holding out the key card towards the reader.

'Yeah,' the man in the helmet grunted, but as Isom looked up he immediately realised the man wasn't Emmett or Holland. Panicked, Isom reached for his gun, but as he did the captive lowered his hands. The right hand went behind his back and reappeared holding a Glock. Isom's mouth fell open in surprise, and before he could even touch his own weapon the other man's gun barked twice.

CHAPTER 67

Colin Bell heard the *crack-crack* of pistol shots from the direction of the main entrance. He took his transceiver from the holster on his belt and put it to his mouth. 'This is Charlie Bravo, come in Alpha India.' He released the transmit button, but there was no reply. He tried again. 'Come in Alpha India, I need a sitrep.'

Again there was no reply. Bell cursed and put the transceiver back in its holster, and began running towards the main gate, pulling his Glock from its holster.

The main gates were closed and there were no vehicles on the drive. The gatehouse door was open and the lights were on inside. Bell slowed as he got closer to the building. He moved to the left and saw a figure lying on the ground by the pedestrian gate. It was Andy Isom, he realised. A man was reaching through the barred gate. There was another man in fatigues and a Kevlar helmet standing behind him, holding a Heckler. Bell frowned, trying to understand what he was seeing.

The first man locked eyes with Bell and he said something to the man behind him. The second man looked up and Bell realised it was one of the jihadists. The white one. Bell reached for his gun. He brought it up but before he could fire the man's carbine kicked and three rounds buried themselves in the grass by his feet. Bell dived to the side, came up on one knee and fired two quick shots. He was unlucky and both ricocheted off the bars of the gate.

The carbine fired again but Bell dived and rolled, and he was able to use the gatehouse as cover. He ran towards the building, bent at the waist.

CHAPTER 68

'Did you get him?' asked Raj. He was pulling at the body of the guard he'd shot, trying to get the key to open the gate. 'I don't think so,' said Sid. 'He's behind the building.'

'Keep an eye out, I'm an easy target here.'

Raj managed to grab the key card. It was attached to a chain but he pulled it hard and the chain came away from whatever it had been attached to. He tapped it against the card reader and the lock clicked.

As he pushed the gate open with his left hand, the hinges of the gate squeaked and the man appeared from behind the gatehouse. Raj recognised him immediately – it was the grey-haired man with the hook, the one who had seemed to be in charge.

Raj fired two quick shots and the man ducked back. He kept his Glock trained on the wall where the man had been and motioned for Sid to step through the gate. They both moved forward cautiously. Raj waved for Sid to go wide. Sid had a Heckler and the grey-haired man had a handgun so firepower was on their side.

They shuffled forward. Raj's heart was pounding; he knew that he would have to react instantly. He turned his head from side to side, listening intently.

Sid had the better viewpoint and Raj looked over at him. Sid gave a small shake of his head. Raj frowned. Sid was only a few feet from the corner of the wall so he should already be able to see around it. He took a step to the side, keeping low. He looked at Sid again. Sid had his Heckler up against his shoulder, crouching as he moved forward. The Heckler was trembling in Sid's hands, his finger tight on the trigger.

Sid took a deep breath and Raj realised he was about to charge forward. He opened his mouth to tell him to hold back but it was too late, he was already past the point of no return. Raj moved forward with him.

Sid stepped around the corner and immediately fired two three-shot bursts. Raj rounded the corner, swinging his gun around, but there was no one there. 'Did you see him?' he asked Sid.

Sid shook his head. 'I just fired. Better safe than sorry.'

Raj looked over at the main house. It was too far away for the grey-haired man to have reached it. He'd either gone inside the gatehouse or taken cover at the other end of the building. He waved for Sid to approach the doorway. He held his Glock with both hands as he moved forward. As the door came into view he could see inside. There was a high-backed chair and a number of large monitors showing views from the CCTV cameras covering the estate.

Sid shuffled into Raj's line of fire and Raj hissed at him. Sid turned to look at him, frowning. Raj opened his mouth to say something but before he could the grey-haired man appeared from around the corner of the building. He fired immediately, two quick shots, both of which hit Sid in the vest. Sid roared in pain and swung his Heckler around but the man was already firing again and the second double tap blew away Sid's face. Blood splattered across Raj's arm. He tried to get a bead on the man but Sid was still in the way.

Raj ducked to the left as Sid's legs collapsed. He was low when he fired and his shot hit the man in the leg, just above the knee. The leg buckled and it threw off his aim so the two shots he fired both ricocheted off the gatehouse wall.

Sid hit the ground and his carbine slipped from his grasp. The grey-haired man took aim again and Raj dashed for the gatehouse doorway. As he reached it two more shots thudded into the wall above his head. Raj turned and took aim. There was a sudden look of panic in the man's face as he realised he was out in the open. He fired again and a round whizzed by Raj's head and buried itself into the wall inside the gatehouse. Raj had the Glock in his right hand and the position he was in meant he couldn't get his left hand up to support it. He aimed it as best he could and began pulling the trigger. The first shot went wide, to the right, and the second one went high.

The man returned fire with two shots, one of which nicked the material of Raj's shirt. Raj had to fight the urge to duck for cover; he knew that his best chance of survival was to keep firing. He fired a quick double tap and both rounds thudded into the man's chest. The man took two small steps back and fired but the shot went way high. Raj fired again but missed – he was aiming for a head shot but his marksmanship wasn't up to it. The grey-haired man had stopped returning fire and Raj took the opportunity to step out of the doorway, bring his left hand up to support his right and to fire continuously, shot after shot until the clip was empty. It was only when red roses blossomed on the man's shirt that Raj realised he wasn't wearing a vest. The man staggered back, his mouth open in shock, and then he fell to the ground.

Raj kept the gun aimed at the man as he cautiously approached him, but there was no movement and his shirt was now soaked in blood that glistened under the overhead floodlights.

Raj took deep breaths to steady himself, then walked over to Sid. Sid too was obviously dead; most of his face had been blown away. 'Sorry, mate,' said Raj. He dropped his Glock and picked up Sid's carbine.

Raj looked around but no one seemed to have reacted to the shots. He went into the gatehouse and stood in front of the CCTV monitors. He ran his gaze across the screens but couldn't see any other guards.

He left the gatehouse and walked up the drive. As he got to the front of the house, he realised that the front door was ajar. He held his carbine at the ready as he approached. He didn't see any movement but he decided to enter through the rear of the house, just to be on the safe side.

He kept on the grass as he moved around the side of the

building. Most of the downstairs rooms were in darkness. He rounded the rear of the house. There was a large terrace, with stone steps leading up to it, illuminated by what appeared to be ornate street lamps. Raj took a good look around to check that all was clear before heading up the steps. He walked by a massive BBQ pit and threaded through the wooden seats and tables towards a door that led to the kitchen. He gently turned the handle and pushed the door open. There was a man in grey fatigues sitting at the kitchen table, his head bobbing back and forth. Raj frowned, wondering why the man hadn't reacted to the shots; then he realised he was listening to music through noise-cancelling headphones.

Raj walked on tiptoe, his carbine aimed at the man's head. The man saw the movement and jumped to his feet, ripping off the headphones. 'Hey man, be cool, I'm just a fucking pilot!' he stammered.

Raj didn't recognise him, but when he'd been flying the helicopter he'd been wearing a helmet and dark glasses.

'I'm not armed,' said the pilot, raising his hands. 'I'm just a hired hand, I fly the chopper for Mr Van der Sandt, you don't have any beef with me.'

'Van der Sandt, that's the name of the guy that's been hunting us?'

The pilot nodded nervously. 'Jon Van der Sandt. He's richer than God.' He pointed at the ceiling. 'He's upstairs.'

'You knew what he was doing, right?'

The pilot looked away and didn't answer.

'You dropped us in that clearing, you knew exactly what he was doing. You were part of it.' Raj raised his carbine.

'Please, my wife's pregnant . . .'

Raj stepped forward and slammed the stock of his Heckler against the pilot's head. He went down without a sound.

Raj put his carbine on the table. He went over to the counter and took the leads from the kettle and coffeemaker. He used the leads to bind the pilot's hands and feet, then picked up his weapon and tiptoed over to the door that led to a large hallway lined with abstract paintings. To his right was a massive dining room with a gleaming oak table surrounded by dozens of chairs. To his left were a set of double doors opening into what looked like a ball-room with a raised stage and a piano.

The corridor led into a double-height hallway with a huge chandelier above a marble staircase. The main door was ajar. Raj moved into the hall, his gun at the ready. He walked on tiptoe to the front door and looked cautiously outside. Nothing.

He looked up the staircase, which was two metres wide and curved around the chandelier to the upper floor. At the top was a huge painting of Van der Sandt and his family, a beautiful woman maybe twenty years his junior and three good-looking children. That was what all this was about. His wife and children had been murdered and he wanted revenge. He'd got what he wanted; Sid and Jaffar and the rest of them were dead. But at what cost? He kept the gun trained on the landing as he took the stairs one by one. He reached the top and listened carefully. There were hallways leading left and right.

The left was where he'd seen Van der Sandt at the window, so he went that way. He moved cautiously. There were doors to the left and right, all closed. He reached the middle of the corridor. He eased open a door to his left. It was a bedroom, straight from the pages of a design magazine, and it looked as if it had never been slept in. He closed the door.

He reached the end of the corridor and paused as he considered which way to turn next. He figured he should go left, but first he needed to check that both hallways were clear. He stood at the junction and peered around to the right. It was clear. As he started to turn to look the other way he heard the crack of a Heckler and a bullet thudded into the wall above his head. As he jerked back, another round hit a light fitting and blew it apart.

Raj crouched down. He listened. There was no footfall so the shooter was staying put. He shrugged off his backpack and stood up. He held the gun in his right hand and the backpack in his left. He took a breath to steady himself, then tossed the backpack into the corridor. As he stepped around the corner he had the

Heckler up to his shoulder. The shooter was midway down the corridor, his Heckler at waist level, the barrel pointing towards the bag. Raj saw the man's eyes widen in surprise, and he recognised him immediately. He was the one who had cold-cocked Raj in the hangar. The man's mouth opened as he started to swing his Heckler across but Raj had already pulled the trigger. The round hit the man's vest and Raj took a step forward and fired again, two quick shots that both hit the vest but higher up this time.

The look of surprise had turned to terror and the man pulled his trigger even though the carbine was still pointing down. A bullet ricocheted off the floor and whizzed down the corridor.

Raj didn't have time to use the sights as he walked towards the man. He pulled the trigger twice and both shots went high and to the left, slamming into the ceiling. He adjusted his aim, still walking, and both shots hit the man in the centre of the vest. The man staggered back and his left hand slipped off the carbine.

Raj fired another double tap. He tried to aim higher but he was closer now, just fifteen metres away, and he hit the vest again.

The gun was now swinging from the man's right hand but his finger was still inside the trigger guard.

Raj stopped, his feet shoulder width apart, and he fired twice. The first shot hit the man in the forehead and the second one missed, but one was enough. The man fell backwards, rolled against the wall and slid down, smearing the wallpaper with blood.

Raj took a deep breath. The man had been standing between two doors, and he figured he had been guarding Van der Sandt. He put his ear to the door on the left and heard faint footsteps inside. He used his left hand to slowly turn the handle. He pushed the door and it opened. He stepped back and kicked the door, hard. It flew open. Van der Sandt was standing at a window to the side of a massive fireplace, looking out over the gardens. He was holding his rifle in his right hand and he started to turn towards Raj.

'Drop the gun!' shouted Raj, his finger tightening on the Heckler's trigger as he walked into the room.

The man ignored the command and brought up the rifle as he continued to turn. Raj pulled the trigger. It clicked but didn't fire. He pressed the trigger again. He was out of ammunition.

Van der Sandt smiled. 'That's unlucky,' he said. He gestured with his rifle. 'This one is fully loaded. Trust me on that.'

Raj tossed the carbine onto a sofa made from zebra skin. He raised his hands but he doubted that surrendering would improve the odds of survival, not after everything that had happened that day.

Van der Sandt's finger tightened on the trigger and Raj tensed, expecting the worst. Then just as quickly the man relaxed. 'Toss that knife, and get me a drink, will you?' he said, waving at an oak drinks cabinet. 'A whisky. You'll see the bottle. Macallan in Lalique.'

Raj threw the knife onto the sofa, then went over to the cabinet and opened it. There was a selection of spirits including a bottle of Macallan.

'I'd say help yourself, but obviously you don't drink,' said Van der Sandt. He walked behind a large oak desk and sat down in a high-backed leather chair. He swung his feet up onto the desk, keeping the gun aimed at Raj.

'I drink,' said Raj. He took out two chunky crystal tumblers and poured large measures into both. He walked over to the desk and put one down in front of Van der Sandt. He raised the other in salute. 'Cheers.'

Van der Sandt looked at Raj curiously, then picked up the tumbler with his left hand and clinked it against Raj's glass. '*Sláinte*,' he said. The rifle continued to point at Raj's chest.

They both drank. 'This Macallan is sixty-two years old,' said Van der Sandt. 'I've always made it a policy never to drink a whisky younger than I am. It gets harder the older you get, obviously.' He waved his tumbler at the drinks cabinet. 'That bottle cost me more than a hundred thousand bucks.'

'It's a good whisky, no question of that.' Raj walked over to stand by the fireplace. At first he had thought he was in a study, but he realised it was a trophy room. There were elephant tusks forming an arch around the man's chair, and all along the walls were heads of animals – deer, big cats, and even a rhino. The room was huge, almost the size of a tennis court, dotted with sofas, winged chairs and coffee tables, and scattered around were stuffed big cats in various poses, including a male and female tiger standing together.

'My name is Jon Van der Sandt. I figured you should at least know that.'

'I know who you are,' said Raj.

'And you? Who are you?'

Raj raised his glass. 'Rajesh Patel. My friends call me Raj.'

Either side of the drinks cabinet were two lights, each formed from an elephant's trunk holding a bulb. There were half a dozen animal skins on the floor, including that of a polar bear and several leopards. The heads had been left on and glassy eyes stared back at Raj. On the far wall a crocodile that must have been almost six metres long had been stuffed and mounted, its jaws agape.

'And who the hell are you, Rajesh Patel? How did you come to be fighting for a terrorist group in Syria?'

'I'm not a terrorist,' said Raj. 'I told you that when this all started.' He held up his tumbler. 'When was the last time you saw a Muslim drinking a single malt?'

'So what are you, then?'

'I'm a Brit.'

'Religion, I meant. What religion are you?'

Raj shrugged. 'I'm an agnostic, pretty much. But my parents are Hindu and I'd go to temple with them.'

'So you're Indian?'

Raj frowned. 'I'm British. I was born in London.'

'But your parents are Indian?'

Raj shook his head. 'Wrong again. My mum was born in Leeds, my dad was born in Uganda. My dad's family were forced to leave in 1972 when Idi Amin expelled all Asians from the country.

They were forced to leave behind their chain of supermarkets and rental properties and had to start again from scratch in London. Dad had it rough, he was just a kid at the time. But he's a Brit now. And he's never even been to India. Mum's the same. Her parents moved to the UK in the fifties. So I'm British, mate. It's the only country I've ever known.'

Van der Sandt frowned. 'Then what the fuck were you doing in an ISIS camp?'

'They'd kidnapped me,' said Raj. 'They'd had some sort of accident involving a suicide vest and they needed me to patch up the survivors. I did what I could and then they said I'd have to stay the night, and that's when your goons moved in. They wouldn't listen to me.' He shrugged. 'And here I am.'

'What do you mean, patch up survivors?'

'I'm a doctor. I was working at a local hospital. They took me away at gunpoint.'

Van der Sandt snarled at him. 'Bull-fucking-shit,' he said. 'You're no doctor. You've had military training.'

'Sure, I was a Royal Marine Commando. But I'm a doctor too.'

'So you were a medic?'

'Not just a medic. A doctor. I did my medical training and commando training.'

'And you were in Syria with the Marines?'

'No, I left the Marines a few years ago. I was working for a humanitarian agency.'

Van der Sandt drained his whisky and held out his glass. Raj took the bottle over and refilled the tumbler for him. 'You want to tell me why?' asked Van der Sandt.

Raj tilted his head on one side. 'Why I left the Marines, or why I was doing humanitarian work?'

'Both.'

'The people of Syria need help,' said Raj. 'What's happening to the Syrians is a tragedy. A true tragedy. And the world is turning their backs on them.'

'Had you served as a soldier in Syria?'

'No, just Afghanistan. But when I left the Marines I worked

at a hospital in London and I met a few doctors from Syria. They told me the horror stories of what was happening there and I wanted to help.'

Van der Sandt sipped his whisky. 'And why did you leave the Marines?'

Raj shrugged. 'It's a long story.'

'Are you in a rush?'

Raj smiled thinly. He sat down in one of the winged chairs and took a long drink of his whisky. It was smooth and warm, though he couldn't see how it could possibly be worth a hundred thousand dollars a bottle. 'I had a run-in with the powers-that-be over the value of human life,' he said. 'I wanted to treat an Afghan casualty, my sergeant disagreed.'

'You were an officer?'

'I had the rank of lieutenant. But my combat experience was limited so often I would defer to my sergeant. We'd been in a firefight and I wanted to treat an injured Afghan. My sergeant told me not to. I ignored him and said sergeant put two rounds into the man's chest. It was murder. Cold-blooded murder.'

'It was war.'

Raj shook his head. 'The firefight was over. No British lives were at risk. The Afghan was no threat and he needed my help.'

'And?'

Raj shrugged. 'When we got back to base I reported the sergeant. But no one cared. The rest of the men who'd been on the patrol backed up the sergeant. Said he'd shot the Afghan because he was about to fire his weapon. It was bollocks, his AK-47 was on the ground. The top brass knew they were lying but no one cared. So I quit.' He shrugged again. 'It wasn't how I'd planned to end my military career, but I didn't see that I'd any choice.' He drained his glass, then stood up and refilled it. He sat down again and sipped his whisky. 'What you said in the hangar, when you first brought us here: I get it. You wanted revenge. But you've got the wrong man.'

Van der Sandt grimaced. 'It looks that way,' he said quietly. 'I owe you an apology.'

'And what about the families of the men I had to kill to get here? Are you going to apologise to them, too?'

Van der Sandt drank his whisky. 'This has turned into what my military friends would call a clusterfuck. It's not what I intended.'

'What did you think this was going to achieve, anyway? Did killing them make you feel any better?'

Van der Sandt nodded. 'Actually it did. I couldn't have lived with myself if those animals had continued living. You know what they did, right? They attacked a beach resort. They shot at women and children with Kalashnikovs and they kept on killing until they ran out of bullets. How would you feel if your family had been killed like that?'

'I hear you,' said Raj.

'My wife, my son, two daughters. Butchered on a beach. And for what? What did they ever think that would achieve? If they attacked an army base, or assassinated George W. Bush or your Tony Blair, then I would have understood the logic. It would have made some sort of sense. But what they did?' He took a long drink of whisky. 'They deserved it. And yes, I'm glad they're dead and I'm glad that I killed them. But about you, what can I say? I'm sorry I dragged you into this. But sorry really doesn't cover it, does it?'

He pulled open a desk drawer and took out a cheque book. He picked up a pen and began to write on a cheque.

'I didn't think anyone used cheques these days,' said Raj.

'Well the Queen of England does, and this is the bank she uses,' said Van der Sandt. 'The men who were working for me, their families will be well looked after. They all have iron-clad contracts and if anything happens to them . . .' He shrugged. He finished writing the cheque and stood up. He picked up the rifle and walked over to where Raj was sitting. 'Maybe this will go some way to making up for what I put you through,' he said.

He handed the cheque to Raj and went back to the desk. Raj's eyes widened when he saw it had been made out for five million dollars. 'I can't take this,' he said, looking up. 'And even if I could, it wouldn't make it right. You're going to have to pay for what you did, and not with money.'

Van der Sandt waved away his protests. 'Give it to the hospital in Syria. Do some good with it. I don't expect you to forgive me. That's not what it's about. I know there'll never be any forgiveness for what I did. I did it because I had to, because I wouldn't be able to live with myself if I didn't get revenge on the men who took my family. Now I can die a happy man.'

Raj looked down at the cheque. Five million dollars. He shook his head in disbelief, then flinched at the sound of a gunshot. He looked up and saw Van der Sandt staggering back, the left side of his head blown away by a shot from his own rifle, which clattered to the ground. He fell against the desk, blood pouring from the fatal wound. Raj jumped to his feet but realised immediately that there was nothing he could do. Van der Sandt was dead before he hit the floor. Raj's hands were shaking as he put the cheque into his pocket.

He went slowly downstairs and into the kitchen. The pilot had regained consciousness and he glared at Raj. 'Why the fuck did you hit me?'

Raj ignored the question. 'I need to get out of here,' he said. 'Will you fly me? Or do I just leave you tied up here?'

'Where do you want to go?'

'Where's the nearest police station?' asked Raj.

'About seventy kilometres away,' said the pilot. 'Next to the hospital.'

'Can we land there? At night?'

'Sure.'

'And you'll fly me?'

'Yes, if you untie me.'

Raj knelt down and untied the leads from around his wrists and ankles, then helped him to his feet. 'What do you need?' asked Raj.

'Nothing. The chopper's fuelled and ready to go.'

They went out of the kitchen door and across the lawn to the helicopter landing pad. 'You knew what was going on, didn't you?' said Raj.

The pilot shook his head. 'I'm just a hired hand. They tell me where to fly and I fly.'

'Come on, you saw what they were doing. The way they kicked us out in the middle of nowhere. And the guns they were carrying, they weren't for fun, were they?'

'I was told that Mr Van der Sandt wanted revenge for what happened to his family.'

'And you were okay with that?'

The pilot shrugged. 'An eye for an eye?' he said. 'I don't see anything wrong with that. If more people had to bear the consequences of their actions, maybe they'd behave better.'

They climbed into the helicopter. The pilot took the left-hand seat and Raj sat next to him. The pilot looked at him, eyes narrowed. 'Did you kill his family?' he asked.

'No, I didn't.'

'So why are you here?'

'Wrong place, wrong time.'

The pilot picked up his helmet and put it on. 'I'm in trouble, aren't I?'

'Not necessarily,' said Raj. 'You weren't shooting at me and like you said, you just fly where you're told to fly.'

'What will you tell them? About me?'

'Mate, I don't intend to even mention you. In fact you can just drop me at the police station and fly off to wherever you want. What happens then is up to you.'

'Thanks.'

'Don't thank me. Just get me the hell out of here.'

The pilot smiled gratefully, went through the pre-flight checks, and then started the engines. As they rose into the air and banked over the garden, Raj looked down at the house. He folded his arms and took a deep breath. He was going to have to do a lot of explaining.

THRILLINGLY GOOD BOOKS FROM CRIMINALLY GOOD WRITERS

CRIME FILES BRINGS YOU THE LATEST RELEASES FROM TOP CRIME AND THRILLER AUTHORS.

SIGN UP ONLINE FOR OUR MONTHLY NEWSLETTER AND BE THE FIRST TO KNOW ABOUT OUR COMPETITIONS, NEW BOOKS AND MORE.